MY SINFUL NIGHTS

BOOK ONE IN THE SINFUL MEN SERIES

LAUREN BLAKELY

AUTHOR'S NOTE

I originally wrote Sweet Sinful Nights in 2015. In 2019, as I reread the book, I saw an opportunity to improve aspects of it. But improvements are never simple. Once I went into the story to change how it started, nearly everything changed.

If you've never read this sexy, emotional, and suspenseful romance, I hope you savor every page. If you're reading it again, I hope you love the new characterizations of the hero and heroine, as well as the motivations, tension, and conflict. While the underlying details of the characters' professions, hometown, relationships, and circumstances remain the same, nearly everything else is new—including the dialogue, how they interact, and why. All told, this reimagined storyline contains about 80 percent new material.

ABOUT

A sexy, emotional, heart-stopping romance novel from #1 New York Times Bestselling author Lauren Blakely...

Ten years ago, I let the love of my life slip through my fingers. It's my greatest regret, especially since she's all but disappeared. When she walks back into my world unexpectedly, I have one mission — win her back. Whatever it takes.

But the gorgeous, brilliant, tough-as-iron Shannon has secrets of her own, and a family past she's trying to escape.

Slowly but surely, I break down her walls over our sinful nights together, with a connection more passionate than ever, an intimacy more fiery than it was before.

But the past can only stay behind you for so long. And when the people who want a piece of her family start circling her, I'll have to prove I'm the man to protect her from her suddenly dangerous present.

MY SINFUL NIGHTS

By Lauren Blakely

Want to be the first to learn of sales, new releases, preorders and special freebies? Sign up for my VIP mailing list here! You'll also get free books from bestselling authors in a selection curated just for you!

PRO TIP: Add lauren@laurenblakely.com to your contacts before signing up to make sure the emails go to your inbox!

Did you know this book is also available in audio and paperback on all major retailers? Go to my website for links!

This is an emotional, suspenseful series, with high-stakes action and consequences. For content warnings go to my web site.

HIS PROLOGUE

Ten years ago

Here's the thing about long-distance relationships.

No one ever tells you how painfully hard they are.

We're talking run-an-ultra-marathon hard. Learn to write in Mandarin hard.

I was seven months into one, and I still wasn't used to the missing.

Would I ever be?

On Friday afternoon, I stared at the picture on my desk of my fiancée, gazing at Shannon's bright blonde hair, short and sleek, pushed back in a slim silver headband. I took in her vibrant eyes, her smile.

A smile I knew I'd brought back to her face, and damn, did that ever make me happy.

To be the person who'd done that for her.

One day more, and I could make my way to see her again.

Twelve more hours till my flight.

A knock sounded on the plastic wall of the tiny cube I called home from nine a.m. to midnight most of the time.

There was always a rap on the proverbial door. There was always something I needed to do. There was never time to linger on Shannon, to think about her, let alone see her.

The thing I wanted most in the world.

I looked up from the picture and into the unshaven face of Jed Hawkins, head writer on *Late Night Antics*. He smiled, the kind of smile that said *I'm about to ask you for a big-ass favor.*

Since I was the new kid on the block, and more than thrilled to have that position here at a late-night comedy show, I put on my most professional grin. "What can I do for you?"

I said it before he even had the chance to tell me what he needed.

That was how you rose in this field. You did it by jumping on opportunities before they even came your way. Otherwise, you were too late. I'd learned that in the first six months at this job. There was always someone waiting in the wings.

Jed scratched his jaw, heaving a sigh, like it pained him to ask the next thing. "Here's the thing. That series of sketches on the new Marvel flick?"

I nodded. I knew the sketches. I'd worked on them, written a few jokes for them.

"The host wants us to rewrite them," Jed said with a *what can you do* expression. His eyes were dark—or maybe it was the bags under them.

There was nothing I could do about that.

What I could do was *this*.

Don't let on that the request drives you crazy.

It was just par for the course. Rewrites landed on your plate hourly. As a junior writer on a TV show, you just did them.

"I'll get started now," I said.

"And . . . we need the first one by morning. The second by noon. The third by—"

"Tomorrow at this time," I said, masking the heavy weight in my gut.

I had a plane to catch in the morning.

A plane I didn't think I was going to make now.

Story of my fucking life. I'd had to cancel the last three trips. Shannon had offered to come here each time, but work had piled up and I wouldn't have been able to see her even if she did.

Just like I couldn't see her now.

Because of those damn sketches.

But that series of sketches was the linchpin of the show, so I didn't have a choice. Jed swiveled around, took a step, then spun back and said with a sigh, "One more thing. Host is going to need you on set this weekend after all. In case there are any other last-minute changes."

That weight? It was an anchor now, sinking me. Sinking my long-distance love affair. "Got it."

Jed had the decency to look rueful. He shrugged. "Sorry. I think you were going out of town, but—"

"It'll be fine. I'll take care of it."

He left, and out of habit, I glanced at the clock. But I knew it was already the middle of the night in London.

Too late to call.

Instead, with my shoulders sagging, I sent an email to Shannon, telling her I would have to reschedule my trip. After I hit send, I gave myself a minute to be annoyed.

It had been seven months like this. Seven months since college ended. Seven months since we'd promised to find a way to stay together. We'd known it wasn't going to be easy. We lived thousands of miles apart, a country and an ocean between us. But we'd had a plan. When school had ended, we'd figured a once-a-month visit was doable. She'd fly here. I'd fly there. Every other month one of us would travel, maybe only for a weekend. But a weekend was worth it.

When you loved someone to the depths of your soul, a weekend was worth it. That was what I told myself over and over and again and again.

The problem was we'd only managed one damn weekend in seven months. All the every-other-month plans had flown out the window. Our schedules had never aligned. Our days off were never the same. And work kept shoving itself in the way, the bully in the lunch line.

You had no choice but to let the bully cut in front of you.

That was how it went at age twenty-two, cutting your teeth after college.

Shannon had scored a golden opportunity as an assistant choreographer for a dance company in

London, and I'd landed the chance of a lifetime as a writer on a late-night comedy show. These were the chances we had to take, even if it meant being apart.

Those chances also meant missed chances.

In the break room, I poured myself a cup of coffee.

I returned to my desk, draining the coffee as I stared one more time at the picture of Shannon.

Gritting my teeth, I cursed under my breath, shaking my head in frustration.

This was what seven months of working my ass off had come down to. One opportunity to see my woman and many more canceled ones.

And I had to get her out of my mind or I'd never get my work done.

I dug into the script, shoving Shannon aside.

HER PROLOGUE

The phone rattled on the table of my flat in Bloomsbury. Brent's name flashed across the screen.

Maybe it was the time of night—seven. Maybe it was the last few emails he'd sent— canceling trips, saying he was working late, telling me he wished he could see me, but he couldn't make it work.

Whatever it was, I *knew*.

I just knew.

With dread coursing through my veins, I picked up the phone. Swiped *answer* warily. "Hi."

"Hey Shan," he said.

And there it was. The apology in his voice already.

He'd already told me he couldn't come here this weekend. I knew he wasn't apologizing

again. This was about something else.

"Hi Brent," I said, bracing myself.

"So, listen, I was thinking about things…"

I squeezed my eyes shut. Grabbed the edge of the counter. It was coming, and it was going to hurt.

"Okay," I said carefully.

"And I miss you so damn much that I don't want to do this to you."

With a heavy weight in my gut, I sank down to the floor. "Do what?"

"I just can't make this work, babe," he said, and he sounded awful. Truly awful. But I felt awful too, knowing what was coming.

"And what does that mean?" I asked, voice tightening.

He sighed heavily. I hated that this was hard for him. Too bad that didn't make the inevitable end hurt less.

"I just think maybe we should try again when we're in different places in our careers," he said, like he was devastated.

But resigned too.

I bit my lip to bite back tears. He was right. I knew he was right. We weren't working. There wasn't a way for us to work. We were pushing a boulder up a hill, only to watch it roll back down.

Every. Single. Time.

But there were things I needed to tell him. Things I couldn't bring myself to tell him now.

"Sure," I said, choking out that one word past the tears.

The longer I stayed on this phone, the more I'd break down, the more I'd tell him now. And I couldn't. I needed to wrap my head around what this meant.

And I didn't want to trap him.

I'd tell him in person. I'd have to. That was the only way.

"I have to go," I said.

I burned everywhere.

I hurt in every cell.

A torrent of misery whipped through me.

I hung up and called my older brother. Through the tears, I told him I had to see him. He booked me on the next flight out of London.

The lights flickered across the night sky as I peered out the window. I tapped my nails against the armrest. I needed to be home. Needed to see Michael first. He'd know what to do. He'd been my rock for years. The one I relied on the most.

When the plane landed, I headed to baggage claim, where I fell into my brother's arms, a fresh round of tears cascading down my cheeks. He patted my hair, drew me into an embrace, and whispered, "It's okay. Tell me what happened."

I sobbed, hurt clogging my throat as I choked out, "Brent and I broke up. And I'm pregnant."

Michael's eyes widened, and he gritted his teeth. Then his jaw clenched. But his voice was steady and comforting as he said, "Tell me how I can help you."

"I don't know how to tell Brent. I don't want him to feel tricked into staying," I said.

He nodded intensely. "Tell him that, Shan. Tell him *that.*"

He was right. I just had to do it.

A little later, in the quiet of Michael's condo we talked it out, as we always did. How to say it, when to call, what to do.

But a pang of regret crashed into me. Should I ask Brent if he wanted to try again? For the baby's sake?

Oh God. This was so damn hard.

I set a hand on my stomach.

Closed my eyes.

Gazed heavenward.

Asked for strength.

My throat hitched, clogged with emotions I didn't want to feel.

I took a deep breath, picked up the phone, and started to dial his number, but my stomach roiled. I couldn't do this tonight. I needed a clear mind. I'd tell him in the morning.

* * *

But in the morning, I wasn't able to get to the phone for a long time, as waves of sickness crashed through my body.

And soon, there was no reason to call.

1

────────

SHANNON

Present day

"He's not going to be there tonight." My twin brother spoke as if he were a soothsayer, as if he'd spoken to an oracle and been granted a view into the future—three hours from now when we were to meet with Edge nightclub to seal the deal.

But his certainty didn't quell the vicious butterflies in me.

Because holy ten years.

It had been ten years since I'd seen him.

"How do you know for sure?" I asked as I rested my ankle atop the barre in the studio at the Shay Productions offices, a few miles from downtown.

I peered outside. The late-afternoon sun dipped in the sky, blasting blinding light through the floor-to-ceiling windows that looked out on, oddly enough, sidewalks and trees. Outsiders were often shocked that my

Vegas-based company was actually located in an office park, not amongst the glittering skyscrapers and hotels that greeted visitors with neon and lights. No need for spark and dazzle during the day though.

Besides, Vegas was so much dirtier than the night led us to believe.

I looked at my brother as he answered me with a soft, understanding smile. "I know he won't be there because the meeting is with James, his business advisor and main investor. James is the guy at Edge who I've been working the deal with," Colin said. A venture capitalist, he ran his own firm but also handled the business partnerships for me, including a potential one with Brent's nightclubs to integrate my choreography into their in-house shows.

Such a strange thought to be doing business with Brent. I stared at my left hand, my ring finger as bare as it was the day I twisted off the ring and sent it back to the person responsible for the second shattering of my heart.

The first time it broke was in a driveway late one night when I was thirteen.

And Brent took the healed remains and stomped on them.

I drew a deep breath, shoving that far behind me.

He was the past.

I hadn't followed my ex's every move, but I was well aware that after a wildly successful career in comedy, during which he'd moved from junior writer to late-night host himself, he'd opened a string of popular nightclubs. Those clubs needed dancers, and dancers needed routines.

"So it's just James going tonight?" I asked, triple confirming. I didn't care if James brought his poodle, if he had one. As long as Brent wasn't present, I'd be good to go.

"Just James. Besides, he said Brent's not even in town. He's in the Caribbean or something, and I have a date at nine, so it'll be short and it'll be just the three of us," Colin reassured me as he tugged at his wine-red tie, already close to unknotted.

I rose, walking to him. "Stop it," I said, tsking my brother gently. "You always do that."

"Do what?"

"Tug at your tie."

He scoffed. "I hate these stupid things."

"Then why do you wear one?"

Colin shrugged and ran a hand through his dark, nearly black, hair. "It's expected," he grumbled, as I straightened the knot. "I swear sometimes you treat me like I'm still the baby of the family."

"You always will be," I said with a grin, as I finished the task and held up five fingers. "You're five minutes younger than I am."

"Thanks, as always, for the reminder. Anyway, James wants to meet you, since you're the face of the company. You're the star."

I stretched my neck from side to side. "I'm absolutely not a star," I said, though I'd once wanted to be the one on stage, dancing for audiences. "Does this investor guy know it's me though?"

Colin arched an eyebrow. "As in, does he think he's contracting entertainment services from Shay Sloan, or from the woman who's the object of Brent's desire in 'King Schmuck,' one of the most popular viral videos in the last year?"

At the mention of the video, I rolled my eyes and walked to the other side of the room to grab my water bottle. "I presume he knows the first," I said, taking a sip. "How about the second?"

Colin laughed. "I'm guessing no. Ironic, huh? Brent has no clue you've been under his nose all these years."

"I had no clue he was here either, until you started talking to his business guy. I didn't go looking him up," I said, though that wasn't true at first. For the first few awful months after we'd split, I'd googled Brent nearly every day. Devastated in too many ways, hungry for breadcrumbs, I'd gobbled up each and every bit of information I could find, reading posts here and there in the entertainment trades about his show.

But in time, I'd stopped searching for him regularly. What was the point? And eventually, I'd stopped looking him up.

Then earlier this year, the *"King Schmuck"* video had surfaced, making the rounds online and catching Colin's eye. He showed me some of it too—a bit of Brent at a comedy club talking about Facebook-stalking his college girlfriend who he let get away, then getting busted for said stalking in the middle of a business meeting.

But I was secretly delighted in the wild-goose chase he'd taken himself on via Facebook. He might have found Shannon Paige-Prince and been checking out her profile, but I wasn't that person anymore, and I barely maintained that page. I didn't even have the same hair color.

That was the real King Schmuckery.

Take that, Brent Nichols.

I didn't maintain any profile, because I didn't want to be known, or to be found. I preferred my new name and my new life—and living it off the internet.

"Anyway, *Shay*." My twin brother lingered on my business name, mocking me playfully as he said it. "The guy you hate won't be there."

"I don't hate Brent," I said quickly. But maybe I did? After all, I hated that he didn't fight for me. I hated that I wasn't enough for him. I hated that I'd lost once again.

"And no, I didn't tell James you were engaged to King Schmuck back in college." But even those words and the weight of our promise—*engaged*—seemed like a terrible understatement of what we'd shared. We'd been everything to each other. "It's not germane to the business deal we're striking. It's a private matter. Like other things that are private."

"Other things," I echoed, and those things mattered deeply to the four of us siblings— matters of privacy.

"Then let's go to this meeting tonight and seal the deal to bring the hottest dance show around to the hottest clubs worldwide," he said, holding up his fist.

I bumped my fist to his. "See you in three hours."

As I left the offices and headed to my nearby home, I drove past a billboard of the Wynn, the place that had put Shay Productions on the map three years ago when

I'd choreographed a sultry extravaganza of the senses for the theater housed inside that upscale hotel. That production had enabled me to quickly build my business, to take my choreography well beyond one stage to worldwide venues.

I turned onto my block, a trendy street not far from the Strip. I drove past the organic breakfast café and the hipster coffee shop, then pulled into the parking lot of my condo. As I locked the car door, I reminded myself that my career had given me freedom and distance from the past. It had let me leave Shannon Paige-Prince and all the pain, scandal, and tragedy that came with that name far behind.

That was a dream come true.

On the way upstairs, I snagged my mail, spotting a familiar postmark that made my stomach twist—that always made my stomach twist. A letter from my mother.

History told me waiting to open it wouldn't make it any easier to read her words. But I didn't think I could handle it right then.

Especially when I turned it over and saw a note also scrawled on the back of the envelope. A plea.

Love you, baby, love you so much. Miss you like crazy. Miss you to the moon and the stars. Come see me soon.

The desperation in it tugged at me.

My stomach roiled, but now was not the time for this letter.

I slapped it on the kitchen table to look at later.

I showered, blow-dried my hair, and applied fresh makeup, twisting my long chestnut locks into a neat updo. I slipped into a sleek black dress that zipped up the side, then into a pair of four-inch red suede shoes with ties that went all the way up my ankles to my calves. Vegas nights could be chilly, so I grabbed a shimmery silver wrap for my shoulders.

I looked the part. I *needed* to look the part. I might not have been the one onstage, but I still looked like a dancer.

Hell, I *still was* a dancer, even if I'd never dance again the way I wanted to.

I'd gotten over the ACL tear in college that had made me change my dream.

I'd gotten over the loss of the pregnancy, the breaking of my heart.

I'd gotten over Brent.

I knew how to get over stuff. I'd done it since I was thirteen, when my father was murdered in the driveway outside my childhood home while I slept.

2

___

BRENT

At one thousand feet, the plane started getting service again, so I tapped the screen on my phone, ready for the barrage of messages to load. Wireless had been down on the return flight from St. Barts, and I was antsy to know what I'd missed. Edge had been expanding rapidly in the last year. My company was like a busy airport with jets lined up, taking off and landing every fifteen minutes.

As the plane dipped closer to the runway in Vegas, the emails loaded onto my phone. I scanned quickly for James's name, since my right-hand man was tasked with keeping me apprised of the latest deals, problems, and opportunities—that was what he'd done since he'd convinced me to jump ship from late-night comedy on TV to the nightclub business a few years back.

Fortunately, the email that awaited was of the opportunity variety.

.   .   .

Meeting tonight with Shay Productions. Should be able to sign them up.

Excellent news.

James had assembled that deal for background dancers in record time—less than one week—while I'd traveled to St. Barts.

The Caribbean club opening had gone so smoothly that I'd returned one day earlier than planned. Hearing that the next deal was falling into place was music to my ears, especially since Edge's expansion into New York had been hitting roadblock after roadblock. I yawned as I began to reply *Good luck*. I hadn't slept in my own bed in ten days, and I was ready to crash.

But I covered my mouth, stifled the yawn, and reminded myself that businesses didn't grow if the CEO made sure he got a good night's sleep. Edge had thrived because I'd burned the midnight oil and kept a laser focus on the company. That included meeting all my business partners when I was in town, and making sure everyone was on the same page.

The second the wheels touched down in the city I called home, I dialed James.

"Hey, where's the meeting?" I asked as we taxied.

"SkyBar at the Waldorf Astoria," James said in his always calm, always on-top-of-everything voice. "You keeping tabs on me?"

"Yes. Of course. I have spies everywhere."

"I'll be on my best behavior."

"I'll warn everyone, then," I joked.

"Yeah, you do that," he said, since we both knew he was as straitlaced as they came.

"Seriously though. I'm going to join you. I know you can handle it on your own, but when I can, I like to meet the people we're doing business with before we sign off."

"That's why you're the boss. I'm sure Shay will appreciate you taking such an interest in those finer details."

"I'm stoked to close this deal soon." That was what I needed—a surefire win.

Soon, I made my way off the plane after grabbing my bag from the overhead and headed down the escalator toward the terminal exit, where my regular driver waited. The black town car zipped along the highway as the sun fell below the horizon, and twenty minutes later, I'd reached home.

After a quick shower that both perked me up and washed off the remnants of cross-country travel, I pulled on jeans and a button-down, adding a tie.

I grabbed my helmet, locked the door, and hopped on my bike. As the engine purred to life, I mentally prepped for the meeting tonight with the dance company.

There'd once been a time when my life was all about dancing. Or rather, one particular woman and the way she moved.

What was Shannon up to these days? Was she still in choreography? Had she moved beyond London? Had she found a boyfriend? A husband?

The thought curdled my stomach and made me gun

the engine and ride faster, the cool evening air whipping past as I drove to the hotel.

I didn't know the answers to those questions.

Once I came up for air after our breakup, I'd tried to track her down. I'd called her. Sent her another email. Even tried calling her brother Michael.

Her number had been disconnected.

Her email bounced back.

Her brother hadn't taken my call.

All I could figure was I'd hurt her too much. I should have fought for her, and I didn't.

Regret, thy name was Brent.

Had she moved on too? And if she had, who kissed her tears away when she received letters that tore her up? Letters she'd once asked me to open? To read?

The notion that someone else was there to do that now was like a fist in the gut.

When I reached the Waldorf Astoria, I kicked her out of my mind once more; said hello to Sean, the valet guy; and headed to the elevator, ready to turn my focus back to business and away from the past.

The sleek metal elevator shot up to the twenty-third floor, and as I checked my phone, I saw I was early for the meeting. When I reached the SkyBar, the hostess greeted me and said that James Foster was already there. Exactly as I'd suspected. James was beyond punctual, and I was grateful every day to have such a steady guy as my lead investor and business partner.

I scanned the bar for the Donald Glover doppel-gänger, who was seated in an oversized red leather chair by the floor-to-ceiling windows that showed off the city. I made my way to James.

"I see you're late as always."

"I see you're full of shit as always." He reached out a hand to shake and welcome me back. "Also, nice tan. Clearly means you spent the whole time slacking," James said as he sat down again, gesturing to the booth on the other side of the table.

"Yep. Drank piña coladas poolside and napped in a hammock."

"Just as I suspected."

I scanned the room for the server. "Maybe I need a daiquiri to bring back those island memories."

"The waitress should be right back. She'd just stopped by before you arrived," James offered.

I gestured to the square bar in the middle of the space. "I'll just grab a drink myself. You want something?"

"Vodka tonic would be terrific."

I threaded my way around the leather chairs and chrome tables to the towering shelf of liquor that framed the bar, then ordered a scotch on the rocks and James's drink too.

"Coming right up," the bartender said.

I drummed my fingertips against the steel countertop as he headed to the other end to pour the drinks. Turning around, I leaned against the bar and stared out the windows, where the entire city stretched far beyond the glass. City of sin. City of secrets. City of endless opportunities. Whatever bout of exhaustion had threatened when I'd landed had vacated the premises. I was wide-awake and energized, ready to sign deals, to grow Edge, to keep on building the business.

Glass clinked against metal, and I turned to grab the drinks and start a tab. A minute later, I had a glass in each hand and was making my way back to the table when I stopped short.

My pulse pounded.

My throat went dry.

The floor tilted and loomed closer. The glass walls zoomed in. I blinked.

I was seeing a mirage. Either that or I'd slipped back in time, because there was no other explanation.

After all those years, there she was, in the flesh. A vision in black and red—and a brunette now. I stared from across the room, trying to process what I was seeing.

Shannon Paige-Prince.

The biggest regret of my life, more stunning than she'd ever been, and she wasn't alone. She was with one of her brothers, and they were both focused on James. Heading for our table.

As she turned in my direction, she looked up and we locked eyes.

The woman who got away.

My drinks slipped from my hands, crashing onto the dark wood floor and shattering.

3

SHANNON

The waitress swooped in quickly with two new drinks.

She was so fast I barely had time to think.

But my ex? He had no problem not only thinking, but *quipping*.

"That answers my question. Those glasses are indeed breakable," Brent said, tapping on his glass as he sat back down with his new drink and raised it in a toast.

James laughed, and the men clinked their glasses. "Good thing you tested it. I was so darn worried," he said, flashing an *isn't it funny that Brent is a glass-dropping klutz* grin. I faked a smile, still shaking in my skin. The entire bar seemed to sway and bob, like a boat on the seas. I dug my fingernails into the leather of the armchair I'd claimed—a necessary stake in the ground because it gave me distance from that man. That man I wasn't supposed to see tonight. Who wasn't supposed to be here. Who'd been just as surprised to see me as I was him. And who was clearly doing a much better job at covering it up than I was, with his little jokes.

Everything was so easy for him.

The man was a master at ad-libbing, at covering up the hole in the routine.

I hated that he had the ability to patch a gaffe so quickly by mocking himself. With that endearingly self-deprecating tone and expression he'd mastered. The one that had worked its way into my heart in mere seconds and made me fall in love with him when we were younger. He was so damn charming when he owned every bit of who he was.

Just a guy navigating the world.

But another part of me was decidedly pleased that he'd been so shocked to see me that he'd dropped the glasses.

"In any case, now that my CEO has finished his quality control inspection of the Waldorf Astoria's glassware, I'd like to introduce everyone," James began, gesturing to my brother and to me. "This is Shay Sloan, the founder and head choreographer for Shay Productions. And her brother, Colin Sloan, a financier who advises Shay Productions. Shay and Colin, allow me to introduce Brent Nichols, who runs Edge."

"Good to meet you. I've heard a lot about you," Colin said, going first, no doubt sensing I'd need a moment to collect myself. He extended a hand to the man he'd met at Christmas the year Brent had proposed. But my twin knew how to cover up the past, and knew intuitively that I'd want him to.

"All good, I hope," Brent said, with a quirk to his lips, though he had to know it couldn't be good. Colin, Ryan, and Michael knew exactly how the engagement with my college love had ended.

They had nothing good to say about the man across from me—the man who was looking far too handsome to be believed. Broader, sturdier, and older. A decade older, and he'd aged well. A line here or there, a crinkle in the corner of his eyes—it all worked. He dragged his hand through his hair, all that dark, soft hair.

I knew how it felt in my hands.

The sensory memory swept through me.

"And—" James began, gesturing to me, but before I could say a word, Brent jumped in.

"Great to meet you, Shay."

I blinked, surprised he went so quickly to my new name, but grateful too. I gave him my best professional smile. "Good to meet you. I wasn't expecting you to be here tonight. But it's a delight." *Delight, my ass.*

"I wasn't expecting you either," he said meaningfully, and James shot Brent a strange look as if to say, *Of course you were.*

When Brent shook my hand, a million things zipped through my body. *Memories, feelings, promises.* He never once took his deep brown eyes off mine as our fingers met. I drew a breath and wished I didn't feel a slight charge in my body from the way his gaze held mine. How could my body betray my heart like this?

"Hi there," he mouthed quietly.

I said nothing as a fluttery sensation spread through me with every breath. For a second, maybe more, we were the only ones there. We lingered on this connection, and the handshake went on longer than it should have. Longer than it should have with a man who broke my heart.

I let go of his hand like it was on fire.

James tilted his head to the side and gestured from Brent to me, curiosity etched in his eyes. "Brent, you've been holding out on me. Do you two know each other?"

Worry gripped me instantly, breaking the moment. Would Brent feel tricked or hoodwinked that I was the face behind Shay Productions? I gulped and parted my lips to answer.

But Brent jumped first. "We both went to school in Boston, I believe. Isn't that right, Shay?"

"Yes," I squeaked, breathing easier. He seemed to be guiding the awkwardness out of the way so neither one of us had to admit how we'd known each other—or how well.

"Yes. I went to the Boston Conservatory," I said, shrugging off my silvery wrap.

"And I was at Boston College. We had friends in common, didn't we, Shay?" he asked with a slight smile, keeping it casual, making it easy for me.

Maybe because he wanted this business deal.

That had to be it.

He was skirting over the past to win a negotiation.

Fine by me. Our past didn't need to play into this partnership, no matter how genuine he'd seemed when he asked how I was.

"We did. It's good to see you again," I said. I hardly knew if that was the truth or a lie.

His eyes never strayed from me, and he lowered his voice, speaking in the barest whisper. "Is it?"

My chest rose and fell, and I didn't know how to answer. How was it possible to be attracted to someone who broke you? Seeing him again stirred up so many memories, not only of the way we fell apart, but of the way I'd leaned on him so much in college, and how he'd been there for me every time. He'd been my rock.

He'd held my hand through all those devastating letters.

Every damn one of them.

I glanced down, adjusted my skirt, and reached for a glass of ice water, the cubes hitting my teeth as I knocked back half the liquid.

"Yes, what a small world."

"Let's get down to business, then," James said, and for a while, Colin and James did most of the talking while Brent leaned back in his chair, crossed his legs, and raked his eyes over me.

What was that about?

He was undressing me again, drinking me in, cataloging my hair, considering my bare shoulders, roaming his eyes over my breasts, landing on my legs.

I had to collect myself. Standing, I grabbed my purse. "Excuse me, gentlemen. I need to powder my nose."

I walked past the hostess stand and around the corner, trying to calm my quickening pulse with steady, measured breaths. I grabbed the handle of the ladies' room door, when a hand came down on my shoulder.

I whirled around, coming face-to-face in the darkened hallway with the man I'd once planned to marry.

"Shannon." My name sounded rough on his lips.

"Brent." I did my best to keep my tone cool.

"How are you?" he asked again, his eyes locked on mine.

After all those years, after all the pain, that was what he asked? How the hell I was? That was what he wanted us to be? Two adults practicing benign civility outside the ladies' room?

"I'm fine." It was better this way. Better to be able to stand near him and manage the basics. Even though the basics were stretching me thin.

"You mean it? You're fine? You're doing okay?" He sounded genuinely concerned. How did he manage this double act?

"I'm great." I was, for all intents and purposes. And what else was I going to say?

He stepped closer. I retreated against the wall, pulse pounding viciously.

"I can't believe it's you. James told me he was talking to Shay. I've heard of your shows. But I never knew you were Shay Sloan. I guess that makes me a world-class idiot. But then, I think we both *know* I'm a world-class idiot."

I sighed, my heart heavy at his words. Was this deal even worth it? "Is this a problem? Is it better if we step aside so you can find another company to work with?"

"Better?" he asked, as if my question didn't compute.

"Yes, would you prefer to work with another dance company?" I asked.

He didn't answer immediately. His eyes were still locked on me. I wanted desperately to look away.

Instead, I noticed every detail. The way he swallowed. The line of his jaw. The intensity in his gaze.

The tension that radiated from him.

My nerves were frayed thin from the battle inside, from the tug-of-war waged between heart and body. I was comprised of two opposing desires. Something soft and needy and desperate in me wanted to throw my arms around him and ask how he'd been and where the years had gone. Something hard and angry and bitter wanted to lift a knee and kick him right in the balls, then slam my fists into his chest and tell him how everything had hurt so goddamn much when he'd stopped fighting for me.

And for our baby.

The baby he didn't know about.

The baby I lost the morning after I went home to Vegas.

Finally, he answered my question. "No, it's not a problem. I want the best for my business. James tells me you're the best."

My business.

Everything was about work back then.

Everything inside me snapped. That tight line of tension was severed. Like when a tightrope is chopped in half and the acrobat tumbles wildly to the ring. I let loose. "Doesn't matter whether you're in comedy or clubs. Glad to see it's still business first," I said harshly, wanting to slice him with words.

I pushed hard on the ladies' room door. But his hand wrapped around my wrist, and he yanked me back, spinning me in one quick move, so I was chest to chest with him. His breath ghosted across the skin of my neck.

"That's not fair," he said.

I fumed.

What gave him the right to say what was fair? Not in love, and not in life. There was no such thing as fair. "You want to talk about fair? Go ahead. Try me. I'll tell you what's not fair. I've got a long list of what's not fair, and it starts with a body in a driveway and keeps on going all the way to a prison in Hawthorne," I said, but before I could say more, he reached for me, wrapping his arms around me, and this time, his touch wasn't sexual. It wasn't lustful. It was an embrace from someone who knew nearly everything about me, and my throat clogged with emotions.

"Are you safe?" he asked in a whisper into my hair. "I'm so sorry. I'm still so sorry about everything that happened to your family. I'm so damn sorry."

A tear had the audacity to slide down my cheek and fall onto his shoulder. It was a Pavlovian reaction. Too many tears had fallen on that shoulder. "Is anyone threatening you? Are you okay?"

"Yes," I said quietly, with a nod, wishing his arms didn't feel so good, so true. "I am. It's fine. It's all fine."

He pulled back, tucked a hand under my chin, and lifted my face. I was so close to him I could trace the outline of his jaw, could run the pad of my finger over his stubble, his unbearably sexy eight-o'clock shadow.

"Are you sure?" he asked, so much tenderness and worry in his tone.

He made all the sense in the world to me, and he made zero sense at the same time.

I gathered myself, and willed that obstinate organ in my chest to stop beating at double time. I ordered my traitorous body to cease trembling just from being near him. "Yes. I'm sure."

He let go and tipped his forehead back to the bar. "I should get out there. They'll start wondering. See you in a few."

And he walked away.

He was always good at walking away.

My head hurt, and I couldn't grasp the situation at all.

I pushed open the ladies' room door, walked to the sink, dropped my hands onto the cool tile, and let out the longest, hardest breath. I hoped to hell this was the only time I'd have to deal with Brent Nichols.

When I was near him like that, I couldn't think straight. I could only feel. And I felt too many emotions. Too many emotions that were far too dangerous for my heart.

There were no two ways about it—I had to leave, and I had to leave right then.

4

———

BRENT

I couldn't let her leave.

Now that she'd reappeared in my life and we were within the same fifty-foot radius, I had to secure time alone with her. Without James. Without Colin.

A few moments outside the restroom weren't enough.

There was too much to say. Too much that had gone unsaid for far too long.

And seeing her reminded me how stupid I'd been, how foolish I'd been to let her go without a fight.

That was the biggest regret of my life.

I'd chosen badly at the end.

Now, I could say all the things I didn't know how to say then.

But I'd need to get her alone to do that.

On my return from the hallway encounter with Shannon, I pressed my fingertips to my temple, weighing my options.

Then I spotted a shimmer of silver on the floor

under the table. A long shot, but it was my best opportunity, so I grabbed the edge of the fabric as James and Colin focused on business matters.

An hour later, the four of us held glasses and raised them high. The deal was done—all that was left was the signing.

"We'll draw up the papers this week, and get this show on the road," James said, then snapped his fingers. "Oh, and Shay, can I get your number too?"

I reined in a grin. He didn't even know he'd just become my wingman and secured the ten digits I had most wanted in the world. As Shannon rattled off her number, James tapped it into his phone, and I repeated it in my head. James looked at his watch. "And on that note, I have a wife waiting for me and a two-year-old who likes for his daddy to say good night to him. And I believe our friend Colin has a date."

I clapped my business partner on the back. "Get the hell out of here. I'll see you tomorrow. I'm going to catch up with Miles over at the bar," I said, gesturing to the baby-faced bartender I knew. "And Colin, I hope the rest of your night goes well too."

"Thank you," Colin said as he stood. Shannon did the same.

"It was great chatting with you. I look forward to the partnership with Shay Productions," I said, extending final handshakes to them both.

"As do I," she said, flashing that same professional smile she'd given me earlier.

As she reached for her purse, my shoulders tensed. I hoped she wouldn't realize what she was missing. But she hadn't noticed all through the meeting, so perhaps she wouldn't notice now.

The three of them left.

Shannon weaved her way through the tables to the exit. The black dress she wore looked as if it had been painted onto her luscious body. Those red shoes, with the crazy crisscross straps, were a beacon, guiding me to where I wanted to be—home.

With her.

Neither my body nor my heart had forgotten Shannon Paige-Prince.

Not one bit.

She turned the corner to the elevator banks, out of sight now. I leaned back in my chair, trying to catch one final look at her. No such luck.

I hated that I had to let her walk away, but if I was going to talk to her again—the way I wanted to—I had to play it smart. After three minutes, I figured she was down the elevator and walking across the lobby, but not yet gone. I texted her.

You left your scarf. Want me to bring it by your office tomorrow, or do you want me to bring it down to you now?

I waited.

She might not respond. She might text me immediately or in the morning. She might simply send a messenger service to pick it up.

My phone buzzed, and I slid open the message. All it said was *Hold onto it for me.*

I stared at the screen for several seconds. What the hell was that? That answer was not in the multiple-choice rubric. I squinted and reread it, as if that would translate her words into a clue as to what might happen next.

Ah, hell. Maybe tonight wasn't the best time to talk to her.

I stood, pushed away from the table, and grabbed the scarf that had been under my leg. If she wanted me to hold onto it, that was what I'd do. I'd figure out how to meet her alone and talk to her without her brothers around. Hell, I could probably benefit from some time to plan what I wanted to say. She was the last person I'd expected to see tonight, so I hadn't scripted my lines. How did you apologize for the kind of idiocy you'd perpetrated when you were twenty-two? I'd been young and selfish—I'd wanted everything that was in front of me. *Hey, Shan. Sorry I didn't hop a plane to London, find you, and tell you I was never going to let you go.*

I went to the bar to close out my tab with Miles and plot my next steps. I should sit down with my good friend Mindy and ask for her advice. Mindy was as solid and straightforward as they came, but she was diplomatic too. She'd guide me through this unexpected reunion.

But when I tucked my credit card into my wallet and

turned around, I came face-to-face with my own lack of planning.

Shannon held out her hand. "My wrap, please," she said, her tone even, her face unreadable. "It's my favorite."

"I didn't think I'd see you again tonight." I clutched the fabric, as if that would tether her to me for longer. It felt like a lifeline as my heart sped up just from being so close to her. The bar was filled with patrons, the tables packed, the stools taken.

"I'd like the wrap," she said crisply, the meaning clear. She only wanted the scarf.

"Have a drink with me, please," I said, opting for honesty first. And serving up the truth. "I'd love to talk to you. There are things I need to say."

Her jaw tightened, ticking. Her green eyes went as hard as stone. "Isn't it kind of late?"

Too late for us? That had to be what she meant, and that wasn't good. But I wasn't above begging.

"Please," I said. Fate had given me an opportunity, and I had to take it.

Had to right the wrongs of the past.

The last time I'd talked to her, I'd failed. I'd sat out a round.

Tonight, I wasn't going to make that same mistake.

"Besides, it's barely nine. Hardly late at all," I added, attempting a joke with a thread of sincerity. Perhaps it wasn't too late for us at all.

She sighed and shook her head. "Listen, I'm sorry I made the comment about comedy or clubs, and your focus being business, but even so, it's been a long day."

I was not going to let her go. "One drink. I just want to talk to you. Tell you things."

She licked her lips and exhaled, but said nothing. In her silence, I sensed an opening. A chance to earn a laugh or two. With complete honesty.

"Fine. Confession time." It was all I had. "I held onto the scarf to see you again. I saw it on the floor, took it, and hid it. I'm a thief, I'll admit it," I said, holding my arms out wide, one hand still gripping the silvery fabric. I wasn't letting go of the only thing I had that she wanted.

She furrowed her brow. "You took my wrap on purpose?"

"Yes. You always left them behind when we were together," I said, stopping briefly when she winced at those words—*when we were together*. "When I spotted it on the floor, I grabbed it when the guys weren't looking, and I hid it. I sat on your scarf." I kept my eyes fixed on her, admitting the full truth even if it made me look like a complete ass.

Her lips quirked almost imperceptibly, but it was enough for me to think that I was gaining ground. I tried to build on it. "It's a nice scarf. Do you think I could pull it off for a meeting tomorrow with my real estate guys?" I tossed it around my neck and adopted a pouty stare.

She rolled her eyes, and I was ready to declare victory. "You're the worst," she said, laughing. "Stop it."

"You don't like the way it looks on me?" I continued, deadpan.

"It looks ridiculous on you, Brent," she said, but she

didn't stop smiling. "And by the way, it's a *wrap*. Not a scarf."

"So . . . you really like this . . . *wrap?*" I asked, as I removed it from my neck.

"I do. I like it so much I came back for it."

I raised an eyebrow. "Only for the wrap?"

"Only for the wrap," she said, enunciating each word, but the hard edge had evaporated. In its place was something . . . almost playful.

"What about a trade, then? Wrap for a drink?" I asked, dangling it in the air, the metallic fabric shimmering under the lights in the bar. Vegas had coasted into nighttime, ushering in all the possibilities of the town, all its risks, all its opportunities. I held up the long scrap of material, my whole body poised on the edge of something. "You'll notice I used the proper name this time. *Wrap.*"

I handed it over. Whatever she decided next had to come from her, not from me holding a piece of her wardrobe hostage.

Time slowed to a crawl as she held my gaze, her green eyes giving nothing away. The straight line of her lush red lips revealed no hint of her intent. Perhaps she was toying with me. Torturing me. I probably deserved it.

I definitely deserved it.

She raised a finger. "One drink."

I could breathe again. I'd been granted a reprieve. And I was taking it.

I guided her to a quiet table near the corner of the SkyBar, with the city spread out far below us. She sat first, and I was torn between trying not to stare, and watching every move she made. But I'd never been good at looking away from her, and now was not the time to learn new tricks. She crossed her legs, one bare-skinned calf sliding against the other. My breath hitched. *Those legs.* Those gorgeous, sexy legs. They were my downfall, my weakness, and my complete obsession. They were an altar I'd pray at. I'd spent countless hours caressing them, touching them, and tasting them. If I were an artist, I'd have drawn them over and over. I hadn't been able to keep my hands off them when we were together. I hardly knew how to keep my hands to myself now.

"So," I said, breaking the silence between us as I tore my gaze back to her eyes. "You've done well for yourself."

I hated that we were talking like any other man and woman without a history, but I sensed she was something of a wary animal around me, and she needed to be coaxed out of the corner.

She nodded. "Thank you. It's been quite rewarding building the business."

"It's very impressive what you've done with your company." I had half a mind to kick myself as soon as I said it. What I wouldn't give to turn this conversation around to something that mattered. But I was going in cold, navigating without a road map and hoping I wouldn't crash.

"Can I get you something?"

The waitress had materialized at our side, giving me some breathing room. "We have some fantastic cock-tails," she said, then waxed on about several concoctions. Shannon opted for the house martini and I ordered a whiskey. As the waitress walked away, Shannon folded her hands across her lap, shooting me another closed-mouth smile. "And you're doing great too. I'm so pleased that Edge is faring well."

"It is," I said.

Shit. This was not how I'd wanted to spend time with her. It was so fucking formal. So immensely fake. So not us. But I didn't know how to steer the conversation out of this pothole.

But she knew how. She did it, veering back to the question she'd slung my way outside the bathroom door. One I knew I'd have to answer. "How did you decide to switch to a whole new business? You were pretty committed to comedy way back when," she said, a note of restraint in her voice, but her curiosity evident too.

Her keen interest made perfect sense. My job had been a wedge that drove us apart.

"The show was canceled. The show's creator had a huge falling out with the network, so he pulled the plug when the contract ended."

"And that was it? You jumped to nightclubs?"

"I was looking for something new, but truth be told, the jobs in comedy weren't that stable long-term. James came to me with this opportunity, and I saw a chance to mix both comedy and clubs. Some of our clubs host comedy acts in the late afternoon and early evening. Turned out that was a void in the entertainment world, so I filled it. And sometimes I moonlight. Do stand-up once or twice a month at my venues."

She nodded, like she was taking in all this new intel. "You loved performing. Is that enough to satisfy your comedic thirst?"

"Yes," I said, smiling. "I had a good run, but this situation works for me now. And the occasional gig is enough. That's when I did the King Schmuck bit. I don't know if you saw that one online," I said, because it was better to get that out in the open.

"Hmm." She looked up at the ceiling as if she was trying to recall, then shook her head. "Doesn't ring a bell. I must have missed it. But I've been pretty busy too, and I don't spend much time on the internet."

Soon, the waitress returned with our drinks, and Shannon raised her glass in a toast. "To business."

"To reunions."

I knocked back half my drink, letting the burn fuel me.

Screw this small talk. I didn't want to be polite with her. I wanted to *know* her. To understand why she'd never picked up the phone when I called in those first few weeks, why she'd been so hard to find, and why she'd changed her name. I scooted closer. "Shan, I'm sorry I didn't try harder."

She blinked, like I was speaking Portuguese. "What?"

"Try harder," I repeated, reminding her.

She narrowed her brow. "Why would you have tried harder?"

"Why wouldn't I? That's what I should have done," I said emphatically, owning it.

She shrugged nonchalantly. "You were busy."

"With work, yes, but that was no excuse," I said, trying to lay it on the line with her.

I squeezed her thigh. "I know. And not a day goes by that I don't regret it."

"I need to go." Her voice quavered, but her words cut me like knives.

She walked out.

This time I let her.

Because now was not the time to say any more of my piece.

5

SHANNON

I marched into the gym. I was one of only two women in this place, and the only one wearing heels. But there was one person I needed to see. The person I relied on most in the universe.

Ever disciplined, Michael was exactly where he usually was at ten thirty at night—lifting weights, after having logged an hour on the cardio machine. Michael owned a security conglomerate and ran it with our brother Ryan. Michael arrived at the office at eight every morning after his five-mile run, worked a full day, then headed to the gym nearly every night for a second workout. Call him a workaholic. Call him an athlete. Call him a machine. He was all of that, and he was also the moral compass of our foursome.

The eldest of us siblings, he'd been our rock.

And right then, I needed my rock.

He hoisted the barbell high above his chest with a measured exhale. A few feet over, a beefy guy in a muscle tank grunted as he raised his weights then dropped them in a loud clang on the floor. With pinpoint precision, Michael lowered the bar to his chest, inch by inch, then pushed up again, setting it down on the metal holder the second he saw me.

He sat up straight as I parked myself on the end of the bench.

"What's going on?" His voice was etched with concern.

I shook.

My shoulders quaked.

My breath came fast.

Michael wrapped me in a hug. "What is it, Shan?"

I was choking with memories, with mistakes, with regret.

I told him everything. What Brent said. How he apologized.

The entire night.

When I was done, Michael scrubbed a hand across his face, took a beat, measuring his words. "But here's the thing. You two were falling apart," he said, reminding me with a controlled breath of what had been happening ten years ago.

"I know," I said in a tiny voice, my head lowered, my hair falling in a curtain around my face. I'd unclipped my French twist on the drive here, gunning the gas and blasting pop music to drown out my thoughts as I sped along the highway, putting distance between Brent and myself.

But really, the space I needed was between my own assumptions and the person I wanted to be. A person who should be in control of her emotions, of her feelings, and of her hasty reactions.

"But does it change the score?" Michael asked. "Does it change what happened during the seven months after college and before that night? Does it change what happened the next morning after you came to my place? Does it change the fact that he didn't fight to win you back? He's a man. That was his job. Win his woman. Not ask to see her again in a year." Michael was emphatic. This was black and white to him.

I drew in a deep breath, trying to make sense of all this new information that had tipped my world upside down, that had changed ancient heartbreak into a fresh new round of remorse. "Was it?"

Michael nodded vigorously. "He never should have let you get away."

"But what about me? Didn't I let him get away too?" I asked, needing to hear it from him.

He stroked his chin as if deep in thought. "Let's see. You were both twenty-two. You were fresh out of college. You were young and in love and living six thousand miles apart. I'd say the cards were not in your favor and the deck was stacked against you."

"But what about now? I walked out tonight," I said, my chest tightening. "After Brent and I talked. I just left, and we're doing business together."

Michael's eyes darkened momentarily. "Then you go see him tomorrow." He pointed at me as he spoke in that gentle but authoritative tone he had. "And you be businesslike. You be a professional. Be a Sloan."

"A Sloan," I repeated.

That was who I was.

I'd taken my cues from Michael. We all had. He'd been the first among us to change his last name to Sloan, and had suggested we all do the same. Sloan was an everyman name. It had no history, no notoriety. We could slip easily through this town and live free of all those questions from people who remembered who we had been long ago. With new names, our old life had faded away, receding far into the rearview mirror.

My brothers and I had risen above our roots. As the Paige-Prince kids, we'd grown up lower-class and hadn't known anything beyond the outskirts of our dangerous Vegas neighborhood. Now, we were better than that. We'd refashioned ourselves into upstanding citizens, business owners, successful adults. We were the restrained, sophisticated, successful Sloans.

And the four of us had resolved to deserve our good name.

To earn it.

To live up to it every day.

In our father's memory.

We might not carry on his name, but with our new name, we had vowed to carry on his love, his grace, his strength.

I had to be strong.

I had to behave like a Sloan.

And Sloans did not walk out of business deals because of emotions. "I'll see him tomorrow," I said, giving myself a pep talk. "Let him know the deal is on. I'll say I'm sorry I walked out like that."

He rubbed my back. "You've got this. Now, call me

tomorrow," he said, pinning me with wide blue eyes until I nodded.

"I will report back," I said with a crisp salute, then hugged him goodbye, feeling more centered and calmer than when I'd pulled into the gym.

But as I drove the final blocks home, that feeling vanished and a deep shame washed over me.

I couldn't believe I'd simply walked away.

I parked and walked into my condo.

My gaze landed on the picture frame on my kitchen counter. An image of sunflowers. I brushed it lightly with my fingertips, whispering, *"Miss you, Daddy."* Then I slumped into a chair at my kitchen table and untied the crisscross straps of my heels, heaving a sigh as I dropped one red suede shoe on the cool tiled floor.

I let the memories of my one great love affair come back to me. Memories of the man I'd adored. The man I was still wildly attracted to.

Wanting him was easy. Wanting him felt good.

When I was younger, Brent was my good drug—one hit and he'd washed away all my troubles.

He'd been the only thing that had felt good after far too long spent feeling nothing but bad. Nothing but the black mark of my family that trailed behind me all through my teenage years. Nothing but being one of the Paige-Prince kids.

Before him, I'd only had dance and my brothers, and they'd been amazing, but they hadn't been enough. Then Brent came into my life, and I had something pure and unsullied by the cold, cruel world. He was my sexy, sinful addiction, and I rationalized that it was much healthier to need him than the bottle or a needle.

But it wasn't just the sex that had burned brightly between us. It was everything. He'd made me laugh, he'd made me smile, and he'd brought me so much happiness. I hadn't been close to anyone like him since.

While I hadn't turned into a nun when we'd split, I hadn't been busy fornicating during the last ten years either. My list of lovers was remarkably short—no one had compared to Brent because no one *could* compare to him.

I'd spent the last decade mostly alone. I'd had dates here and there, and a few longer-term relationships. But sex and love residing in the same person? That had happened to me once in my life, and it had been with the man I'd wanted to go home with tonight. That moment in the hallway had reminded me of how much I'd needed him, relied on him, and *healed* because of him. And how I'd cratered when we fell apart.

Our end was like punching a hole in my chest. It was like turning off my gravity.

I stood and removed the silvery wrap. I was tempted to bring it to my nose, to catch a final trailing scent of that man who still affected me.

I resisted, letting it drop on the chair.

I walked into my bathroom, washed my hands and face, brushed my teeth, then stripped off the rest of my clothes.

But I couldn't stop thinking of Brent.

Seeing him brought everything to the surface.

* * *

The next morning, I headed into the kitchen, still unmoored.

I needed something to get my mind off Brent for a little while.

I spotted the mail I'd brought in yesterday. On the top of the pile was the letter from my mother. I picked up the white envelope. It bore the same return address my mother had had since I was fourteen.

Dora Prince

Inmate #347-921

The Stella McLaren Federal Women's Correctional Center Hawthorne, Nevada

Might as well get this out of the way. Better to read it now and put the past behind me, then focus on the day ahead.

I took a deep, fueling breath, steeling myself for the latest round of unstable, needy, borderline insane words. With a hard stone residing in my gut, I pushed my finger under the flap and ripped it open. I took out the letter and unfolded the lined paper, girding myself for what lay on the page.

Baby,

. . .

How are you? How are your dance shows? Are your dancers as talented as you were? Sometimes at night when it's quiet and everyone's asleep, I close my eyes, and I swear I can see you onstage, with a smile so bright you light up the whole recital hall, like you did when you were my little girl in her candy-pink tutu, doing your pirouettes.

I know it's different now, but in my mind, you're still dancing. You'll always be dancing. Just like someday I'll be free. You'll get your knee fixed, and I'll get out of here, and life will be as it should again.

That's what I hold on to when it gets all dark and black in my head, because I swear, it gets darker every day. It's been almost eighteen years now in here, and the light is fading. I thought I'd be out of here. That they'd see I didn't do it. I didn't. I swear. I wish someone would find the people who did.

Can you come see me again and help me, please? I'm not that far away. It's less than a five-hour drive. I had my visiting hours cut—I'll explain why when I see you in person—but they can't take away my rights. The law allows me four hours per month, and they're granting me two to see family on June 30th. You are my family, baby. See me. See me. See me. I'll write to you for a thousand years if I have to. I swear, baby girl, I swear.

. . .

Help me.

Your loving mommy

Years of practice didn't ease the heavy knot in my gut. Letter after countless letter didn't make the words hurt less. Every note I read was a piece of my flesh being sliced open.

You couldn't hide from that kind of hurt, I'd learned. You just had to let it bleed, and hope it didn't bleed out what was left of your heart.

Folding up the letter, I slid it back into the envelope, then tucked it away in a kitchen cupboard.

I was half her, but I was half my dad too.

And today, I had to act like my father's daughter.

I had to be stronger.

I wasn't the twenty-two-year-old pregnant, emotional woman worn down by a relationship that was no longer working.

I'd remade myself. I'd shrugged off who I used to be. I'd risen anew from the ashes of my family.

From my mother, who had killed my father in cold blood.

But some days, I wasn't so sure if I could ever outrun my history.

The past kept coming back.

And now, the past was in my present.

I had to do what I had to do.

Go see Brent again, and do it like a Sloan.

6

BRENT

As we waited to be seated at breakfast, Mindy shot me the most sympathetic look in the history of such looks. The sound of early-morning slots soundtracked her *Oh, that sucks* as I gave her the SparkNotes of last night's tale of misunderstandings and mistakes.

She offered up a smile. "On the bright side, at least you didn't put your foot in your mouth last night."

I plastered on a grin. "Gee. I'm super grateful for that."

"Well, it's something you've been known to do," she said as the hostess at the Wynn's breakfast café walked over to us.

"Right this way," the hostess said. "We've got your regular table for you, Mindy."

That comment eased some of the overhang of what-the-hell-do-I-do-now that I was facing. "You're royalty here," I whispered to my friend. "The security chief who's treated like a queen."

"My tiara will arrive any day."

"Along with a scepter," I added.

The hostess led us to a green upholstered booth in the classy breakfast spot in the middle of the hotel on the Strip. A former soldier, Mindy ran security at the Wynn. She was also one of my closest friends, and we'd been buddies since high school. When she'd lost her fiancé in Afghanistan, I did all I could to be a shoulder for her to lean on, like she's always been for me.

The hostess handed her a menu, but she waved it off with a smile. "Don't you know I have it all memorized by now?" Mindy grinned, tapping the side of her head.

"Of course you do. I'll send the server over shortly to take your order," the hostess said with a smile, and handed me a menu.

I rolled my eyes. "Like I said, royalty."

"And today, I will be your royal advisor," she said, returning to her shoulder-to-lean-on mode.

My confidante on all matters related to Shannon, Mindy had been briefed chapter and verse from the start. She knew the good, the bad, and the ugly. She'd helped me pick the diamond for the ring when I was getting ready to propose in college. She knew, too, about the breakup. She'd encouraged me then to try to make it right. But Shannon's phone had been disconnected, and she hadn't returned my emails.

And I wasn't going to let Shannon wriggle away again.

"Good. Because I need a royal decree or something telling me what to do next. I've got nothing," I said, laying myself bare. "I've been racking my brain all night and all morning, and I don't know where to start with her. But I want to, Min. God, how I want to. Seeing her again was a reminder that letting her go was a colossal mistake. And how the hell do I fix it? I don't have a clue."

"That's because everything comes easy to you, Mr. Lucky," she said, and I couldn't argue there. Great family, great parents, great job. The only glaring misfortune was losing Shannon.

Still, I said, "I'm a lucky cat."

"Exactly. You're happy and healthy and you have some kind of Midas touch with your business."

"Sorry, not sorry. But what does that have to do with the Shannon situation?"

"A lot, actually. Your charmed life is the kind everyone longs for. But it's also why you're coming up empty. You've never had to fight too hard for anything. It's not a character assassination. It's just true," she said, her light-blue eyes kind and honest.

"I get it. And I get that's not often the case," I said.

"It's not." Mindy knew loss; she knew pain. "But don't worry. I can help you. Pick your breakfast, and then we'll get started."

When the server swung by with coffee, we ordered, then I locked eyes with Mindy. "So, swami, tell me what to do."

She set her hands on the table, folding them. "I'm not even going to say you need to apologize. Because you need to do more than apologize. You need to prove yourself."

"And how do I do that?" I let out a long, deep, frustrated stream of air. "I don't even know if she wants to talk to me."

"Here's the deal," she said as she poured a white packet of sugar into her mug. "You have two things you need to do. One, you need to remind her how good you were together. And two, show her you're serious now. Show her you won't give up. Show her you're the kind of man a woman like her needs."

I wiped my hand across my brow. "That's all? That's a piece of cake." Then I turned serious. "Okay. Lay it on me. How do I show her I can be the man she needs?"

She laughed softly. "There's no formula. Look for signs—do you think you affected her in any way last night?"

I raised an eyebrow, a burst of confidence speeding through me as I remembered the way Shannon had shuddered in my arms last night. "I think I did," I said with a wide grin. "She didn't seem to mind when I wrapped my arms around her."

She rolled her eyes. "Well, there you go. Just keep hugging her, Brent. See where that gets you."

"You're saying I need more than hugs?" I joked.

"Call it a long shot, but hey, maybe start with the basics. Like an apology."

"Ten-four, but how exactly do I apologize for making the dumbest mistake of my life? Because that's what letting her get away was."

She pointed at me, her eyes lighting up. "That," she said excitedly. "What you just did. Say that. That would be a good start. Let her know in a way that will show her you're being completely honest." She took a sip of her coffee. A minute later the food arrived, and Mindy flashed a bright smile. "And maybe get her a gift too, King Schmuck."

The answer hit me.

* * *

After I finished my scrambled eggs and toast, and downed a hearty dose of coffee for fuel, I headed to my next meeting at the Luxe. Once there, I made a quick detour into a boutique inside the hotel.

I scanned the shop quickly, spotting in seconds something that would be perfect for Shannon. She wasn't a flowers-and-chocolate kind of woman. And while I doubted a material object would be enough for the mea culpa I needed to pull off, I had to start somewhere. I wasn't going to wait in my office and stare dreamy-eyed at my phone, wishing for a call. No, I was going to do everything I'd failed to do years ago.

There was no way on earth, no way in heaven or hell, that I would let the woman I wanted slip away from me again.

I had the opportunity for a second chance. The game was on, and I was going balls to the wall to win my woman back.

* * *

As the meeting with our real estate team drew to a close, I was eager to burst out the door and turn on my phone. To call her. Ask her to get together. If that didn't work, I'd head to her office and begin the grovel fest. I'd make my first apology. I'd probably have ten thousand more to make, but if that was what it took, I'd do it. I was heading to New York tomorrow to deal with the hurdles Edge faced there, so I had to move fast.

"That's the plan for the next six months now that we've got Shay Productions on board with its dance shows. And that's what we need from you as we expand overseas," James said as he shut his leather folder and laid his pen on the conference room table with gusto.

"Love it," said Tate, the lead real estate attorney, who was tasked with handling our deals for new facilities. "I've got some properties in mind. Let me scope them out and we'll reconvene in two weeks."

As we weaved through the casino on our way out of the meeting and over to Edge, James lowered his voice. "What was the deal with you and Shay last night?"

I turned to him and shot him a curious look. "What do you mean?"

"Just seemed like there was some vibe between you two."

I shook my head, cutting that conversation off at the knees. Shannon was a private woman. She clearly wanted her carefully constructed present identity kept secret. My first step in proving I could be the man she needed would be to protect who she was.

"Like I said, I knew her vaguely in college," I said, giving nothing more away as we reached the front door to our flagship club on the property of the Luxe Hotel.

Edge was quiet now in the late morning, since it didn't open until five. Much later, there would be a line snaking along the velvet rope by the brushed steel exterior wall. The purple sign bearing the club's name in crisp, clean letters would be bright and beckoning, calling out to the clubgoers of Vegas who were eager to party, to lounge, to dance, to drink, to be treated to bottle service from gorgeous bartenders, and to move and sway. To celebrate pending marriages, weekends away, or just nights on the town.

"Maybe you'll get to know her better now," James said. "Because there she is."

As I turned the corner, Shannon was waiting by the front door of Edge.

7

SHANNON

I surveyed Edge to ground myself. Clubs had a different energy during the day. No music played. The lights were bright, shining in every corner. I felt as if I were wandering backstage and peering at all the pulleys and levers, sets and costumes that made a Broadway show go round. Because there were no smoke and mirrors now. Those would only come with an audience or a crowd in the evening.

Even with the lights switched on, Edge still possessed the sleek sensuality it was known for, with its silver bar, low divans, gauzy curtains, and rich colors—colors of desire, like wine reds and deep purples.

My footsteps echoed across the black tiled floor that would be lit up tonight, illuminated by rays of smoky light from the ceiling, by crescents of blue from the stage, by shimmery gold beams.

The click of my high heels punctuated the strained silence between the two of us, James having left us for a prior engagement.

I rehearsed the words in my head—why I'd come to see him.

I had to be smarter this time around. I had to be careful so I wouldn't misstep again. So I wouldn't let emotions get the better of me, like I'd done for so many reasons so many years ago.

Drawing a breath, I spun around then smiled. This was a start with my new business partner.

He grinned back, and hell, did that ever make my heart flutter.

"It's like seeing how a magician pulls off a card trick," I said, gesturing around the empty space.

"Speaking of, I've been working on card tricks. I'll have to show you some of them."

"You do card tricks now?" I asked with a note of delight in my voice, because I could picture it. It seemed like his style. He'd always loved cards and had played in poker games at school. I could see him brandishing a deck with a "now you see it, now you don't" sweep of his hands.

"I'm not going to give Copperfield a run for his money. But yeah, I can do some basic stuff."

He took a few steps to the bar and rooted around, finding a deck easily.

"Pick a card, any card."

I ran my fingertips along the top of the deck, settling on the ace of diamonds.

A few cuts of the deck later, he brandished it.

I clapped, pleased as a kid at a birthday party. As he put the deck away, I sneaked a peek once more at the man with me—so much taller, so much bigger than my small frame. My eyes definitely hadn't been playing tricks on me last night. He was still devastatingly handsome, looking sharp again today in jeans and a navy-blue button-down. The shirt was untucked, and with the cuffs rolled up, his strong forearms were revealed, along with some of the ink he'd gotten in college. I'd gone with him to get his first tattoo, the black sunburst just above his wrist. I'd joked that it fit his "sunny disposition," and he'd promptly scowled and glowered. But then he'd draped an arm around me and flashed me his winning smile.

The one he was giving me now.

"Can I get you something, Shan? Water? Soda? Wait." He held up a stop sign hand. "Do you want me to call you Shay?"

I shook my head. "When it's just you and me, Shan is fine."

"Shan it is, then. For you and me," he repeated, like those words were a delicacy.

"And I'll take a Diet Coke."

"Coming right up," he said as he walked behind the silver bar. A small red gift bag was on the counter, as well as the usual accouterments of cocktail napkins and straws.

I took a seat at the bar, while he poured a soda from the tap. He handed me the glass. "I'm not a bartender. I just play one on TV," he said, imitating the deep tones of a TV announcer. I smiled.

I downed some of the soda. I'd never been so grateful for a sip of Diet Coke before. It quenched my thirst and gave me some newfound courage to own up to my actions last night—walking away. I held the glass in one hand and parted my lips to speak. But he was already talking as he rounded the bar to stand next to me.

"Shannon," he said, his voice intensely serious, his deep brown eyes focused on me. "I need to apologize for so many things. And first, I need to apologize for letting you get away. I need to say I'm sorry for not trying harder. Hell, I should have flown to London and found you and wrapped you in my arms."

I froze, my fingers gripping the glass. All the words I'd wanted to hear years ago. My heart caught in my throat.

I wanted to bathe in those words.

Roll around in them.

But I was here to right my own wrong. I shook my head. "I came to say I'm sorry too. I shouldn't have walked away last night. I shouldn't have cut our drinks short and taken off like that." I put down my glass then fidgeted with a silver bracelet on my wrist. "That was unprofessional. You're a business partner now, and I hope you'll still be one."

He tilted his head, then laughed. "Yeah, I need to tell you—I never thought you walking away would change the deal. I hope that doesn't make me cocky, but it's the truth. I figured your feelings for me and for the deal were separate."

"They are." I let out a long, exaggerated breath. "Also, whew. Glad to hear that."

"But I'm glad you felt the need to come back," he said, a wry grin on his face.

"You are?"

"I could tell you needed some time and space last night, but I'm glad you're here, and I'd love to keep talking."

A smile tugged at my lips.

Talking.

It seemed so normal.

Maybe necessary too, after the way we didn't talk for years.

Talking and touching—that was who we were back in the day.

Now, we could do *one* of those things.

Talking sounded like the right idea.

There were things I wanted to tell him about, things I wanted him to know. But today was not the day to serve up that terribly sad story.

There would be time.

I took a breath to center myself, then looked in his eyes. "I'd love to talk, Brent."

"Good. Let's start with clothes." He lifted a hand, lightly fingering the strap of my silky black tank top. "What do we call this? A shirt? A tank?"

I laughed. "Top will do," I said, enjoying the way one little touch sent heat scampering across my bare skin.

"Excellent. Then I have something for you, and I think it'll go with this top," he added, a glint in his eyes. "I wanted to give you something."

He reached for the bag on the counter. "I picked this up this morning. Dropped it off here before my meeting," he said, handing me the shiny red shopping bag with slim handles. My heart beat faster. He had always given me little things when we were together. Pretty postcards of London, Paris, Vienna, and all the places I wanted to go someday. A song I'd heard at a coffee shop and wanted to listen to on my computer. A mini lemon cupcake, for when I permitted myself little treats.

I opened the bag, rustled around in the tissue paper, and pulled out a thin blush-pink silk scarf. I didn't even try to contain my smile. "This one's a scarf," I said playfully.

"And I bet it looks as amazing on you as the wrap did. I also thought if you wanted to leave it behind, I can steal it again, so I can say 'I'm sorry' another time. I'll say 'I'm sorry' ten thousand times if I have to."

But I had to apologize too. "I'm sorry too. I should have tried harder too."

"Yes and no," he said, his eyes locked with mine. "Because I was caught up in work. That was the bigger issue. I couldn't figure out how to make us work. You were trying harder. You were shouldering the weight of us. And you were willing to bend to my schedule."

There's some truth to his words. He'd canceled three trips, and I'd offered to come see him instead, but he couldn't fit me in. But now isn't the time to pile on the guilt. "It was hard for both of us," I said diplomatically. "We were both at our wit's end, trying to make it work."

He blew out a long stream of air. "I wish I had tried harder. That's what I'm most sorry for. And I know this scarf doesn't even begin to cover up all my regrets, so I hope you'll take it in the spirit I've given it. I thought it was pretty, and I thought it would look good on you.

But then, everything looks good on you," he said, his eyes never straying from mine.

Picking up the scarf, I tossed it around my neck, striking a pose. I was flirting, and surely I shouldn't be. But it was so easy, so familiar to play like this with him. And it felt so good, even just for a moment.

"Thank you. I love it," I said, stroking the fabric. His breath hitched as I touched it, and I let go quickly, reaching for the glass of Diet Coke and taking another sip. My hands felt unsteady. I looked at him again. He was shifting back and forth on his heels.

"But, Shan, that's not all I have to say. That just barely scratches the surface," he said, holding my gaze. "You know I never talked about the specifics of our relationship when I was doing stand-up in college." His voice was stripped bare, the way he'd always talked to me when he wanted me to know he was serious. I trusted that voice, and I remembered the promise he'd made to keep the details of our private life out of his comedy. So I'd never be that girlfriend a comedian used as the butt of a joke in his routines. "That remains the case. But there was one bit I did, and I suppose I always hoped you would see it. I did it so you might see it. But you told me last night you never did, and I'd really like to show you a small part because I think this says everything I want to start to say. Will you watch it?"

I gulped and nodded. I didn't push back like I had when Colin had first wanted to show me the video. I didn't resist. Maybe that made me a fool, or maybe it just made me ready. Four million others had seen it, but

I was the only one who'd watch it as the intended viewer.

"Show it to me," I said, my voice soft, nerves trickling through it. He dug into his pocket for his phone. I wasn't sure what to expect, but I was incapable of staying away from Brent, not when he showed this sweet, tender, loving side. I'd come here only to apologize, never expecting he'd feel the need to do so too. But now that he'd begun his apology, I wanted all of it. Craved it.

I leaned against the bar as the clip began—the part I'd seen about Facebook-stalking his college girlfriend.

The on-screen Brent tapped his chest, the look on his face one of utter disdain for his own antics. "Ever done that with your college girlfriend? Searched for her on Facebook? I did that. Spent a ton of hours trying to figure out what she was up to. Translation—is she still hot and gorgeous, and did she marry some other guy?" He paused, shook his head. "Because I'm the guy who still pines for his college girlfriend."

A rush of heat spread across my chest at those words. Meaningless words, but still, the compliment thrilled me, and I turned to him. He was watching me, cataloging my reaction. I returned my focus to the phone, more interested now in on-screen Brent.

"But in my defense, if you saw her, you'd pine too. She was . . ." He stopped walking, stopped talking, and for the briefest of moments, he was not onstage—he was lost in time, it seemed. The next word seemed to fall from his lips with regret and wistfulness. "Perfection. She was perfection. She was the one."

I brought my hand to my mouth, covering my trembling lower lip. I sucked in my breath, holding in all that I felt, the overwhelming rush of emotions. It was just a comedy routine. He was great onstage, even when poking fun at himself. But even so, I was flooded with so much possibility at the way he talked about me.

When I'd originally watched the first half of the video, I'd wanted to reach my hands through the screen and throttle him.

Now, I wanted to squeeze my own heart for the stupid way it dared to beat the tiniest bit faster when he'd said *perfection*.

Because I was where I'd always wanted to be—believing him.

Believing in the man I'd loved.

My throat tightened.

Silence cloaked us both. I stared at the screen, not quite ready to meet his eyes, too afraid of what I'd see. I'd only come here to clear the air for our business deal, and now I was spun back in time, feeling so many things again.

Lust. Desire. Sadness. Hope too. So much hope.

Without looking up, I asked quietly, "What part?"

"What do you mean—what part?"

"What part did you want me to see?" I asked, keeping my voice steady so I wouldn't reveal the cascade of emotions waterfalling through my chest.

I kept my head down. If I looked in his eyes, I'd lose myself. I'd lose my center. I'd lose every ounce of strength I'd relied on during the last ten years.

His voice was a confession. "*She was perfection . . . She*

was the one." Then his fingertips brushed against my wrist. I lifted my face and looked at him. His eyes were serious. I believed him, just like I believed in my body.

I'd always listened to my body, had always been deeply in tune with its wishes and wants.

Since I was four years old, I had wanted nothing more than to dance. I had danced every day, harder, faster, better, until I was at the top of my game, and then I tore my ACL one day during a rehearsal. But still, I remained a physical woman. And now, my body and my heart wanted the same damn thing.

"You know what else you used to say was perfection?" I asked.

He nodded. "I absolutely do."

8

BRENT

Perfection.

That was how I'd always described kissing her.

That was what I said to her after our lips met.

Now, she slid off the stool, into my space.

Exactly where I wanted her.

Neither one of us said a word. Her green eyes were dark and intense. Her lips were so close. The inches between us were swallowed whole by the connection that crackled hot. She seemed to sway closer, and I moved in, seizing the moment.

I lifted my hand to her hair, pulled back in a messy bun, different from the shade she'd had when I knew her, but beautiful just the same. A strand had fallen loose, chestnut brown and curled. I touched it, ran my finger across the single lock. Time melted away as I leaned into the familiar crook of her neck. The craving for her ran so damn deep it lived inside my bones.

I inhaled her, that honey scent, a new smell that imprinted on me in an instant.

"Shan," I whispered, rough and gravelly, filled with so much want for her, which had built over the years, grown higher, spread farther, formed roots. Inhabited me. I was desperate to have her in my arms again, to smother her in kisses that erased all the years.

"Brent," she whispered, my name sounding like sugar on her tongue.

I buried my face in her neck, layering kisses on her soft skin. "Where have you been?" I asked, though it was entirely rhetorical. She hadn't been with me. I hadn't been with her. That was the answer.

"Where were you?" she countered softly.

I lifted my face and looked her in the eyes as I brushed the back of my fingers along her cheek. "Thinking of you," I said. I cupped her cheeks in my hands. "You're so fucking beautiful," I rasped out, and then I crushed my mouth to hers. I consumed her lips. I kissed her hard and greedily, and the world around me faded into a speck of nothingness because there was room for nothing else in my world but her. Nothing but the utter perfection of Shannon Paige-Prince wrapped around me where she belonged.

No time had passed.

No years had gone by.

No regrets had dug deep inside me.

We kissed like it was the first time, and the last time, and like it was for all time. We kissed like two people who wanted to climb into each other's skin, to smash into the other person. It was crashing back into orbit. It was gravity reinstated. In the press of her lips, in the slide of her tongue, in the gasps she made, we hurtled back in time. All mistakes were erased in that moment. There were no doubts. No questions. She had to feel everything I felt. She had to want a second chance too. I dropped a hand to her lower back, yanking her close, but not close enough. Kissing was not enough. Lips would only get us so far. I had to feel her, touch her, taste her.

She pressed into me, a full-body collision, grinding against me. I groaned as I reclaimed her mouth, my entire being consumed with a desire so powerful I didn't know how I'd make it through the rest of the day.

As she rubbed her body against me, I imagined the heat between her legs. It fried my brain and short-circuited my skull. The desire to touch her enveloped me. I wanted to watch her undress, to stare at that to-die-for body that I'd missed so terribly, to roam my eyes over her curves.

To touch her everywhere.

To have her, take her.

Hell, the way she fused her body to mine told me all I needed to know. She wanted the same things.

I kissed a line along her jaw to her ear as she breathed hard. "What do you say we have a do-over of last night? How about we get another drink tonight and then end the night properly? With another kiss," I said, skimming my hand along the outside of her thigh.

Her smile lit me up, but her answer was what gave me hope.

"Yes."

9

SHANNON

For our do-over that night, we met at a low-key bar off the Strip. A neighborhood joint called The Depot that was the opposite of the glitter and glitz the city was known for. Brent knew the owner, he'd said. That was his style—knowing people, making friends with them.

We ordered the same drinks as last night. Martini and whiskey again for our mulligan.

We toasted, and he nodded at the pink scrap of fabric wrapped around my neck. "Nice scarf. Did some guy who's really into you give you that?"

I wiggled my brow. It was surreal to hear Brent say these words. "Maybe."

"I bet that guy wants to get to know you again." He barely waited a second before diving into a litany of questions. "How is your family? How is your grandmother? Your grandfather? How is everyone?"

"They're great. They're all great," I said. "I'm going to see my grandma tomorrow. We do yoga together. She's still as amazing as ever. So is Grandpa. He dotes on

Grandma. Loves her madly." I waved a hand in front of my face, as if it were a magic wand. "Enough about me. Tell me something happy. Your family was always the happy one. Your mom and dad were still together and actually liked each other—and still do, I presume. How's your brother?"

He caught me up to speed on his brother, Clay, who'd been married for a few years and had a baby daughter now.

"I can't believe you're an uncle," I said, shaking my head in wonder.

"My niece is adorable." He took out his phone, clicked open the galleries, and showed me pictures, including one with the girl and a black-and-white dog. My stomach tightened for a moment as I thought of the pregnancy I'd lost, but I shoved that aside. I'd learned to live with the pain, and now it was barely a dull ache. It was a memory, one that didn't have the same power it had years ago.

"That's Ace. He's the border collie mix they adopted a few years ago."

My heart skipped a beat because he looked like a dog I knew well. "Ryan has a dog like that," I said. "Named him Johnny Cash. Because he's mostly black. The Man in Black and all."

"Great name."

"Ryan treats him like a king. I think he even cooks him steak on Sundays."

"Lucky dog," Brent said with a smile.

"Have you been back in Vegas long?" I asked, before taking another drink of my martini.

"A little over a year. I returned to start the clubs," he said.

We chatted about the city, work, and our new businesses. As we drained our drinks and started a second round, I realized he was staring at me, like he had a secret.

"Why are you looking at me like that?" I asked, swiping my fingers across my lips.

"I'm still thinking about kissing you," he said, owning the glint in his eyes.

That kiss this morning had brought so many feelings flooding back.

Feelings I'd locked up for years.

I wasn't ready to jump back into a relationship. I wasn't prepared to put the past behind me yet. We had a long way to go. Trust wasn't restored in a day, and faith didn't heal with one earth-shattering kiss.

But *need* was another matter. It roared back to life.

No surprise there.

When Brent and I had been together, he'd fucked all my troubles away. Every kiss, every touch, every taste was the antidote to a painful memory. Sex with him was exhilarating. It was the greatest rush, the sweetest high. It was ecstatic amnesia. When he fucked me, I was no longer one of the Paige-Prince kids. I was not the left behind, the whispered about, one of those kids whose mother murdered their father for money.

With Brent, I was muscle and bone, solid and strong. I was a woman wanted by a man.

I wanted that man too. With everything inside me. The desire burrowed into my blood. It called out insistently, like a beating drum, like a fire in my veins. I might regret this later. I might regret it in a few minutes. But in that moment, I didn't feel regret. I felt hungry. I felt greedy.

I felt justified.

I reached for the collar of his shirt. "You said you know the owner, right?"

He just grinned. "I do."

My meaning was clear.

And Brent knew what to do with it. Holding up a finger, he stepped away to talk to his friend, then returned to me a minute later. He tipped his forehead to the back of the bar, guiding me to a cramped office by the restrooms.

Cramped worked just fine for my needs.

In seconds, we were inside, Brent shutting and locking the door behind us.

I leaned against it.

He inched closer. "You," he said in a low rumble that sent goosebumps over my skin, a promise of other things he'd say in that wickedly sexy voice. "You are perfection. And like I told Mindy this morning, I can't stand the thought of you slipping away again. I will do whatever it takes to keep you," he said, and the words torched my heart. They started a bonfire in my belly.

I wasn't ready to be kept. I wasn't making promises. But I was ready to *feel.*

So I pushed back with a tease, tugging at his shirt, toying with the buttons. "But you don't even have me."

His eyes darkened. "I am well aware of that. And I intend to change it."

He kissed me, sending me to that druggy, blissed-out state in seconds, like he'd done this morning.

This man, he knew what I needed.

He slipped a hand under the soft material of my top, pressing gently against my belly. I murmured my intense appreciation for his hands as he kissed and touched. And while he kept my lips occupied, his fingers danced lower, down my skirt, then up, traveling along my thighs.

I ached for him. The kisses that morning had lingered with me all day. I was a woman on edge, operating at high levels of lust.

His hand made its way inside the waistband of my panties, then lower and lower still, and . . . oh dear God . . . his fingers were on a fast track for my hot, wet center. When he glided them across me, my knees nearly buckled.

"Oh, babe, was it all that kissing that got you this hot?" he whispered as he stroked.

"Yes. It was . . . *perfection*," I answered quietly as I shuddered in his arms, dying for more of his touch, for him to get me off as only he could.

"Good. Because this wetness is fucking perfect for my fingers to slide through," he said in my ear as he stroked. "All this fucking beautiful wetness. For me. Just for me."

I rocked my hips into his hand. "Yes," I said softly, my voice trancelike, my body overcome with silver sparks of desire as he rubbed his fingers across my heat. "It's all for you."

10

———————

BRENT

She was hotter than she'd ever been. Slippery wetness coated my fingers. Her slick heat was all over my hand.

I was wound up, turned all the way on, but there was one thing I had to have. I moved my lips along her neck, then whispered in her ear, "You have to be quiet, but you need to say my name when you come."

I needed to hear it on her lips. Needed her to feel me owning her body. Needed to use the physical part of our reconnection to show her we could be as good as we were before.

"Yes, Brent," she said with a moan, rocking against my hand.

Her panties were useless. I was dying to rip them off her, spread her wide, and properly worship her gorgeous body.

But this was a high too—a quickie of sorts in an office with paper-thin walls. It was such a thrill. Her need to come was intoxicating.

I slid my fingers across her, so wet and warm and

inviting. She trembled against me as I stroked, hungry for my touch.

I could feel the way tension tightened in her body as she neared the edge.

"You're so close, babe. I know you want to moan and cry out, right?"

"Oh God, I do."

"And it'll be even harder for you to hold back when I slide my fingers into you," I said, doing just that. Her beautiful body was strung tight, stretched to the limits of her own desire, her own sexuality. I loved knowing how to play her, how to touch her, how to send her into a land of bliss.

Some things didn't change.

She rode my fingers, her breath coming fast, like she was seconds away from nirvana. "Come for me, babe. Let me feel you come all over my hand," I said, and she clenched tightly around me, her body shuddering in my arms.

I watched her face, her gorgeous, beautiful face, as she squeezed her eyes shut and nearly sealed her lips together to zip up her cries as she came on my fingers. Right as she reached the crest, she whispered in a broken, beautiful pant, *"Brent."*

It was everything I'd ever wanted to hear from her.

As she trembled, I kissed her lips once more, feeling like maybe, just maybe, I was starting to prove myself to her.

But orgasms didn't cure everything. There was so much more I needed to do.

Later, I took her home, dropped her off, and said I

wanted to see her again. "I have to go to New York tomorrow. I want to see you when I come back," I told her.

"Sounds promising."

I arched a brow. "More than promising?"

Her lips curved up in a grin as she took the scarf off her neck, wrapped it around me once, and held the ends. She looked me square in the eyes. "I love this scarf, but I'm leaving it behind. So you can find me again."

Then she left, heading into her house.

And the scarf was so much more than a scarf.

It was a promise between the two of us.

The next night, I listened to the comedian working the stage at Bob's Beer Haven and Comedy Club in Soho. The dimly lit venue off Spring Street had a been-there-for-years vibe that I dug.

I'd be meeting my brother here shortly, then tomorrow I'd see the owner of the building where I'd leased space.

Until then, I was enjoying the young comic. He had a Will Ferrell style, and I liked his set. When he finished, I nodded my appreciation to Bob.

"He's a good find," I said.

"Yeah, he's not too bad," Bob said as he wiped down some glasses.

"The place is still bringing it." I looked around,

checking out the crowds, still sardined into the place with no signs of leaving.

"But not for much longer." He sighed.

"Sorry to hear about your landlord. Who the hell needs a quadrupling in rent?" I asked, still shocked the landlord could be so grubby.

"Things I ask myself every day," he said. He was shutting down operations soon, and the location had been leased to a chain restaurant.

"Don't stress about it, man. We've got plans," I said. Bob was a solid businessman, and I'd promised him a job managing my club in New York, provided we got the approval from the city to open it. With two kids in college now, the man had needed to find a new gig quickly, and I'd been glad to potentially offer him something.

"And I'm looking forward to those plans," he said, then tipped his forehead to the end of the bar. A man in a cap had sat down, looking in need of a beer. "I'm going to take care of some customers."

"Keep up the good work," I said, then stepped away a minute later when my brother and his wife arrived.

We ordered burgers and caught up on family and work. Then Julia studied my face. "You look particularly . . . happy."

"Do I?" I asked.

Her eyes twinkled with delight. "I bet there's a new lady in your life."

I shook my head, but my smile gave me away.

"Serve it up," Clay said, wiggling his fingers.

I shrugged. "Not new. It's Shannon."

My brother nearly dropped his glass. "The one you fucked up royally with?"

"Thanks for not mincing words."

"I never mince words. But now I'm going to need the full story."

I gave them the basics, then figured this was a chance for me to gain further wisdom in the art of pursuing this woman. Mindy's advice was a terrific foundation, but I could definitely add to my education with Julia. "So, I'm on this whole prove-myself-to-her kick. To show her I can be the man she needs. What do I do?"

Julia replied immediately. "The answer is simple. You need to focus on what matters to her. How can you show her how important she is to you? Where did you fail in the past in that regard?"

I scoffed, thinking of my canceled trips and focus on work. "That's gonna be a long list."

"Then take it item by item, step by step, and follow her cues," she said.

When we left, I hailed a cab and headed to my Midtown hotel. As the cab ambled through traffic, I unlocked the screen on my phone and opened up a new text message to Shannon. Keep it simple, keep it direct. That was what I'd do.

Brent: I'm in New York . . . thinking of you. I fly back late Saturday. Can I see you Sunday night?

. . .

Shannon: I don't know. Can you?

Brent: May I?

Shannon: What will you be wearing?

Brent: What do you want me to wear?

As the cab weaved through traffic, I clutched the phone and peered out the window, forcing myself not to simply stare at the screen and wait for a reply. As I scanned the billboards and neon signs, I spotted one up ahead with a body in motion. A dancer leaping through the air. I read the details on the sign, and something clicked.

"Yes," I said triumphantly, and I had the answer to the question Julia had posed to me—about what matters most to Shannon. I was about to begin a quick Google search when she replied.

Shannon: Honestly, you're pretty hot in nothing. But I don't think you should parade around naked at dinner, and I keep hearing the new restaurant in The Cromwell is fantastic. There's a four-month wait though. And I know you hate waiting. But maybe you can get us in . . .

. . .

Like there was a chance in hell I wouldn't.

Brent: Consider it done.

The cab arrived at my hotel, and several phone calls later, I'd pulled it off. I knew enough people in Vegas, so I'd called in some favors and secured the reservation for the woman I wanted most in the world. I also had something else for her, thanks to a couple of extra minutes spent googling and ordering, but I'd wait until dinner to give her that gift.

Now I couldn't wait for dinner.

* * *

Tanner Davies snapped his fingers to get the waitress's attention the next day at McCoy's in Midtown. The woman with the bouncy ponytail doubled back to our table. "Yes?"

"I said I wanted sweetened iced tea. This is unsweetened. Take it back," he barked, making a get-this-out-of-my-face gesture with his fingers.

"Right away, sir," she said with a deferential nod.

"Anyway," he said to me, "like I was saying, the neighbors are worried about you, man. They think you won't address their concerns properly."

"With four clubs opened in the first year, I think I've shown how serious I am. We just opened St. Barts, which followed our new clubs in Miami and San Francisco, and of course our first club in Vegas," I said, carefully detailing the progress my business had made during the first twelve months of operations.

Tanner shrugged dismissively. I wasn't so sure if he was the enemy or just the gatekeeper of all the problems the city kept heaping on me. Permits were shooting up in cost. The zoning commissioner threw up roadblocks. But New York was a linchpin in my plans for Edge.

"What's the real concern?" I asked, opting for directness. "And what can I do to help ease it?"

Tanner scratched his jaw, then cleared his throat. "Look. I'm just the messenger here, so don't shoot me. But the neighbors worry you're just some former TV celebrity, living it up now in Sin City, who's going to bring a lot of noise and crowd and trouble into their neighborhood at night. The whole Vegas thing doesn't sit well with them. Vegas isn't exactly a family town," Tanner said, and I reined in the flash of anger I felt at the way he was insulting my city. Any city had its troubles, including New York. Vegas had plenty of good in it too, just like New York. "And they want to know why they should allow another club in their neighborhood."

"The location is zoned for a nightclub," I said, pointing out the obvious, because that was the reality of the property. Rather than dealing with intangibles, or the Vegas disdain, I wanted to try to focus on the facts. "You had one in the building before mine, and it went out of business."

"That's what I've been saying to them," he said. "But they want to know why *you*."

The question was entirely personal.

But I kept my answer on business.

"Because we don't attract a raunchy crowd. You won't find clubgoers puking outside these neighbors' loft apartments at three in the morning. My clubs are upscale and classy. They have a certain mystique, a lush sensuality, but it never crosses over into trashy."

The waitress returned with a fresh iced tea for Tanner. "Here you go, sir. Sweetened, as you requested."

My lunch companion grunted, then spoke to me. "That's what we need the neighborhood association to see." He lowered his voice to a whisper. "And it wouldn't hurt if you threw in a few thousand to have some of the Tribeca parks redone. There are a couple in need of a makeover, and that would make the residents happy."

I wasn't entirely fond of the payola approach, but he wasn't asking me to grease his palm—he was asking to build a park for kids. "Easy enough. I'll be glad to do that. Anything else?"

"Yeah, how about you peel off a little extra for me? The ex is trying to take me to court for alimony payments." I didn't answer, but Tanner quickly waved a hand and flashed his yellowed smile. "I'm just kidding. I won't let the bitch have a dime of my money. And I'll help you with all this. I want your club in my building."

"Great. And I want Edge there too. So let me know if there's anything else you need from me."

"That's all for now. But I'm sure there will be something else soon. That's how it goes in New York. You gotta do whatever it takes."

That seemed to be the new mantra in my life, whether with a certain woman or with business.

11

SHANNON

I extended my arms high above my head, my palms flat together, my fingers pointing toward the sky. Solid warrior pose. Just like my grandmother beside me.

"You're a yoga badass," I said to her.

"Just like you," she answered.

At age seventy-three, Victoria Paige showed no signs of slowing down. She was fit, trim, muscular, and determined to keep up with anyone and everyone.

"Even the dog is getting jealous of my yoga skills," she said with a wink as we shifted poses on the sun porch of her ranch home in one of the nicer areas in the Vegas suburbs, a house that we four grandkids had bought for her. Her boxer mix raised his snout at us then returned to lounging in the sun.

"As well he should be, Nana. Your downward dog is the best," I said as we both planted our hands on our mats.

I peered into the backyard, taking in the familiar family scene on a Sunday. Michael was fixing a fence-post with our grandfather, while Ryan and Colin tended to the grill. The homey scene was almost enough to make anyone forget why the six of us were so close.

When my mom was arrested, social services sent my brothers and me to live with our paternal grandparents. They did their best to finish the job their son had started, seeing the four of us through the end of our high school years after our mother went to prison for conspiracy to commit murder, sentenced in a swift and speedy trial mere months after her arrest.

My stomach clenched, as it often did, just thinking about the last moments of my father's life. Thomas Paige was shot four times in the driveway of our own home, a run-down, ramshackle house in the worst section of the city, which was riddled with crime. He'd been found with fatal gunshot wounds and an emptied wallet, as if a robbery had simply gone wrong. A robbery was plausible enough in that neighborhood.

We didn't come from means. We came from desperation. We were bred from broken dreams, from a mother who'd wanted to be a Vegas star but never had the talent, so instead eked out a meager living as a seamstress, and from a father stuck driving cabs on the night shift. But his situation had started to change, and he'd thought he'd finally caught his lucky break when he began driving limos. He started making more money, and after a couple of years at his new gig, the future looked bright.

But there was no lucky break that June night he was shot after eight hours of chauffeuring rich kids from the swank suburbs to their after-prom parties.

He was my hero, and losing him tore my world apart, ripping the fabric of my life to tatters.

It tore my grandma to shreds too, but the woman had to buckle in and become a parent again to four broken kids.

At the time I'd never fully comprehended how horrible my grandparents must have felt. Their son was dead, his life taken at the hands of his wife—the very same woman who'd carried these four messed-up, troubled kids who had been dropped on their doorstep as teens.

As I grew older, I came to understand the terrible balancing act that my father's parents had had to pull off to raise us with love and kindness during those last few critical years. My brothers and I were grafted by murder, united by death and prison, into their home.

Some days, I still missed my father fiercely, in the same raw way I'd missed him in high school.

Today, I felt that empty longing envelop me for a split second as I stepped out of the final pose, finishing our yoga session, and looked at a sun-faded photo of my father in his early twenties that hung above the end table on the porch. Sepia now in tone, the image showed his hands wrapped around Michael's waist as he hoisted the toddler onto a slide.

My heart squeezed at the sight of it, but I felt love too—love for him, and love for my grandparents. They were the heartbeat of our fractured family. A few years ago, my brothers and I had bought them this new house in a safe and affluent section of Vegas. I was so damn glad we could do that. We'd made a pact as teens to live differently than our parents, to pull ourselves out of the terrible circumstances we'd grown up in.

"We'll become Sloans," Michael had said, the night he'd suggested we change our name, taking on Victoria's mother's maiden name—our connection to her and to him. Turned out the name meant more. "The name itself means 'warrior.' That's who he was for us," Michael had said. "That's who we will be for him."

Our way of honoring him.

Our lives honored him too. We'd made a vow to give back as much as we could, to support charities, and help others improve their lives.

Remembering my daddy, I pressed my fingers to my lips, then touched my dad's photo in the frame.

Victoria did the same.

"I love that picture," she whispered. "That's how he always was with all you kids. Spending time with you. Loving you."

My throat hitched. Even now, eighteen years later, I still felt so much emotion welling up inside me. "I know, Nana. I remember that about him. That's what I remember most."

When she squeezed my arm, her eyes were veiled with a sheen of tears. But her voice was strong as she shifted the topic of conversation. "I hear from Colin that you're doing business with your old flame," she said.

Grateful to focus on the present again, I answered her, "You hear correctly. He hired my company to arrange for some dancers and choreography at his nightclubs."

We walked across the cool tiled floor to the kitchen. She turned on the tap and poured some water, handing a glass to me, and I downed half of it quickly. She glanced left and right, as if checking to see if my brothers were in earshot. "He's a sweet boy."

"Boy," I said with a laugh. Brent was hardly a boy. He was all man, and the memory of how he'd touched me in his friend's bar the other night crashed back into me like a comet of lust.

"He came back to bring me my ring, you know," she added, leaning her hip against the counter as she pushed a hand through her silvery hair.

"He did?" I asked, flashing back on how I'd given him the ring when he saw me in London. It had needed resizing and he said he'd take care of it, so it was with him when we broke up. "You never told me that before. I thought he'd mailed it here."

"I did try to tell you at the time, sweetheart. But you didn't want to hear a word of it. You weren't interested in any news about Brent, so I let it go. The ring doesn't fit me anymore, but he came by and dropped it off himself several months after you split. You were still in London."

A strange sense of shock raced through my system. I'd always figured the ring had arrived by mail, never by personal courier in the form of Brent Nichols.

"He called me in advance. Made sure I was here. Said he wanted to return it to its rightful owner," she continued, as she poured herself a glass of water.

"He came to see you at your house?" I asked, processing this news for the first time.

"He did. Pulled up on his bike and came inside. I offered him some tea and sat with him for a few minutes. Russ was at work, so it was just your boy and me. He said he didn't want to risk putting the ring in the mail, or FedEx, or any of those services," she said, and that little detail somehow worked its way into my heart, chipping away at the tiniest piece of ice still coating that organ to protect me from Brent.

"That's actually really thoughtful," I said softly.

"He asked about you. He wanted to know how you were doing."

My heart beat faster. I wanted to grab it and tell it to settle down. "He did?"

"I think he just wanted to make sure you were okay," my grandmother said, stopping to take a drink of water.

That lump in my throat resurfaced, and tears threatened my eyes. I blinked, holding them in. What was wrong with me today? I needed to get a grip. That was ten years past, and this was now.

"I'm seeing Brent tonight," I blurted out, desperate to tell someone I could trust.

"You are? About the business deal? Or maybe about more?" my grandma asked in a sly tone.

I went with it, turning the moment playful. "Maybe more. We'll see."

"For what it's worth, I always liked him."

"Liked who, Nana?" Michael's voice carried across the room. I straightened my spine as he sauntered into the house with the toolbox, heading to the garage.

"Liked you, my love," she said, patting her eldest

grandson on the cheek as he passed by. "I've always liked you."

Michael narrowed his eyes. "Hmm. Doubtful," he said skeptically, but continued into the garage.

Once he was out of sight, my grandma hugged me. "Some secrets are just between us girls."

"Girl power," I whispered, and she winked in response, then headed to her room to change out of her yoga clothes. I turned the other direction to go hang out with my brothers in the backyard, passing Colin and my grandfather on their way into the house.

"Just going to make some more marinade," Colin said, with culinary bravado. "My marinade rocks."

"No way is it better than mine. And to prove it, we're going to have a taste test contest," my grandfather chimed in, and I smiled at their competitive ways then joined Ryan by the grill. He pressed a spatula on top of a burger.

I bumped my shoulder to his. "Hey you. Are you going to take one of those home to Johnny Cash?"

"Of course. Nothing but the best for man's best friend," he said with a grin.

Like all my brothers, Ryan towered over me, but I was used to being surrounded by these sturdy men. Ryan's brown hair looked lighter in the noonday sun, as if several strands were streaked with gold.

He flipped a burger, then glanced carefully at the house. "Hey," he said in a low voice. "Did you hear from Mom?"

I nodded heavily, thinking of her letter. "The other day. It's the same old, same old."

"But is it?" Ryan asked, holding up the barbecue tongs as if punctuating a point. "What if she's right?"

I sighed and placed a hand on his shoulder. "Ry, we can't do this every single time she writes to us."

He narrowed his gaze. "But what if she's right that there were others involved?"

I shot him a stern look. "Well, there *were* others involved. The other guy is also in prison because his fingerprints were all over the gun." The details had been splashed across papers and the news at the time, and the specifics of how the local detectives had followed the trail of evidence to our mother was in black and white for anyone to find. Ryan and I had hashed this out a million times, and probably would a million more. It was an endless cycle with no answer, but the facts were these: Twenty-two-year-old Jerry Stefano, card-carrying member of the local gang the Royal Sinners, had pulled the trigger. Jerry Stefano had been in touch with Dora Prince many times, and was instructed to make the crime look like a robbery gone too far.

But the murder was never about the money in our father's wallet. Our father had a five-hundred-thou-sand-dollar life-insurance policy. Dora Prince was the beneficiary. And Jerry Stefano had been promised ten percent if he could get away with it.

Murder for hire, plain and simple.

Our mom had wanted the money.

It was murder in cold blood.

Ryan shook his head. "I know, but *what if*, Shan?" He dropped his voice to the barest whisper. "Listen, a buddy of mine in the DA's office said one of their attorneys visited Jerry in prison recently. They haven't been there in years, but the attorney went to ask him some questions. See if he knew about some other crimes. Doesn't that say something?"

I groaned, frustration coursing through me. Ryan had a hard time letting go. He was obsessed with possibilities. "Jerry Stefano was a Royal Sinners gunman. Of course he knows about other crimes. He was probably involved in them. I'm sure that's what the attorney wanted from him—information."

Ryan was undeterred, smacking the spatula against the burger for emphasis. "We should at least visit her again."

I dragged a hand through my hair. "She'll do her usual routine. Tell us there were others. Tell us they're still around. Like she did at Christmas. She'll try to manipulate us."

I didn't share Ryan's sympathies, but I harbored guilt. Too much guilt over my mother and all those years when we were as close as a mom and daughter could be. Like my dad, my mom had been there for me, for every dance, every recital, every performance, every moment. Maybe that was why I'd had such a hard time severing ties with the woman now in orange. Or maybe it was because I believed that my mother, in some bizarre way, loved me and my brothers.

Deeply.

Ryan seemed to sense an opening because he pushed on. "Look, if you don't want to see her, why'd you give her your new address when you moved back to town a few years ago? So she could write to you. Michael and

Colin never did. They cut her out completely. They never see her," he said, then leaned in closer and clasped my shoulder. "I'm not saying she's innocent, Shan. I just think she's our goddamn mother. The least we can do is go see her again in jail."

I gritted my teeth. Visits with my mother were exhausting. They wore me out. But as that kernel of guilt pulsed through my veins, I threw him a bone. "I honestly don't know if I'm up for it again so soon. But let me know when you go, okay?"

He gave me a hopeful grin. "I will."

As I headed into the house, I glanced at the time, grateful that the clock was ticking closer to my date. I wanted to speed up the next several hours, run through them in fast forward, because I needed something that felt good. Something that was the complete opposite of my twisted family story.

Speak of the devil.

When I returned home and grabbed my mail from yesterday, there was an envelope.

Another letter from prison.

My mother had drawn hearts on the envelope flap this time.

My stomach roiled.

I didn't want her drama before a date. Ironic, though, because Brent was always the one who'd opened the letters when she sent them to me in college.

He'd been my shoulder, my support, and I'd desperately needed him then.

I set the envelope down.

Maybe he'd play that part again.

Was I ready for that?

Was I ready to trust him a second time? Would he walk away if things got tough? Could I trust him with my heart again?

I asked myself those questions as I got ready to see him.

After I showered and dried my hair, I tied the slim strap of my charcoal-gray top at my neck, then smoothed my hand across my black skirt, which hit just above my knees.

Trust.

How did you get it back? Michael may have been right when he said I had a pass, but that pass no longer applied.

Now that Brent and I had reconnected, no matter where we were going, I needed to tell him the full truth.

We had a ways to go.

But one thing was still certain. I loved touching him, and he loved touching me.

As I ran my palm across the fabric of my skirt, I closed my eyes and imagined the feel of Brent's hand. He had strong, solid hands that knew me. That had mapped every inch of my body. That had traveled across the terrain of my skin. He was my magic pill, my sip of champagne, my bite of smooth dark chocolate. He was an endorphin, the most powerful, potent one I'd ever had.

When I opened the closet door, I made a mental note to ask Michael to fix it. The dang thing was still loose. I perused the racks of shoes, then selected a pair of plum-colored pumps with four-inch heels. Walking past my bureau, I stopped at a frame on it—another shot of the sunflowers I loved.

I trailed a finger along the top of the frame, smiling wistfully at the image of the flowers next to a stone.

There was a photo behind the frame too, but I didn't need to look at that right now.

I headed into the kitchen, and my phone buzzed on the counter. I grabbed it from its spot next to the sunflower frame I kept there. A text from my driver said he was one minute away. I shut and locked the front door, then nearly smacked into Ally, who lived two flights up. Laughing, she glanced up from her phone to smile at me.

"What's so funny?"

"Cat videos, obviously." Ally looked up toward her condo, the broad smile still on her face. She pushed her big round sunglasses high up on her head.

"But of course," I said.

She thrust her phone at me, showing me a clip of a tabby kayaking with his owner. "This cat hikes with his person. I wish my cat would just cuddle with me at night."

"Keep dreaming," I teased.

She raised an eyebrow and looked me up and down. "You look gorgeous. Date tonight?"

I grinned, feeling a little sassy. "As a matter of fact, yes. And thank you. I better get going. My ride is here."

"Your date won't know what hit him. You look gorgeous, Shay."

I blew her a kiss in thanks, then she called my name again.

"Yes?"

"I have a date too. It's probably going to be a sleep-over. If you're coming home, any chance you can feed Nick later tonight?"

"Yes, I'm coming home. And of course I'll feed him. Nick is so cute. I love that tomcat. Cats make me happy."

"He's a total ladies' man," Ally said with a wink. "He ought to make you ecstatic."

Sounded like someone I knew. I smiled at the private joke as I walked down the steps.

When I slid into the air-conditioned white Nissan, I confirmed my destination—The Cromwell near the Bellagio—with the Uber driver.

"Can I interest you in a candy or a water?" the driver asked.

I shook my head, but thanked him.

On the way there, my mind returned to the inevitable. To the weight I carried with me.

Words I knew I'd have to say soon.

I swallowed and parted my lips as if to speak. *I was pregnant with your baby. Then, my body failed me.*

The words were awful, like jagged glass in my mouth. They hurt so much. Too much. I'd put it behind me, as much as one can—I'd processed that loss. He'd have to do it for the first time.

He'd have to feel the hurt.

Was it wrong to want a night that didn't hurt?

Tomorrow. I'd deal with it tomorrow. Truths like this were best delivered in the morning, right? I could have this evening with him, then in the morning, I'd discover the right words.

In the morning, I'd be ready.

I wanted dinner without tears or sadness, so I forced myself to focus on the opposite.

On laughter, happiness, and sweetness.

That made me think of candy, and it gave me an idea.

I knew someone who loved candy.

12

——————

BRENT

Temptation got the better of me as I walked toward the hostess stand at Giada in The Cromwell, a trendy, boutique hotel on the Strip. Shannon was waiting in the entryway, her back to me, looking far too sexy for me to keep my hands to myself.

Because . . . that ass.

Small, but firm and round.

And absolutely delicious.

I knew precisely how fantastic it felt to grab that flesh while I sank deep into her. I shook my head, like a dog shaking off water, but it didn't deter the dirty thoughts that invaded my brain. Hell, they launched a full-scale attack, completely taking over my sense of propriety as I strode up to her. No one but me should be allowed to see her in a skirt that hugged her ass like that. But then, she couldn't hide that perfect body in a burlap sack if she tried, and I couldn't hide my rampant desire for her either.

The hustle and bustle of the evening crowd

surrounded me as I crossed the final distance to the restaurant entrance.

Three more steps. Two more steps. One more step.

My hands reached out. I couldn't help myself. Well, I *could*. I chose not to.

I cupped her ass, and she flinched for a second, but then I brushed my lips against her neck, and whispered, "You are so unbelievably beautiful that I hope you'll forgive me for not being able to keep my hands off you."

She trembled, leaning into me. "You aren't winning any medals for self-restraint tonight."

"I'm not competing in that event."

"You never could keep your hands to yourself in public," she said, but she wasn't swatting my mitts away, so I ran my hands along the sweet curves of her body.

"Or in private either. But can you blame me? Have you looked at yourself lately?"

She turned around, breaking contact. Her lips curved in a small grin. "Yes. Why?"

"If I were you, I'd never be able to resist touching myself."

She playfully rolled her pretty green eyes. "Amazingly, I can find the will to resist incessant self-touching," she said, but she wasn't moving away. It was almost as if we'd slipped back in time, forgotten the way we'd split, and had returned to the way we were—*good together*.

"Do you have a reservation?"

The sweet, cheery voice of the hostess broke the trance Shannon was putting on me. I was like a man hypnotized who'd just snapped out of it. I turned to the ponytailed, fresh-faced young lady in a black dress, and said, "Nichols."

The hostess scanned the computerized list, and then tapped the screen. "There you are. I see Mario has requested one of the best tables for you," she said, dropping the name of the restaurant manager I'd called in the favor from. "You'll love this table."

Shannon turned to look at me, her lips forming a puckered O. *You're fancy*, she mouthed.

"Thank you so much. I really appreciate him doing that," I said to the hostess.

"Right this way, then, Mr. Nichols."

The hostess guided us to a table on the terrace with a view of the fountains at the Bellagio.

"Your table," the hostess said, then walked away.

I pulled out a chair for Shannon, and she smiled at me once more. "This is lovely. Even though there are no tablecloths," she said seductively.

A rumble worked its way up my chest, and I looped a hand around her waist, tugging her close. She didn't resist. She moved with me, aligning her body with mine. "I was thinking the same thing," I said low in her ear, then kissed her there, nibbling on her earlobe.

"Or we could just get a room . . ." she said sexily, letting her voice trail off.

I wrenched back, looked her in the eyes, and grabbed her hand. "Let's go. Now."

"I was only teasing. I'm terribly hungry," she said as she shook her head and dropped my hand, then settled into her seat. "Besides, I've been waiting for a long time to come here."

I kept my eyes on those luscious lips I hoped to see parted in pleasure later on. If I had my way, she'd be coming more than once tonight, whether here or back at my place.

* * *

Over appetizers and a bottle of wine, I learned about the productions she'd choreographed, her career path, and how she'd started Shay Productions.

I asked her questions, eager to hear what she'd been up to since college. Like a paint-by-numbers artwork, I was beginning to see all that I had missed. She'd worked on *West Side Story*, *Anything Goes*, and *Chicago*, had logged a gig as a behind-the-scenes choreographer on a reality dance show in Los Angeles, then spent some time with a Cirque du Soleil production, before returning to Vegas and working on a dance revue at Planet Hollywood. That show was the launchpad for her company and the production she'd staged for the Wynn.

"The show at the Wynn really put me on the map," she said, as she took another drink of the wine.

"That's a great venue and a great opportunity."

"It's funny because I've never really thought of myself as a lucky person," she said, looking philosophical as she stared off in the distance for a moment. "But I've had a few lucky breaks in my career—meeting the right people, getting the right introductions—and it's made all the difference. Like the reality show I worked on. I might do some more work for them. I've got a meeting in LA with the producers tomorrow about staging a one-night reunion show with some of the former winners, so there's another bit of luck," she said, rapping her knuckles on the table. "Knock on wood."

"Hey. You deserve some luck," I said, meeting her gaze, making sure she knew I meant that from the bottom of my soul.

She shrugged and waved a hand dismissively. "I don't really subscribe to the notion that someone deserves good things in life. Things just happen. Some people are lucky and some aren't."

"And some people are immensely talented and recognized for their talent. And that's you," I said, keeping my eyes firmly on her. I wanted her to know how much I admired her work, especially since I hadn't done the best job of showing respect for her career when I was so focused on my own back then.

"Thank you. I love what I do, and I wasn't sure I would. I didn't think I'd be able to survive without being the one dancing."

"I know." I covered her hand with my own, memories of her devastating pain still fresh.

"I do love choreography now though," she said, and a gleam was in her eyes, hinting at her resilience.

"Tell me what you love about it," I said, resting my elbows on the table as I listened to her share her passion.

She tilted her head to the side, as if she was briefly considering my question. But she didn't seem to think about it for long. "I love being able to have a vision. To imagine what something beautiful will look like," she said, talking animatedly with her hands. "And then to make that vision become a reality onstage. I love what my dancers are capable of doing, and being able to take a kernel of an idea and translate it into this moving, fluid entity in front of an audience." She stopped, took a beat, then added, "And soon, that audience will be your clubgoers."

I shot her a small grin. "Can't wait to see that."

"The show we have planned for Edge is amazing," she said, enthusiasm latching onto her words. "It's going to be so sensual and lush. We're rolling it out in San Francisco first, I believe?"

"Yes. I have no doubt it will be great. Thanks to you," I said, then I linked our fingers together, twining them. It felt so right. Even better when she gave my hand a squeeze. "You've accomplished so much," I said. Would she have found her way down this career path if we'd stayed together? Between flights and opposing careers and love, perhaps not. "I'm really proud of you."

"And you have accomplished a lot too."

"Shan," I said softly. "I'm not saying this makes up for how we fell apart, and if I could go back in time, I would completely do the whole thing over and find a way to be with you. But I'm so damn glad that you've been able to achieve all that you have."

She didn't speak at first, and I wasn't sure if I'd said the wrong thing yet again. Tension flickered through my bloodstream as I waited for her to pull her hand away or shoot me a harsh stare. Instead, she cast her eyes down at the table. When she raised her face, she swallowed. "My grandma told me you went to her house. To return the ring in person."

My shoulders tightened, but I went with her segue, nodding and acknowledging that moment from years ago. "I did."

She pressed her teeth against her bottom lip briefly, then breathed out hard. "I really appreciate that. You making the effort to get it back to her. To be certain she had it again."

"It was the least I could do," I said, running the pad of my thumb along the outside of her hand, not wanting to let go of her, not wanting to stop touching her.

"Can I ask you something?" she asked softly.

"Of course."

She took a deep breath. "What did you do with the diamond?" Then she snapped her hand away and held both of them in the air, shaking her head. "Wait. Don't answer that. It's nosy. You probably used it for living expenses, and that's what I would expect."

I leaned back in my chair and ran my hand roughly through my hair, wishing I didn't feel so . . . *cheesy* admitting this. But I had to tell her the truth, now that she'd asked. "I didn't use it for expenses," I said in a low voice, as if I had to protect myself from anyone else who might hear.

"You don't have to tell me. Really. You don't," she said insistently.

"I'm going to tell you. Just don't take away my man card."

She laughed, her eyes twinkling. "Did you turn it

into a necklace that you're secretly wearing or something?"

"No. I sold it," I blurted out.

"That's what I expected, but why would that forfeit your man card?" She crossed her arms on the table.

"I'm not done. I sold it in LA to a diamond merchant. And I gave the money to the scholarship fund at Boston Conservatory. The one that put you through school," I said. Somehow I'd managed to avoid ever telling anyone what I'd done with the diamond. Not my brother, not Mindy. It just made me sound like a forlorn guy stuck on a girl.

Even though that was what I'd been back then. And what I still was.

I looked up.

Her mouth had fallen open. She was frozen in place. She must have been thinking the same thing. That I was a sad, pathetic guy. I couldn't believe I'd said the wrong thing again. But then I stopped thinking when she rose, stretched across the table, cupped my cheeks in her hands, and pinned my gaze with her sweet green eyes. "That means so much to me."

She kissed me, softly at first, her tongue darting out as she ran the tip of it across my lips, then more roughly as she gripped my stubbled jaw harder. She kissed me feverishly, crushing her lips against mine, and I groaned as she led, sweeping her tongue into my mouth, diving deeper, consuming me. A shudder wracked through me at her sheer possessiveness. At the feel of her hands on my skin. She didn't hold back, not one bit. She did everything with passion, everything to the fullest, as she fused her mouth to mine. I was reduced to nothing but desire for her as she took a chance—reaching across the table with a basket of bread below her arms, with wineglasses perched precariously on the table, with hundreds of patrons nearby. She didn't care. Nor did I. I was damn near ready to shove everything across the table and forget we were in public.

Then I heard a throat being cleared.

The waiter had arrived with our dishes.

She detached from me, adjusted her top, and smirked just for me. As if we had a secret. Even though it was now a very publicly known fact that the two people seated here on the terrace of this restaurant on a June night wanted each other badly.

* * *

After the waiter served my fritto misto and her tortellini, I broached a subject that had once been a source of friction, but then had brought us closer.

"Is your mom still writing to you?" I asked gently, picking up my fork. I watched her, careful not to push too far.

She closed her eyes briefly, her fingers clutching her wineglass. When she opened them, she was the girl I'd known in college, the one who'd relied on me for everything.

She nodded. "Yes. It was every few months for a while. But lately it's been a couple times a week. She sent me one this weekend. I haven't opened it yet."

I winced, hating that she was going through that. "Babe, I'm so sorry. I know those ripped you apart."

She nodded, pressing her lips together, then breathed out hard. "She still says she didn't do it."

"She probably always will say that," I said softly, wanting so badly to erase all her sadness. I'd always wanted to, ever since she'd finally let me in. She'd been so closed off at first about her family, so secretive, and it had driven me mad. I'd wanted to talk to her, to help her through her troubles, but she hadn't even told me what it was that tore her apart.

Finally, she'd confided in me, telling me all the things that weren't in the press, that weren't public knowledge simply from growing up in Vegas at the time it happened. I'd known her as the girl whose mom had killed her dad, but I hadn't been privy to the backstory, the details that didn't make it into the local news.

The full story had shocked me to the core.

My family was so . . . *normal.* My parents were still married. They were both retired now and played golf together a few days a week in a swank suburb on the outskirts of the city. I tried to see them once or twice a month, and always visited on holidays. I even baked a pumpkin pie every year for the Nichols family Thanksgiving. There was no drama, no dysfunction, and certainly no murder for hire.

Maybe that was why I'd been able to comfort her when we were younger. Maybe that was why we'd been drawn together on some subconscious level. I'd grown up unequivocally happy, and I had extra doses of it. I had a whole storage closet full of additional happiness, and I tried to bring that to her. *Lean on me*, I'd told her. I could handle it. I'd do it again if she needed me to.

"And have you seen her recently?" I asked.

With a shaky breath, she answered, "I went at Christmas with Ryan. She asked if anyone had found the people who did it. Same thing she always says, even though she knows Stefano is behind bars." She lowered her voice to a feathery whisper, her tone confessional. "I still check his inmate number every few months. To make sure he's still in prison. It's silly, I know, since he's in for life. But I just like to know he's where he belongs."

I shook my head, reassuring her, because that's all I could do. "It's not silly in the least to find some kind of comfort in knowing he's locked up."

"It's not like it makes me happy," she said, sadness washing over her eyes. "It just makes me feel as much peace as I guess I can feel."

"You don't have to be happy. You can just . . . be," I said, and that was what I'd told her in college too.

She met my eyes, a sliver of a smile forming on her beautiful lips. "I'm happy right now," she said.

And hell, if that didn't add an extra gallon to all those stores of glee I had.

13

SHANNON

This was what I wanted.

A night that felt good. A night where I could see us coming back together, where trust and faith felt possible again.

Where moving on seemed likely.

And maybe, just maybe, where we might come together in our favorite way.

After the plates were cleared, I declared the meal a feast. "I knew I asked the right man to get me into this delicious restaurant. It was amazing, and everything I hoped it would be," I said, then segued into a new topic. "I watched a funny video before I met you for dinner."

He raised an eyebrow in question. "I thought you weren't into internet videos?"

"I'm not. I only watch videos of my dance rehearsals, and I shoot most of those myself. But my friend Ally showed me a cat video."

"Well, there you go. Nothing better than cat videos."

"And it reminded me of you," I added, a playful grin spreading on my face.

"Am I a cat to you, Shan?"

I laughed, then bit my lip, holding in a chuckle. "Kind of. It's a good thing. Cats make me happy."

He squared his shoulders. "Compliment accepted, then. Also, *meow*."

I laughed again, a ribbon of warmth spreading through my chest. The man had always made me laugh. He was handsome as sin and funny as hell, and that combo had been all I'd ever needed. He had filled the sad places inside me. He'd burrowed into me with his laughter and his wit, replacing my darkness with his light. Tonight, he was firing on all cylinders—his caring, tender side out in full force, along with his clever one, not to mention that handsome side. In his jeans and long-sleeved Henley stretched tight across his chest, he was a sight to behold.

"And since we're talking about things that make us happy," I added, "I remember your sweet tooth."

He let his tongue loll out of his mouth. "Mine is legendary."

"I remember," I teased. "Do you remember that time, all those years ago, when I bought a lollipop from a fundraiser?"

Heat flashed across his eyes. "It's burned in my memory for eternity."

"Same," I whispered, sultry, sexy. He'd pretty much tossed me over his shoulder and taken me to his dorm the second I'd taken my first lick.

Did I want him to do that now?

I wasn't sure if I was ready for sex.

But I was definitely ready for feeling good.

I dipped my hand into my purse and took out the item I'd selected from my very thoughtful Uber driver. I unwrapped it, taking my time peeling the plastic off the lollipop as he watched me. His eyes darkened as I brought it to my lips, gently kissing the sucker.

His breath hissed. His gaze turned feral. I flicked my tongue across the red candy, licking it once as he shifted in his chair. I wondered if he still wore black boxer briefs like he'd worn in college. If he still looked as hot in them as he did then, the outline of him so alluring when he'd take off his clothes for me. My mouth watered as I pictured him unzipping his jeans, pushing down his briefs, his cock springing free.

Ready for me. Always ready for me.

"I fucking love candy." His voice was husky.

"I had a feeling," I said, swirling my tongue across the treat. I watched him as he swallowed, his Adam's apple bobbing up and down. I leaned across the table, lowered my voice to a whisper, and asked, "If I put my hand on you right now, how hard would you be?"

"Rock fucking hard," he said in a growl, the rough and sexy rumble of his admission sending a rush of heat between my legs.

I returned the sucker to my mouth, moving it back and forth between my lips. As I licked and kissed the candy, giving him a hell of a show, he stared at me with hungry eyes. In them, I saw the reel of his desires. All his dirty thoughts, all his dirty dreams—everything he wanted from me.

The waiter rushed by, dishes balanced on his arm.

"Check, please," Brent called out, and the man nodded, then continued on his way.

With my eyes on Brent, I asked, "Do you wonder what my mouth tastes like right now?"

"Spectacular. I bet it tastes spectacular," he answered, his voice strained and full of heat. "Kiss me," he said, giving me a clear order. He leaned across the table and claimed my mouth, marking his territory with a passionate, crushing kiss that made me dizzy.

When he broke the kiss, the haze cleared, and I returned to starring in my show. I kicked back in the chair, striking a casual, seductive pose as I sucked the candy deeply, reminding him of my talents.

He gripped the edge of the table. He inhaled through his nostrils. He looked as if he wanted to rip the table in two.

"We need to go. I need to get you naked, Shan. Will you let me?"

I tensed for a second. Was I ready for sex? But I knew the answer. The answer was no. Once I slept with him again, I'd be all the way in. I wasn't sure I was there yet, not when I still had this secret hanging over me.

But perhaps this could be more. More kisses. More touching and tasting and feeling.

More talking, this time with me telling him the truth.

"Yes, but no sex," I clarified. "I'm not ready for that."

"That's fine, but I am most definitely ready to kiss you all over."

It was my turn to say, *Check, please.*

* * *

We reached my place in record time, and took the elevator up so we could kiss more on the way. Once inside, he set me on my kitchen table and wedged himself between my legs. His dick was hard against my thigh. "I hated not seeing you for the last ten years. It was hell," he said, his voice hungry.

He grabbed my hips, his thumbs digging into my sides. This was our dance. Our foreplay. We knew the steps. "Every day we were apart, I wanted you," he said.

Did I want him when we were apart?

Not always—I'd hurt too much.

But I wanted him now, and I told him as much.

"I want you now," I hissed. He raised an eyebrow, his eyes blazing, his lips rising in the barest of a cocky grin —the one that had always melted me. Its effect was as potent as ever. It seared my body.

"How much do you want me?" he asked.

"More than I should," I admitted, because the full weight of my burgeoning feelings for him was crushing me.

Then I showed him how much. Tugging up my skirt. Pulling down my panties.

Asking.

"Gorgeous," he muttered, grabbing a chair and parking himself between my legs.

Where I wanted him right now.

Where I needed him.

"Do you like what you see?" I asked seductively.

He swallowed thickly, and breathed out hard. "You know I fucking love it."

"How much?"

He groaned as he roamed his eyes over my legs. He brushed his lips across my left ankle, and I shivered, then he licked a path up my calf. His mouth on my skin was divine. It was righting the universe.

But he stopped, standing and grasping my chin in his hand. "Tell me what you want."

"You know what I want," I whispered.

"And you know I want you to say it. Say the words."

My eyes met his. "Touch me. Taste me. Have me."

"More," he said as he held my face. "Tell me exactly what you want."

"Brent," I moaned, writhing on the table, the ache between my legs threatening to take over my mind, to devour my reason.

"You know it turns me on when you say it," he said, grabbing my hand with his free hand and guiding me to his crotch. I gasped as I palmed his erection. So thick and long.

"Fuck me with your tongue," I whispered, and he throbbed even through the denim.

In a blur, he moved back to the chair, his hands circling my ankles. Then my feet were up on the table, my knees raised, and I was spread wide for him. His face was right there, his breath ghosting over me, his mouth so close to my slick heat.

I burned hot when he kissed the inside of my thigh. "I bet you taste like heaven," he murmured.

"Find out."

He dived in, and I moaned—a long, loud cry that carried through the quiet. Pleasure rippled through me instantly. He kissed, he licked, and he sucked. He adored my pussy with his sinful mouth. I threw my head back, gazing at the ceiling as I relished in him, letting him worship me the way he always had.

He licked me mercilessly, his wicked tongue stroking my heat, sending me soaring, flying into a world of absolute bliss.

I trembled from head to toe. I burst with pleasure so intense it blotted out everything but his touch. I arched my back, lifted my hips, and rocked into him in a frenzy.

He'd always said that going down on me was like being fucked too. That I'd get so into it, and it drove him wild. He'd craved it just as much as I had. The evidence, the proof of how I loved his touch lay in the way I moved under his mouth.

"Shan, do that. Fucking go crazy," he told me, and I was right there with his command, thrusting wildly, writhing and wriggling as he groaned and consumed my pleasure with his mouth.

Stars circled my head. The earth fell out of orbit. The sky split open.

I grabbed his hair, screaming in pleasure, calling out his name, as I came on his tongue.

Then, before I let myself get lost in my own bliss, I slid off the table, got on my knees, and showed him I wasn't just a taker. I was a giver too.

And I gave it good.

So damn good, he was grunting my name a few minutes later.

14

BRENT

As she handed me a glass of water in her kitchen, I didn't press. I didn't ask if we were all good again.

I didn't want to assume mind-blowing orgasms all around would restore all that had gone wrong.

Instead, I kept moving forward, because that was what we were doing.

"When I was in New York, I saw a sign for the Alvin Ailey dance company on tour," I mentioned as I took a drink.

Her eyes lit up. "I love Alvin Ailey. It was my dream to win a spot in Alvin Ailey."

"I know. And I remember in college you wanted me to go with you. But I had a gig so I canceled on you."

Her smile fell. The memory of another one of my mistakes must have just returned to her. I kept talking, eager to right that wrong from years ago. "So I bought tickets to see them here next week. I'd really like to take you. And I will keep my promise to take you."

She looped her arms around my neck. "Yes. I would love to go."

I wanted to pump my fist in the air, to shout a victorious *Yes!* Then I wanted to close my eyes and groan in pleasure, because she was running her fingers through my hair. I loved the feel of her hands in my hair.

"You really know how to treat a woman you used to go out with, don't you?" she teased.

"Speaking of that," I said, pulling back and cupping my hands on her shoulders. Tonight had gone so well, and I wanted to build on it. To keep up the momentum. To do that, we'd need to let go of the old wounds. "Shan, how would you feel if we agreed to move on from the past?"

She tilted her head, considering my question. "To put it behind us?"

I nodded, hoping she'd want the same. "Yes."

She smiled, a little sweet, a little sexy, all her. "I kind of thought that was what we were doing."

"Good," I admitted with a relieved grin.

She looked me square in the eyes. The corners of her lips curved up, like she had more to say. I held my breath, waiting.

"I think we could both use a fresh start, so let's focus on the here and now, not the way things were."

I smiled broadly. "Good. So we're dating, then," I said as I drank the rest of the water.

She tapped my shoulder, a chiding look in her eyes. "I think it's best if we don't label what's happening between us."

I could live with not labeling. But I couldn't live with

the possibility that someone else might try to date her. I had to lay down one ground rule. "I'm fine with not labeling, as long as the not-label includes not dating other men."

She arched an eyebrow. "Or other women."

"Yes. That too. I don't want you dating men or women. Good point," I said, in mock seriousness.

She wagged a finger at me. "You know exactly what I meant."

"Yes, yes, I do." I took a step closer, my face serious. "I know we're not labeling, but I still want to support you emotionally. In any way I can."

She drew in a deep breath, indecision in her eyes, before she reached for something on the counter. "Will you open this letter with me?"

"Yes." Reverently, I took the envelope, and knowing she trusted me with her mother's words meant even more to me than her trusting me with her body.

The letter was short. Choppy. Written in a scrawl.

Baby,

I'm thinking so many things.

I lie awake at night, and during the day, my mind is busy, busy, busy.

I think and I work through my thoughts, like they're a pattern.

Life is a pattern, isn't it?

And the pattern on the calendar says June 30th is getting closer. So much to tell you. So much I hope you can help with.

I've been thinking of what to wear when I see you.

Ha ha.

I'm just being silly.

But maybe I'm not, because it is my dream. I wish I could dress up for you, baby. I wish I could go shopping and wear something pretty for your visit. A pink blouse. A white T-shirt. Maybe some nice capri pants. Are they in fashion again?

I'd like a handbag too. Something cute and feminine.

I'd dress up for you so you'd know how special the day is to me.

It's all I want. To see you. To see my little girl, who's now a grown woman. I'm so proud of you, Shannon Bean. So proud, and I wish I could show you. I wish I could take you out to a nice meal and get you a cake and send you flowers. I wish I could be your mom again, letting you know how much you matter to me.

And how proud I am.

So proud.

So incredibly proud.

And I hope, and I hope, and I hope to see you soon.

I'll be in orange, but know in my heart, I'm laying out my clothes and dressing in pink and looking pretty for my baby girl.

Soon. Will I see you soon? I will. I know I will.

I believe. I believe everything can be different.

Your loving mommy

I swallowed roughly, the taste of the letter like sawdust in my mouth. But worse for Shannon, so much worse.

A tear slid down her cheek.

I reached for her, wrapped my arms around her, and

held her tight. I said nothing, because there was nothing to say.

Actions spoke louder.

After I held her for a few minutes, she wriggled out of my arms. "Shoot. My friend's cat. I told her I'd feed him tonight. Let me run upstairs, and then I'll give you a proper goodbye kiss."

She grabbed a key, then darted out.

And I needed to take a leak, so I headed down the hallway, found the bathroom, and took care of business.

When I was through, I washed my hands, left the bathroom, then spotted her bedroom.

It was bright and yellow, like the rest of her home. I'd caught a glimpse of it when I walked in, but hadn't taken it in. Her home had an open, airy feel, even at night.

As I peered into her bedroom, I spotted a frame on her bureau, like the one I'd noticed on her kitchen counter—more sunflowers. This one held an image of bright sunflowers next to a stone.

She loved those flowers. *My favorites*, she'd once said.

Maybe I'd get her some, since they were really her thing now, it seemed. Stepping into her room, I picked up the frame, checking out the photo more closely, when I spotted a date written on it.

A date ten years ago.

That was . . . odd.

Wasn't that right around when we split up?

My skin prickled as I peered at the image. What was that stone?

I didn't know. But when I set the photo down, the frame rattled, like something was loose behind it.

I turned it around.

A flimsy image slipped from the back.

A black-and-white image.

A grainy black-and-white image that could only be one thing.

My heart sped up in my chest, spinning wildly out of control. Blood pounded in my ears, and my throat went dry.

I inhaled deeply, as if the air would steel me, but my breath still came erratically.

Then I did it. With traitorous fingers that dug into her privacy, I pulled out the black-and-white image.

There was one more behind it.

A shot of her looking in a mirror in her London apartment. My heart tripped back in time as I gazed at Shannon, *my* Shannon, from ten years ago. Her hair was short then and still blonde, her face so fresh and young, her expression a half-hearted smile. She had taken the photo of herself. Her belly was still flat.

Shoes clicked on the floor, and the hair on the back of my neck stood on end. I replaced the two hidden images and put the photo down as she called out my name.

But when I turned around, she was standing in the doorway, and I had my hand on the picture frame, as if trying to hide the pictures it held.

Her expression was one of shock. Then disappointment, and next came a trace of grief. Somehow her eyes contained all three.

She swallowed, and her face seemed pinched. But it was her voice that gave her away. A bare whisper, laced with pain, as she closed her eyes, opened them, and spoke. "I was going to tell you tonight."

15

SHANNON

But I had a question for him, as shame and guilt washed over me.

Maybe defensiveness too.

A whole lot of that, for sure.

"Why were you going through my picture frame?" I asked as I stood in the doorway. This wasn't how I'd wanted to tell him. I didn't want him to discover the lone photo of the ultrasound at eleven weeks and the picture of me I'd planned to give him.

His voice was heavy. "The sunflower caught my attention. You always loved sunflowers. And there was a date on the photo. Ten years ago."

"So you looked through the photos?"

"Yes. I was curious. And now I want to know what happened." His tone was no longer barren. It was full of need and fear.

My skin prickled with nerves too, because I was stumbling blindly now. I'd wanted to tell him on my own terms. Not like this. Never like this.

I shook my head, as if I could erase the last ten minutes. Start over—begin at the beginning. Sit down, talk, share the whole sad story, and then feed the cat. I'd never wanted him to discover the truth on his own. A part of me was mad as hell that he'd gone through the frame in my bedroom, and a part of me was deeply ashamed that he'd found the images I'd planned to give him before I had a chance to explain.

The images that were now my private memorial.

I needed to wrest control this second. Straightening my spine, I cleared my throat. "I was pregnant. When we ended. I was going to tell you."

"When? When did you find out?" he asked, as if every word was new and foreign.

I tried to tell the story as clinically as I could. "I missed a couple periods, but that wasn't odd for me. As a dancer, I'd never had a normal cycle."

He pressed on, desperation in his tone. "And then what?"

My heart cratered as the terrible memory clutched me.

This was harder than I'd ever imagined. I knew it wasn't going to be easy to get the awful words out, but being forced to say them tasted even worse. Bitter and acrid on my tongue. I drew in a deep breath and laid them out, one by one in a row of awfulness. "I miscarried when I went home to Vegas. I was with Michael."

"Oh God," Brent said hoarsely, sounding as if he'd been punched.

I had never seen him like this, white as snow, shocked to the bone.

Time crawled painfully to the next second, then the next, and then the next. Soon, he managed to string more words together. "And now I know yet another thing you kept from me."

Something inside me snapped, like an electrical wire sliced to the ground from high above.

"No," I said, shaking my head, with some kind of dangerous cocktail of anger, shame, and hurt mixing up inside me. "Don't pull that on me."

He lifted his chin, planted his feet wide. I knew that stance. Had seen it once before. It meant he was angry, and Brent was rarely angry. The only time he'd been mad was when I'd kept my family secrets private. "But you did it again," he said tightly. "Keeping everything to yourself and punishing me."

I tried to keep the pot on simmer, rather than boil. "That's not what this was about. It wasn't about keeping things from you."

"Like hell it wasn't. You never told me you were pregnant. Why? Why didn't you tell me?"

The pot boiled, emotions bubbling over. "You don't get to claim I was never giving you a chance. That's bullshit. I was eleven weeks pregnant, and I was emotional. I was hormonal. And then I lost the baby."

Brent wobbled. The world seemed to sway in front of him. He grabbed the doorframe, nearly crumpling. I wrapped my arms around him. Thankfully, he didn't shrug me off. In the smallest voice, he croaked out, "But why didn't you tell me *after?*"

My throat squeezed painfully as I gripped his shoulder. "Because we were over then, Brent. When I got home from the hospital with Michael, you and I were over. But the words still came out shaky, marked with tears. "And because there was nothing to tell. It was a miscarriage. It's awful, but it happens all the time. I didn't keep a child from you. I didn't have a child and give it up. I didn't even know the gender of the baby. I didn't even make it past the first trimester. What was I going to say?"

He yanked away from me, pointing at me accusingly. "That. Say that. You should have said that." He looked me in the eyes. His were full of fierce determination. "I would have been there for you. I would have been there for you in a heartbeat."

Emotions roiled in me. "You say that now, but how was I to know? I was going to mention the three canceled trips. Oh, wait. *Four.* Tell me again how I was supposed to know you wanted to be there for me. You didn't exactly demonstrate that."

He huffed through his nostrils. "That's not fair."

"Life isn't fair."

He made a fist, banged it against the doorframe. "I hate that you went through it all alone without me."

"Me too," I gritted out. Then sadly, I whispered, "Me too."

"You should have told me." He shook his head over and over, repeating the same words. "You should have told me. You should have told me. I hate that you went through this alone. I wanted to be there for you, and you didn't give me the chance."

I choked back the tears. "I wanted that too. But how was I to know what you wanted?"

16

BRENT

I'd just learned I was a bigger schmuck than I'd initially thought. I had done something far worse than walk away from the love of my life. Turned out, I'd abandoned the mother of my child when she needed me most.

I pictured her in Vegas, her world changing, and now I couldn't fathom what to do next . . .

I paced the hallway. I opened my mouth, but I had no clue how to respond. I was a fish out of water, gasping for air. Everything had come easily to me. I'd never suffered bad news. I'd never lost someone I loved. But now, I felt the sting of devastation for the first time ever. I was experiencing all sorts of things that had become far too normal for Shannon. Unlike her, I had no road map to navigate this new terrain.

"I don't know what to say," I muttered.

"It's okay. You don't have to say the perfect thing," she said softly. She followed me into the kitchen and clasped my hands in hers, consoling me. "Forgive me."

Our anger was cooling.

But I didn't know what to replace it with.

And I couldn't let her comfort me. Not when I'd failed her abysmally.

When we'd failed each other.

I pushed her hands away because I didn't know how to touch her. I didn't deserve her affection. "I'm sorry I looked through your frame."

She flashed a small smile, absolving me. "It's okay. Though I wish you hadn't, because I was planning on telling you tonight."

In a flash, my guilt vanished because that sounded awfully convenient. I arched an eyebrow in question and shoved all my hurt on her. "Why didn't you tell me sooner?"

She stepped back. "I only started seeing you a few days ago. It's not really the sort of thing you say at a first meeting. 'Sorry I haven't seen you in ten years, but hey, thought you might like to know it turned out I was pregnant when we split.'"

"That's a start," I said, even though those words felt all wrong, out of sync.

"Brent, that's not a start. That's not how you tell someone something hard."

She had a point, but I could barely see it. I was brimming with self-loathing. I hardly knew what to do with all this horribleness, so I threw her apology back at her. "You need to give me a chance."

"I *am* giving you a chance," she said, her voice breaking with tears and anger. "And you know that. I am more open with you than I have been with anyone in my entire life. You just expected it from day one. And I'm so sorry I'm less than perfect at finding the best moment to tell you about the tragic circumstances that have trailed behind me."

I tossed my hands in the air and huffed. "There you go again. It's always about you. It's always about the shit you've been through."

She flinched, as a fresh stream of tears rained down her cheeks. "What? What did you just say?" Her eyes narrowed, and a fissure opened in my chest.

Damn it. That wasn't what I meant.

I had to get out of there.

Because I *didn't* know what to say, what to do.

I didn't have the skills.

I didn't have the words.

I'd just dug a hole so damn deep, and I couldn't scramble out of it in front of her.

"I didn't mean that," I said, grabbing my keys, backing up.

She swiped her hand across her cheeks, wiping away the tears. They seemed to be falling faster now, relentlessly streaking down her face. "I guess it's nice not to have to deal with shit, isn't it? Bet it's nice when everything is sunshine. Maybe if you could think about it, you'd realize it wasn't so easy to tell you on our first date in college that my mother was in prison. That she sent me letters that ripped me to pieces. That prison made her go insane." Her words flew, firing like bullets. "And I'm so sorry that I didn't tell you at the Waldorf Astoria, or at your friend's bar, or at our amazing dinner tonight that I'd lost a pregnancy." She held up two fingers. "If you think about it, we've only had two dates. The bar and dinner. That's it." She took a breath, slowed her pace, cooled her voice. "You need to give me a chance. And if you would, maybe you'd realize that it's hard for me to just serve up more of the pain. But I guess now you know how it feels to lose something. It's pretty awful, isn't it?"

I nodded and clamped my lips shut. I swallowed, and the lump in my throat was like a jagged rock. It cut me to pieces, and I had no clue what I'd say if I spoke again.

Ten years ago, I hadn't done enough for her and for us. Hadn't tried enough before we'd split and after.

But now, in our present, I didn't know what was enough. What was too much.

And what was needed.

All I knew was I was treading dangerously close to fucking up again.

I couldn't chance it happening a second time. I headed to the door.

She followed me, grabbing my arm and spinning me around. Devastation was written in her eyes. "Are you leaving me?"

I took her hand, peeled it off me, then cupped her shoulders. "I'm not walking away," I said, taking my time with each word. "But I'm pissed at myself for not having the right words to say. I'm leaving because I don't want to say or do another wrong thing. I will call you tomorrow. I promise. But if I don't leave right now, I will do the wrong thing. And I can't let that happen."

I opened the door and left.

17

SHANNON

The next morning, I scratched Nick between the ears. The tabby arched his back.

Purring contentedly, Nick rubbed against my legs, a thank you for feeding him again.

"You're a sweetie," I said as I crouched in Ally's condo, stroking the happy creature. My voice sounded empty to my own ears, a hollow noise, mirroring my insides.

Eight hours later, and no word from Brent.

I was a big girl. I could handle eight hours; I could give him time. Even though it felt like an eternity. My body was keenly aware of every passing minute, and each one wore me to the bone. Running a hand down the cat's back, I wished my life were as easy as his—eat, purr, be happy.

But the universe insisted on throwing hurdles and roadblocks at me. The universe kept moving the line. Jump higher. Run faster.

Then it cackled at me and demanded I do it once more.

Right when I'd started to feel good again, considering the wonderful time we'd had last night at dinner. Our date had felt like the true start of something wonderful, the brand-new beginning of us.

That was what hurt so much. After ten years of barely getting over him, I'd let down my guard in just a few days. And here I was with a raw, beating heart, broken thanks to the mess I'd made, with no one here to tend to it.

But me.

"Be a good boy. Ally will be home later today," I told the cat, who answered me with one final silky rub of his head against my leg.

I locked the door and texted my friend.

Shannon: Nick is fed, rested, and ready for your return. Meow!

With a heavy heart, I popped back into my place, grabbed my purse, dropped a big pair of shades over my eyes, and drove to the airport. At the gate, I saw Colin, ready for our quick in-and-out day trip. He leaned against the window looking at his phone. An airline voice blared overhead. "Flight twenty-three from Las Vegas to Burbank will board in ten minutes."

Colin tucked his phone away when he saw me walking to him. "You look like hell," he said.

I rolled my eyes. "Thanks. Good to see you too."

"What's wrong?"

"Didn't sleep much," I said, yawning.

"Is that a good thing or a bad thing?"

I shrugged a shoulder. "Bad thing."

"Man trouble?" he asked, arching an eyebrow.

"Something like that."

"Be a nun. Easier that way."

I narrowed my eyes at him. "You be a monk. How about that?"

He shook his head. "Hell no." He tipped his forehead to a Starbucks across the concourse. "Let me get you a coffee. We can't have you yawning like that in the meeting."

On the short flight to Burbank, I downed my coffee, the caffeine rejuvenating me, temporarily erasing the sleeplessness. I touched up my makeup as Colin walked me through his goals for the meeting with the reality show producers who wanted me to choreograph a one-night reunion, but my mind kept wandering to Brent walking away last night.

It was déjà vu.

The door shutting.

The two of us on opposite sides.

The trouble was, he was right.

We were both at fault.

We'd both made mistakes.

I had assumed the worst years ago because that was what I did. That was my normal, my yardstick, and it had been ever since I was thirteen and lost the person I'd thought would always be there.

Then I'd lost another person to a life behind bars.

After my family was shattered, I'd had no reason to think there were happy endings. Not in life, not in love.

The only love you could trust was brotherly.

I choked up at the thought, touching Colin's arm as the plane hurtled across the sky. "Do you ever feel like we'll never be normal?"

He cocked his head to the side, stroked his chin, then shrugged. "Screw normal. Also, what's going on, Shan?" His tone was kind, caring, reminding me that my brothers were my men. We were each other's rocks. That was our promise to each other.

I sighed heavily, then fashioned words out of my thoughts. "Sometimes I think I can never trust anyone. Do you ever feel that way?"

He rubbed my shoulder. "Sometimes I do. But I hope that changes."

I rested my head against his shoulder. "I don't know how to assume the best."

"When you've had the worst happen, it can be pretty hard to believe anything else. It's taken me a long time to have any sort of positive outlook."

I lifted my face. "But do you now?"

"Sometimes. And sometimes that's all I can hope for," he said, with a *what can you do* smile.

"Is sometimes enough?"

"Maybe it is, Shan. Maybe it is for people like us."

People like us.

That was who we were.

We were broken. We were cleaved down the middle. Our world had been knocked upside down.

Would I ever be able to believe in love?

Part of me wanted to. Part of me wanted to stop assuming the worst. Another part knew I carried the weight of years of doing so with me. Because the worst had happened. The worst was my world.

"Let's talk about something else. Tell me what to expect from the meeting. Business—I can handle that like a Sloan," I said, false bravado in my tone.

He raised a fist for knocking. "Be a Sloan." Then he segued into his advisor role. "The meeting should be short and sweet, and I have some key thoughts on how to make this a good deal for you," he said, then rattled off his thoughts.

I squeezed his arm. "You're the best. Thank you for always looking out for my interests."

He waved a hand as we pulled apart. "You make it easy."

When we landed in Los Angeles, my phone was silent. No messages. No texts. No calls.

My heart sank. Brent had been radio silent all through the night and early morning.

But he'd promised, and that had to be enough.

We deplaned on the tarmac, the sun shining brightly.

Keep on living, keep on moving, and keep on fighting.

18

BRENT

As my real estate attorney talked about neighborhoods in Chicago that were ripe for nightclubs, I stared at an abstract piece of art that hung on the wall—a series of red, gray, and yellow geometric shapes jutted across the canvas at harsh angles. I studied it, as if I could make out the meaning, but I saw nothing. I let my eyes go blurry, let the shapes melt into each other, into a jumbled rainbow. The one color I could still make out was yellow.

Like those damn sunflowers.

Why did she have all those pictures of sunflowers? Where were they taken?

I didn't know. Because she didn't let me in.

Was that her fault? Or mine?

I wanted to blame her, but I had to shoulder the load too. I *had* canceled the Alvin Ailey date in college. I had canceled three trips to see her after graduation.

Most importantly, I had backed out of the last trip.

Ten years ago, I should have said no to that Marvel sketch. Should have said no to Jed.

"So there you go. We should be able to secure the property in Chicago, and I hope we can get that one you had your sights set on in Atlanta. Ten-four, gentlemen?"

Tate raised his eyebrows and glanced around the conference table, waiting for an okay from me and James.

But I was lost in the past, thinking of Shannon. And in the present too. Maybe I didn't know how to handle a complicated woman. Maybe I wasn't equipped to be the right man for someone who'd had so much thrown at her.

Guilt clawed at me. Would I ever be right for her?

Tate and James were asking me questions, but they might as well be speaking Swahili. Hell, everyone was speaking in foreign tongues today. Sanskrit and Latin and Greek rained down on me. I had no clue what anyone was saying.

"Sounds great," I somehow managed to say, finding those words deep within some primordial part of me that remembered how to communicate.

After Tate left, I stood too, but James sat me back down. Concern was etched in his eyes. "Never seen you like this." James gestured heavenward. "It wasn't even like you weren't here—it was like you were on another planet."

I rubbed my hand over my jaw, the day-old stubble reminding me that I hadn't even bothered to shave this morning. I glanced down at my outfit, making sure I'd remembered to put on clothes. The jeans and button-down I wore were the only reassurance that I hadn't gone completely insane. I'd remembered to dress.

"Sorry," I said.

James patted me on the shoulder. "Hey, no worries. I'm here for you. This is your ship, and you steer it. But my job is to have your back. You sure you're okay?"

No. I wasn't.

Only, I had to man up. I had to deal. I had to do a better job. After all, how could I be there for Shannon if I couldn't even assist my colleagues?

But before I could answer, he kept going. "And how can I help?"

Help.

That four-letter word said so much.

Maybe what I needed was help.

Because hand in hand with help came honesty. Openness. Vulnerability.

That was what I'd need with her.

Perhaps I could start in some small way here.

"James," I said, holding up my hands in surrender, owning up to my issues. "I'm someplace else right now. Help me out. What do you need from me?"

"I'm glad you asked."

We sat down and reviewed what the hell that meeting had been about.

I focused on him, shared my thoughts, and made decisions.

When he was through, he clapped my shoulder. "I'm good with this plan, and I'm glad you're on board, but why don't you take the rest of the day off? Whatever business you have scheduled, I can attend to."

"I should cut out early," I said, blinking, trying to focus again on the world around me.

"Do that. Let me know what you need me to take care of. I've got some calls to make."

That sparked a wire in my brain.

Call.

I'd promised Shannon I'd call today.

The day was young, and I was going to make sure I showed up for her.

Like Mindy had said, I needed to prove to her I could be the man she needed.

I might not know how to be there for her, but I would ask, I would learn, and I would listen.

And I would do.

I stood, a blast of necessary energy zipping through me. I went to the Wynn to find Mindy.

19

SHANNON

Colin high-fived me as soon as the glass doors to the network headquarters swung shut. The network had agreed to the terms, and my brother had just booked me a marquee contract for a quick, high-paying, high-profile gig.

The deal-making momentarily took my mind off the sting of last night.

But only momentarily.

"You're a rock star," I told him as we headed down the steps to the waiting car that would whisk us back to the airport, then home to Vegas before the clock struck three.

"No, you are," he said.

As soon as we slid into the air-conditioned vehicle, I checked my phone, hoping for something.

The screen was empty. A lump rose in my throat, but I shoved it back down. I would not cry over a lack of messages. I would not lament the radio silence.

He'd made a promise to call me today, and the day wasn't over. I had a choice before me.

I could believe him.

I hadn't believed hard enough before.

If I wanted this to work, I would have to.

But I didn't have to handle this waiting alone.

I had my brother.

He'd been there for me. I'd been there for him. We'd helped each other through the roughest spots in our lives.

I dropped a hand on Colin's arm. "Hey, you know when you asked about my man trouble this morning?"

"Ah, so that's what it is?"

"Yes," I said, a knot in my throat.

"Had a feeling. What kind?" His tone was caring, gentle.

"It's Brent."

His eyes widened. "Whoa."

"We started seeing each other again."

"After the meeting at the Waldorf Astoria?"

"Yes."

"Damn, you got it bad."

I slugged his arm. "Stop!"

"I'm just saying—I'm impressed." Then he turned serious. "Tell me what's up."

Quickly, I caught him up to speed on the basics, then finished with "And the thing is, I want to change. You know how to change behaviors," I said, since Colin had battled drug and alcohol addiction years ago, finding his way to the other side. "How do you do it?"

He drew in a deep breath and smiled. "You make a choice."

"It's that simple?"

He nodded, clasping my hand. "It's that simple, and it's that hard."

I let those words register. They made all the sense in the world. I had all my options in front of me.

I could choose to change. I could choose to have faith. I could choose to believe.

"I can do that," I said, keeping my voice strong. Brent and I would work it out.

He'd promised.

I believed.

"And I'm here for you. Whatever you need," Colin said.

"I know," I replied softly, resting my head briefly on his shoulder.

Then I opened a new text message and sent Brent a note.

Shannon: *I am thinking of you. I'm always thinking of you. When you're ready, I'm here.*

That was it. That was all. It was time to make a change. It was my turn to believe in hope.

I had history. I had baggage. But I was willing to fight my way to the other side.

20

BRENT

Dolly Parton's "9 to 5" rang out from a nearby slot machine as coins splashed into the metal bucket. A guy in a Hawaiian shirt working the one-armed bandit shouted a triumphant *"Yes!"*

Mindy and I walked past the slot machines while she made her afternoon rounds through the casino.

"I see you are in need of my royal wisdom," Mindy began.

I held up a finger. "Always, Queen."

"Then get ready for some tough love, my friend." She stopped at an empty Cleopatra machine, parking her hand on the historical figure's golden headband.

I bounced on my toes like a boxer. "I'm ready. Bring it on."

"Here goes. You want her back? Then you don't get to step away when shit gets hard."

"I didn't walk away," I said, trying to defend my actions. "I told her I needed time to deal with it."

Mindy nodded a few times, acknowledging me.

"Fine, you needed time. You needed space. I understand. It was a shock. Well, you've had your time and you've had your space. Now, man up."

That knocked me out of my stupor of self-loathing. I had wanted so badly to be everything she needed, but when push came to shove, I'd let pride and fear and a million other things stand in the way.

"Shit," I said heavily. "I've fucked up."

"No. You haven't fucked up," she said, pressing her fingers to my cheeks and turning my frown upside down. "You just took a step back. Now, take some steps forward. This time, instead of walking away, walk back to her. Talk to her. And don't be afraid, because you think you can't handle it. Because you think you aren't equipped." She poked my chest. "Because you are. You worked your ass off to get where you are in business. You did it in comedy, and you're doing it with your clubs. Apply that same tenacity to her."

But did I do that today in the meeting? I raised a hand tentatively. "Confession—my mind was elsewhere in a meeting today. I had to ask James for a recap."

She smacked my shoulder. "Good."

"How is that good?"

She rolled her eyes. "You asked for help. You need to do that with her. Ask her how you can be there for her. Ask her how to be the man she needs. Tell her you might not always know but you want to try."

Mindy's words were ice water splashed onto me. They were the stark reminder that I might not even truly comprehend the scope of Shannon's past and her pain. But that would be all right, if I could be there for her.

The thing I'd failed to do before was what I had to do now. "I need to see her right away."

I cycled back to our last few conversations, trying to figure out where she might be. "I think she's on her way back from LA. I'm guessing that showing up at the airport with a sign isn't the way to go?"

Mindy patted my shoulder. "You are learning. Such a good subject."

And I was learning.

Don't give up.

I reached for my phone, tensing briefly when I saw a text from her. Then grinning as I read it, because her words meant so damn much.

They meant she wasn't assuming the worst.

She was hoping for the best.

I dialed her number. It went straight to voicemail.

But this time around, I would show up.

* * *

I waited outside her building, with a bouquet of sunflowers in one hand.

In some ways, flowers were just flowers. They were an ordinary, average gift. But since Shannon had photos of sunflowers in her home, they were clearly her favorite.

They also said I'd listened. That I was trying to understand the woman I wanted back.

After I parked my bike at the curb, I sat on the steps and answered emails.

I called her again, and encountered her voicemail once more. But that was okay.

There would be no missed calls, no missed emails.

And no mixed messages.

I would be clear.

I stood, pacing back and forth in front of the building. I probably looked like a stalker, and I hoped her neighbors wouldn't call the cops or neighborhood watch on me.

Nobody seemed to care, though, that I was hovering around the entrance. A hipster with huge headphones nodded hello on his way upstairs. A brunette with a yoga mat walked past me and into the lobby.

Some dude in a Buick parked by the curb glanced over at me a few times, giving a cursory *hey there* nod.

I paced up and down the block to kill more time, my phone clutched in my hand. I reached the corner, turned around, and headed back.

The guy was still in his car, his arm hanging out the driver's window, watching Shannon's building.

A bit too closely for my taste.

He'd been there for twenty, thirty minutes, looking like he was reading a book, but he kept glancing up, scanning the street as if he didn't want to miss anything.

It reminded me of a cop on a stakeout, only the guy didn't reek of cop. He was too young.

And something about him rubbed me the wrong way. It was hard to say what it was, but as I neared the

Buick again, I held up my phone as if answering a message.

Instead, I snapped a few pictures of the side of the car, so I could zoom in on the guy's arm, covered in ink.

I tucked my phone away as I reached the open window. "How's it going?" I asked casually.

"Good," the guy grumbled. He had a baby face and looked young enough to be carded if he were at Edge. I continued along the block, and turned around again at the corner. As I returned, the Buick was no longer idling at the curb.

The guy pulled out into traffic and was driving away. I took one more shot, trying to capture his license plate, getting most of the numbers but not quite all.

Probably just some neighborhood guy. But I didn't like the idea of anyone hanging around Shannon's building for too long. Except for me. Call me a hypocrite, but I knew my own motives. Trusted my own motives.

Then I stopped thinking about anyone but Shannon when her name flashed across my screen.

At last.

I answered in a nanosecond.

21

THE GUY OUTSIDE THE BUILDING

I hadn't seen her today.

But still, I watched.

It was my turn.

And I had to take it. To do what I had to do.

I'd seen her before, a couple of times. I'd checked out her hood too.

Nice location, that was for sure.

She was lucky, damn lucky, to live here.

Today, I saw some dude pacing in front of the place, and I made mental notes. Tattoos on his arms. Dark hair. And flowers.

I wanted to know who he was.

What he knew.

What he didn't know.

If he had answers I didn't have.

Someday, I'd have all the answers.

But I didn't need to draw attention to myself, or my mission. I started the engine, dropped my shades, and took off, leaving the guy with the sunflowers behind.

22

SHANNON

My thirsty phone drank its charge on the drive home, waking up near my condo. Glancing briefly at the screen, I saw a barrage of missed calls from Brent.

I squealed.

I called back immediately.

"I'm at your house, waiting for you," he said.

Those words. They made my heart soar. "I'll be there in one minute."

My heart thumped too when I pulled up to the curb. I stepped out of the car, and he was waiting outside my building.

For me.

Looking cool and sexy and so damn caring. Standing in the afternoon sun, holding a bouquet of flowers.

"Hey, gorgeous. I made you a promise," he said, striding across the sidewalk. Our eyes connected.

"Yeah? What's that?" I asked, trying to hide a smile but failing as I got out of the car. The smile owned me.

"That I'd call. That I'd see you. That I'd be here for you," he said, strong and confident.

He stopped inches from me, flowers in hand, and I looked up at him. "I want to be here for you too," I said.

"We'll be here for each other. How does that sound?"

I sighed. Contentedly. "It sounds like . . ." I took my time, enjoying the moment, before I said, "Perfection."

He handed me the flowers. "These are for you."

My smile could not be contained. I wasn't quite ready to tell him why, or all that they meant to me, but I told him enough, saying, "Sunflowers are my favorite."

He slid his arm around my waist. "Listen, I know it takes more than just appearing out of thin air at your house. I know I need to apologize yet again. Because I said some things last night I'm not proud of. I said, *It's always about you.* And that's a terrible thing to say." He stroked my cheek with his other hand. "You've been to hell and back, babe. And all I want is to be by your side. To be your man. I won't always know what to say, I won't always know what to do, but I want to be here. For you. For us. Do you believe me?"

My heart thundered in my chest. "I do, Brent. And I want that too. But I also don't want to be the baggage in your life. I want to help carry yours too. I have been through some tough times, and that means I've got some experience dealing with whatever trouble might come. So if you ever need me to carry your bags, I'll do it for you."

He grinned, a lopsided one. "I'm strong. I've got it."

I set the flowers gently on the ground, then ran my

hands along his arms, strong indeed. "I know you are. But you can lean on me if you need to."

He pressed his shoulder against mine, smiling. "Like this?"

"Exactly," I said.

He wrapped me in his arms. So strong, so warm. "Shan, I wish I were there for you ten years ago. I wish I'd been there because I would have been so damn happy to hear your news," he said, and my throat hitched at his words. "And I would have been sad with you the next day, but I would have held your hand, and brushed your hair, and brought you soup, and taken care of you."

Tears leaked down my face at the sentiment, the beauty of it, the heart of it. I looked up at him. "Thank you," I whispered, barely able to speak. But I had to. I had to find my voice. "I would have wanted all that."

He ran the back of his fingers along my cheeks, wiping my tears away. "But I'm glad we talked about it. And I'm here if you ever want to talk about it again."

I smiled, shook my head. "I'm good. I want to move forward."

"Me too," he said softly.

Then I cleared my throat, because if I was going to make a change—and that was the choice I was indeed making—it had to come with truth and ownership. "But I'm not done yet. Because you were right—I do assume the worst. I do go to the negative. I've done that with you, and it's not fair. I want you to know I'm going to try like hell to assume the best."

A grin was my reward. "I'm all for good assumptions. Like, for instance, you can assume I'll want to see you tomorrow," he said with a wiggle of his eyebrows.

I looped my arms around his neck. "Good. Assume I'll say yes."

"I like when you make an ass of you and me," he said, and I laughed, relishing that we could go from tears to laughter in the span of a few minutes. His hands gripped my waist, and he dropped the teasing. "Shan, I know we've both done things to each other we regret, said things we wish we hadn't said."

"And we've both shut down. We've both turned away," I added, as we laid out our mistakes in the bright light of day.

"We have. But we can *decide* to stop doing that."

I couldn't have agreed with him more. "Yes. Let's have another do-over. Let's do what you said last night. Put the past behind us. For real."

"A clean slate," he said with a smile.

"Want one?" I asked.

He let go of my waist to stroke his chin, like he was deep in thought. "Let's see. Do I want a second chance with the one who got away? I wonder, wonder, wonder."

I swatted him. "I want a second chance with you. Let's label it now—*what's happening between us*. Let's give ourselves another chance. Everything is out in the open, and we're going to talk, to work things out, and to be honest."

His expression turned serious. "Yes."

He dropped a kiss to my lips that sent me soaring.

And I was damn near ready to tug him up to my place, but I had a meeting to go to that evening.

So I broke the kiss and suggested we see each other tomorrow.

"Like a date?"

"Like a starting over," I said.

And that sounded like perfection.

* * *

I held tight to those words—*what's happening between us.*

Labels or not, something was most definitely happening.

We were clearly dating again. I couldn't even try to pretend it was anything but real, honest-to-goodness dating. As if we had just met and were so taken with each other we had to see each other as often as we could. And we'd agreed to dial back the physical, to take our time as we got to know each other again.

It was scary and amazingly fun at the same time.

The next day, I visited Edge in the morning with my assistant choreographer, Christine, to make notes on the space, since the layout of their Vegas venue was similar to the one in San Francisco. James showed us around, but Brent popped out of his office to say hello.

"Hey, Shay. Good to see you," he said as he walked to the other end of the club. After we reviewed the plans for the show, Christine said she needed to return to the studio to rehearse the dancers, and James had other meetings to attend.

As I walked to the exit, Brent caught up with me. "Can I interest you in lunch?"

"*Assume* you can definitely interest me in lunch."

"I assume that's for the best," he added.

"Yes, it is."

Saying yes was easy. Saying yes felt right.

* * *

After we finished pho and chicken dumplings at an upscale Vietnamese restaurant on the Luxe's property, he said he had a gift for me.

"You really don't have to give me anything," I replied as the waiter cleared our plates, even though inside I was delighted. I adored his zest for giving me sweet little things.

"I know, but truth be told, it's not something I can control. My desire to give you gifts, that is." He reached into the pocket of his jeans. "I come from a long line of gift-giving men. It's in my blood, and it can't be bred out of me."

I laughed. "I would never want you to lose that trait, then."

He handed me a small champagne-colored drawstring pouch. I'd never had much growing up, and I'd learned to live with that. But that's not why Brent's generosity had thrilled me so much when we first began to date—I loved his gifts because they were a reminder that he was thinking about me. And my mind was usually on him too.

With quick, eager fingers, I untied the bag and

plucked out a pretty rose-gold bracelet. I gasped. It matched the silver one that I wore every day. Simple and stylish, it was just right for me.

"I noticed you started wearing bracelets," he said as he stretched his arm across the back of the booth, looking so casual and confident, but also hopeful. He clearly wanted me to like his gift. "You never did before, but you do now, so I picked this out for you."

"I love it," I said softly, my gaze on him. "So much."

His brown eyes sparkled at my response, and warmth rushed through me from knowing this simple give-and-take, this little back-and-forth, mattered. It was only lunch, but it was suddenly more.

I held out my wrist, letting him clasp the jewelry on me. Instantly, the moment shot me back in time to another night when he gave me jewelry. A ring.

The night he'd proposed, he'd taken me ice-skating. It was a sport I could still do well enough in spite of my injury. I'd shown off for him, gliding and spinning across the rink while he'd skated . . . well, the way most men who weren't hockey players or professional skaters skated. Clumsily.

It hadn't bothered him though. He'd laughed at his own clunkiness. And then, in a moment of magic, he'd proposed.

Amazing how, in spite of what I saw happen to my parents, I'd never had a single doubt about Brent. I had wanted to be his wife as much as I had wanted to dance —a pure, perfect, passionate love.

A dark thought landed in my mind. Had my mother felt that way when my father proposed to her?

When had Dora crossed the line from loving mother to killer wife? Was there a switch that had flipped in her, or had the possibility always been there, latent through the years? Did she start to change when she cheated on her husband with a well-liked local piano teacher?

I didn't know when the shift happened for her.

And I never would.

But that was her past.

They were her mistakes.

Her life.

This, in the here and now, was mine.

The present was the only thing that mattered.

I focused on Brent, not on my checkered parents and the imprint their ruined marriage had left on my heart.

I ran my finger across the metal. I loved this bracelet because it was from the man I was getting to know all over again.

"What are you thinking?" he asked me, as I stared down at his gift.

I looked up, meeting his gaze. This was a chance to be open. "I was thinking of the time we went ice-skating, and you proposed," I said, a little nervous to admit that. "When you told me that you loved me, that you'd love me always—I don't think I'd ever been happier."

"Me either." His Adam's apple dipped as he swallowed. "When you said yes, everything seemed perfect."

Seemed. We hadn't known then where our future would go. But perhaps it was all leading back to this. This perfect now with this perfect man.

I grinned, wanting to lighten the mood as I remembered his cartoonlike fall to the ice just moments before he'd popped the question. "At first, I really worried you'd hurt yourself. I didn't realize you were working your way onto one knee."

"I'll let you in on a secret—I did that on purpose." He laughed. "Agile AF. That's me."

"I'll make a sweatshirt for you with that title on it," I said, and my nerves were dashed just like that. By the way we could talk like this.

"King Schmuck. Agile AF," he said, like he was reciting his new name.

I shook my head. "News flash. You're not King Schmuck. Not at all."

He arched a brow, looking pleased. "I've clawed my way out of the King Schmuck cave?"

"I'd say you clawed your way out a while ago."

He pumped a fist.

I moved to the other side of the table, ran my hand through his hair, and whispered, "Thank you for the bracelet."

"It looks gorgeous on you," he said, locking his eyes with mine.

I held out my wrist so we could both admire it. "I always loved your gifts, and I still do. Because they're from you."

"Good, then you can assume I'll keep giving them."

And that was a very good assumption to make.

23

BRENT

The next day, I invited Shannon to the Thai restaurant at the Luxe. There was something so freeing, in a way, about the pattern we seemed to fall into with lunch. These moments in the middle of the workday, with a clear beginning and end, were perfect for getting to know her again. That was what we both seemed to crave.

After the food arrived, she jumped into questions. "Tell me more about leaving *Late Night Antics*. You said the show was canceled and the show's creator had a huge falling out with the network. Was that hard for you? You loved comedy so much, and you could easily have found another job in TV," she said as she rested her chin in her hands and looked at me, a curious expression in those green eyes. There was no judgment in her tone. It was just a simple question, and one I'd been asked by many others when I'd announced I was leaving the show that I'd wound up hosting.

But still.

My fork froze in midair over the chicken pumpkin curry. "Was it hard?" I repeated, stalling for time.

She nodded. "You were so successful, so popular. It couldn't have been easy."

My muscles tensed, a visceral response to a topic I didn't entirely want to get into with her. My work had driven us apart, and I was wary to discuss it, because I had loved it.

I feared that the full truth of that love would make me look bad.

Like the kind of guy she couldn't lean on. The kind of guy who might turn away.

I stared at the golden Thai dragon on the wall, at the red embroidered jacket behind the hostess stand, then at the sea of busy tables and booths full of tourists, high rollers, and Vegas businessmen and -women doing deals at the Luxe.

I pulled my eyes away from the crowd and back to Shannon. Her long brown hair fell loosely around her face, so different from the short, fresh-faced style she'd had in college. She was different too. Tougher than she'd been back then, but softer as well. More vulnerable at times.

I could easily spin a quick tale about loving the nightclub business with my whole heart. But I wanted to show her that I'd changed—by giving her the full truth, warts and all.

I inhaled deeply and steeled myself. "Look, I could tell you I love nightclubs like crazy. But that wouldn't be completely true. Yes, I've always craved the challenge of running a club. Yes, I do love Edge, and building it has been exciting, and I've enjoyed it. But absolutely I miss comedy at times."

Her brow knit. "So why didn't you stay in it? You could have worked on another show. I know the entertainment business is fickle, but you were well-liked. You could have found another gig, surely."

She wasn't wrong. I *could* have stayed in TV. I exhaled, because this was the part that was tougher to say, in case it reflected badly on me. "I could have. That's true. But the timing seemed portentous. I didn't want to wear out my welcome."

She tilted her head. "How so?"

"I wanted to go out on top. I didn't want anyone to cringe when I did my monologue. I didn't want anyone to say, 'His jokes are stale' or 'He's phoning it in.' So I made a choice to change careers."

She nodded a few times, as if she was processing my decision. "I get it. You wanted to leave on your own terms. But why do you say that as if you think I won't like it?"

I was going to have to spell it out, no matter how bad it made me look. "Because I was worried you'd think it proves I don't stick around. That I just change my circumstances when I have the opportunity," I said, the words tasting bitter. My own indictment.

She didn't speak at first. I wanted to kick myself for having spoken so honestly.

"Does it mean that?" she asked, but her tone wasn't cutting. It was earnest. "That you don't stick around when things get tough?"

I shook my head several times for emphasis. "I don't

think so. I don't regret choosing to walk away from the possibility of another show, but I think—at least, I hope—I've learned that what might be a good philosophy in business isn't necessarily a good way to approach relationships. Just because I left one doesn't mean I'll leave the other."

She flashed me a smile, and in it I felt exonerated. Not from the choice to step away but from the prospect that she was only going to see me as a certain type of guy.

"Change is good," she said. "Isn't that what we're all trying to do? I know I am. I'm trying not to see people for the things they might do. I'm trying to believe in second chances and, as my grandma would say, focus my energy on that."

"She's the smartest woman I know. I agree with everything she says," I said, slicing a hand through the air as if making a declaration, and Shannon laughed.

"But I noticed one thing about you hasn't changed . . ." she said.

"Besides my stunning good looks, strapping build, and huge cock?"

She rolled her eyes and burst out laughing. "Yes, it is still large."

"Let me know when you need another reminder."

"Sure, whip it out right now, Brent," she said, leaning back in her chair, crossing her arms over her chest. Daring me. God, I loved this about her. She went toe to toe with me.

I lowered my hands to my crotch and pretended I was getting ready to unzip my jeans.

"Kidding! I'm kidding," she said, and I stopped. Then she wiggled a brow. "And yes, I do want to revisit your cock soon. But what I was getting at is this." She stretched to push up my shirtsleeve, her fingers tracing the sunburst on my forearm. My skin sizzled under her touch, and matters south of the border grew harder as she stroked the ink on my skin. She trailed her fingertips across the tribal bands. "You have the same ink you had in college. You never got any more?"

This question was easy as pie to answer. "I got them all with you. You came with me for the first one, and then the others, so it seemed wrong for me to get more without you."

A smile seemed to tug at her lips, like she liked that answer a lot. "Did you want to get more? Was there something you had in mind?"

I fixed a studious look on my face, then said dryly, "A zebra." I held out my arm, pushing my shirt up more, showing her the canvas I'd use, where my upper arm was free of ink. "Right here."

She went along with it, jumping in. "That sounds perfect. You could even have the stripes go all the way around," she said, tracing a pattern on my arm.

"The other option is a badass Pegasus. Breathing fire and all. You see, Shan, now that you're back, all I want to do is just cover myself in ink. Coat myself in it."

"You let me know when you're ready to go under the needle. I'll be there," she said as she danced her fingertips up my arm, hitting the cuff of my shirt from where my sleeve was pushed up. She wrapped her arm around my biceps and squeezed, then let go of her grip.

But now it was time to answer her seriously. "But yes, someday I would like to get something again. If you wanted to come along with me." The words came out vulnerable. They made me feel vulnerable. But they were true. "I always associated ink with you, babe. That's why I stopped."

She flashed a soft smile. "I mean it. If you want to get more, I'm there."

"It's a date," I said, and the date we were on was pretty great today, so I reached for the bag I'd brought with me. It had been next to me in the booth, since this gift didn't fit in my pocket. "I got you something else."

I handed her the bag.

"Brent," she said softly, but a smile spread across her face—that was reward alone. She dug into the shopping bag and took out a box, then opened the top. I cataloged her reaction. Her eyes seemed to twinkle with happiness, then she brought a hand to her chest and took out a pair of red leather shoes with a strap over the arch of the foot.

"You're still a size seven, I presume?"

She nodded as she slipped off her black heels and tried on the new ones. "I can't believe you got me shoes. I love shoes."

"I know you do." I leaned across the table and lowered my voice. "The shoes looked sexy, and you're sexy, and I'd love to see you in them."

She stretched out her leg across mine and modeled the new shoe, then spoke in a smoky whisper. "Do you like them?"

I groaned as I answered, "You know I do."

"Do you want me to wear them on Saturday night? When you take me to Alvin Ailey?" Her tone was inviting, like a promise of what we might do this weekend.

What I desperately wanted to do.

"Yes."

She leaned across the table, dropping her voice more. "And do you want to fuck me on Saturday night?"

I went up in flames. That was all I wanted. "Yes."

"I want that too."

All I could think about now was her in those shoes on Saturday, and what might happen later that night.

I was picturing it all too perfectly.

Too bad my phone rang and I had to think about Tanner when his name flashed across the screen. Perfect boner killer.

"Let me grab this for one minute," I said to Shannon, then answered the call. "Hey, Tanner. What's up?"

The man wasted no time with hellos. "Here's the deal. You need to meet the leader of the neighborhood association. Let him know Mr. Vegas means business. That you won't be bringing trouble to their block. Can you get to New York this weekend? I set up a meeting Sunday night."

I cursed silently. Saturday night was Alvin Ailey. No way was I backing out of that. But I could catch an early Sunday morning flight. "I'll be there in time for a seven p.m. dinner."

"Fine. I'll send you the details," Tanner said in a gruff tone.

Quickly, I circled back to my conversation with him the last time I saw him, catching him up to speed. "Hey,

I put in a few calls to the parks department in the city. I made a donation to have some of the parks in the area revitalized, like you suggested."

"Good. Keep that shit up. You got a long row to hoe."

Thanks for the reminder.

After I hung up, I gestured to the phone. "The neighborhood association in New York is being difficult about my plans to open a club there," I said, telling her about the situation as I paid for lunch.

"Why? What's the issue?" Shannon asked as we walked out of the restaurant.

"Hard as it may be to believe, I don't think they like me."

She scoffed. "They clearly have no taste."

I smiled. "Obviously. But it sounds like I also need to do a dog and pony show so they see me as more than just some guy from Vegas bringing all the glitter and glitz of Sin City to New York."

She arched a brow. "Do you usually wear your Elvis sequined costume when you see them?"

I smacked my forehead. "I knew that was it."

"See? Easy solution. Next time, tone down the bling and feathers, and you'll be good to go."

I draped an arm around her, tugging her close. "You're brilliant."

"Hmm." She tapped her finger against her chin, like she was deep in thought.

"Hmm, what? You coming up with a new Boy Scout outfit for me or something?"

"Actually, I was thinking. Michael and Ryan do some business in New York with clubs and lounges there, handling security. I could ask them if they know anyone or have any suggestions on what might help? Maybe that's a stretch though?"

I raked my eyes up and down the woman at my side. This time, though, it was her heart I was admiring. Her willingness to go to bat for me. "That is sweet of you to offer, but wholly unnecessary. I need to sort this out on my own. And get to the bottom of what the real road-block is."

"The offer stands if you need it."

I pressed a kiss to her cheek.

As we left, I vowed once more to do whatever I had to in order to keep her in my life. Work had won my heart ten years ago. She was more important now.

24

SHANNON

A pink-and-purple illustration of an animal stared back at me.

"I don't even want to ask why you're buying that," my grandmother said with a laugh, pointing to my selection as the cashier at the party store rang up our purchase.

"It's a surprise for someone," I answered with a wink, and snatched the little gift, tucking it into my purse. Brent had been showering me with gifts. I planned to do the same for him.

"That'll be fifty-seven twenty-one," the cashier said, bagging up the balloons, streamers, cups, and party favors that Grandma had picked up for a party she was throwing.

Before my grandma could stop me, I slid my credit card through the machine to pay.

"You didn't have to do that," she said.

I shot her a smile as I tucked my card back into my

purse. "I know I didn't have to. I wanted to." I scooped up the bag and headed to my car.

"And who are you surprising?" she asked as she slid into the passenger seat. "Might that someone be your old beau?"

"'Beau.' 'Boy.' You're so old-fashioned, Nana," I said as I backed out of the lot and turned onto the main drag.

"Well?" she asked pointedly. "Is it?"

I shrugged, but my lips curved into a grin. "Maybe."

She patted my knee as we slowed to a stop at a red light a few blocks from her home. "Excellent. So what are we going to do about your brothers, then?"

"What about them? The fact that all three are total pains in the ass?" I teased.

"Not that. The fact that they're all single. Maybe we need to set up a matchmaking service for those boys."

"Good luck getting those three cavemen married off," I joked as the light changed and I turned left onto her street.

My grandmother gestured grandly, as if she were putting their names in lights. "Matchmakers for the Paige Men."

I startled for a moment at hearing that name.

"I meant the Sloan men," my grandmother quickly corrected.

Just like that, my mind latched onto another Paige man. The one who was long gone. Little things slammed me back in time. Like my old name. Like driving, of all things.

My father's final moments had been in a car, at his

home. The one place where he should always have been safe from harm.

I pressed my teeth into my bottom lip, holding my emotions in as I turned into my grandmother's driveway.

It was a mundane, ordinary patch of concrete. My grandmother didn't even live anywhere near the home where my dad had been shot. But as I cut the engine and looked at my father's mother, I knew without a shadow of a doubt she was thinking about the same thing. She, too, had been jolted out of a festive moment of party planning and pretend matchmaking and hurtled back in time to eighteen years ago. I saw it in her eyes—the same sadness I felt was reflected back at me.

"Sometimes it's hard just turning in the driveway," I said softly. "Makes me think of Daddy."

She clasped my hand. "I know. Every day I think about him."

I looked down at our hands, a swell of sadness in my chest. "I miss him."

"I do too, sweetie."

I probably always would.

After I walked her inside and said goodbye, I shut the door behind me, waiting till I heard her lock it. Then I scanned the surrounding area as I returned to my car. It was my habit. Something I always did. Looking for eyes on me. For anyone watching, scoping out the hood, as the shooter had done before he'd killed my father.

But Jerry Stefano was behind bars, I reminded myself.

He was locked up where he belonged.

Surely the DA hadn't been visiting him to talk about freeing him of the *murder*. The evidence against him was cold and hard.

Whatever the DA had discussed with the gunman had to be about other crimes. He was a gang member. He was a career criminal.

But still, I had to be smart. Had to be alert for anything amiss, listening for those footsteps crunching on the grass, seeking the shadow of someone who wasn't supposed to be there.

Stefano was in orange, but that didn't make me feel entirely safe.

Those bars that held in the shooter didn't hold back his friends, his associates.

Those bars didn't mean he wouldn't have people on the outside looking for vengeance.

Wanting to settle the score for their friend who was locked up.

My eyes roamed the sidewalk, the house, and the garage before I unlocked my car door, breathing again.

No one was here. It was morning. I was safe, and my grandmother was fine, and I refused to live in fear. I had to kick the damn specter of hidden guns and gangs and shooters and plots for murder far out of my daily agenda.

I took a deep breath, letting it spread through my body, coaxing it to ease away the stranglehold of the past. Good thing I was seeing Brent that afternoon. He was my antidote. He'd wash away the cruel memories.

I could lean on him for that, as I always had. My sweet, sinful escape.

Even so, as I drove, I called Ryan, asking if he'd heard anything more from his DA friend.

"I'm working on it," he said.

* * *

But leaning on Brent to take away the sadness would be taking two steps back. And I was trying to develop new habits, not rely on my old ones. Brent had always been my magic bullet to extradite the pain. But to truly change, I needed to give instead of take.

Over salad and pasta at an Italian restaurant inside Caesars, I zoomed in on him.

Using that as a chance to learn more about the man he was now.

I asked him more about work, peppering him with questions about his clubs, the expansion, and his vision for Edge, reminding myself the whole time not to be needy. I listened intently, because I wanted this lunch to be about him.

Not about me.

Not about me needing him to lean on.

I knew he was all too happy to be my support. But I wanted to be that for him, even if he didn't need it, even if he didn't ask for it. Just listening, just talking—that was what I could do, what I wanted to do.

"And Edge will keep on growing," I said.

"That's the goal," he said with a wide smile. He truly seemed happy with his new path. That was his special talent—he knew how to find the happiness in every-thing. Someone like him never seemed to need much, while I often felt I required far too much. That was exactly why I'd picked up the gift at the party store. He loved the little things in life.

"Close your eyes," I said, after the waiter cleared our plates and I joined him on his side of the table.

"You gonna blindfold me? I'm game," he joked as he followed my order.

I reached into my purse, rolled up his shirtsleeve to his biceps, and dipped a cloth napkin in a water glass.

"Go ahead. Undress me here. I don't mind," he continued.

"I know you don't, you dirty man."

"You wouldn't have me any other way," he growled.

"You're right," I whispered as I positioned the square of paper on his arm. Then I pressed the wet napkin on top of it and counted to thirty. When I peeled the backing paper off, I told him to open his eyes.

"Ta-da!" I showed him the mark I'd left on his arm, and his big, deep laugh rumbled across the restaurant.

He nodded approvingly at the pink-and-purple temporary tattoo of a little horse I'd fixed to his biceps. "A pony. You got me a pony. It's everything I've ever wanted."

I shimmied my shoulders, pleased that I'd made him so damn happy. "It's not quite a badass flying Pegasus, but if you're a good boy, I'll get you a winged one next."

"Or a unicorn maybe?"

"That could be arranged."

After we left the restaurant, we wandered past the

shops of Caesars, when a flash of color caught my eye. In the midst of all the black and silver high-end items, I spotted an old-fashioned photo booth down a quiet hallway that led to the restrooms. Painted bright red and white, the booth boasted a sign advertising *Four photos for $1.*

"That's a bargain," I said, then grabbed his hand and tugged him toward it. "Let's get a picture to go with your cool new ink."

"We can even put on disguises," he said, rubbing his hands together. "Please let there be a fake mustache. Please, pretty please." He held up his hand and crossed his fingers.

I swatted him and grinned. Today, I didn't need him to blur the memories. This moment was about laughter, and talking, and me giving something to him. Something silly, but then again, I knew he liked those gifts best of all.

I pulled him inside and yanked the curtain closed. "Damn," I said, snapping my fingers when I saw the broken sign slung across the viewfinder. "No wonder no one was down this hallway."

"We can shoot selfies and make our own photo booth picture. You must have some props in your purse."

"Right. Of course. Let me just get out my purple wig. And the fake nose I keep in there," I said, deadpan.

"Now you're talking."

Instead, I grabbed my sunglasses and slid them to the bridge of my nose, puckering my lips. He bared his teeth in an exaggerated grin and flexed his biceps, showing off his new pink-and-purple pony ink. I snapped a picture on my phone and showed it to him.

"We are so sexy together," he said, with over-the-top admiration. He patted his thighs. "Climb up. Take another picture."

"You're just trying to get me to sit on your lap."

"Yes. I am."

I straddled him, the soft cotton of my black dress flaring across his jeans, then held out the phone. "Smile," I instructed.

But instead of smiling, he wrapped his arms around me, planting a soft wisp of a kiss on my neck.

My eyes floated closed as my thumb slid aimlessly across the screen, capturing it. I didn't stop to look this time, because he was brushing his lips along my neck, buzzing a path to my ear. I let the phone fall to the bench, along with my sunglasses, and turned to meet his lips. The goofiness vanished. The silliness evaporated as the moment folded and unfolded into something else, shifting from temporary tattoos and selfies to a hot, wet, deep kiss that swamped my body with desire.

I moaned his name as if he was all I wanted—and he was. "*Brent.*"

"It's hard to take it slow," he said, breaking the kiss for a moment. He ran his hand up my back over the fabric of my dress, and I arched into him, moving in time with his touch. I wanted him too. We'd discussed safe sex the other day, and since I was on the pill and we were both clean, we were physically ready. But I needed to be emotionally ready too.

"It's too damn hard," he added, as he gently tugged

my bottom lip through his teeth, making me moan. He flicked his tongue across my top lip in such a slow, sexy, seductive move that I thought I might reach the peak of climax if he kept it up.

"Especially when you kiss me like that."

"I better do it again, then," he said as he worked his way up my neck, kissing my throat, my jaw, my cheek, then my earlobe. My body practically vibrated from the tender and delicious way his mouth traveled across my skin. The kiss was driving him wild too, judging by the bulge in his jeans and the pressure from his fingers as he dug them into my hips with each lick, each sweep of his tongue.

I could subsist on this moment. I could use it as the balm to my overactive brain, to all the harsh circumstances that rattled into my life from out of nowhere. Out of everywhere. I could keep taking more from him—more kisses, more touching, more contact.

But I wanted to give too. To give to him as he'd done for me.

"My turn," I said, and I returned the favor. I worked my way up his neck, kissing his jaw, then his earlobe. He grasped me harder as I mapped his skin, loving his clean scent, his rough stubble, and his hard body.

"You're quite good at taking your turn," he murmured.

I nibbled on his earlobe, and he pumped his pelvis up into me with a muffled groan. A blast of heat tore through me, as taking and giving smashed together.

"Ride me," he said in a rough, husky voice. We were

wanting all the same things. Wanting the give and the take as well. "Ride me hard. Like I know you want to."

His words ignited me. We'd been taking it slow, but I didn't want to. I wanted him. I wanted my man.

I followed his words to the letter, as we collided in a mad frenzy in the photo booth. Through our clothes, I was grinding against him in seconds, my white panties and his jeans the only barriers. We became a tangle of teeth and heat and madness, as I kissed him ruthlessly and slammed against him. He kissed back the same way, wild and untamed, his hands knotting through my hair, pulling hard. Grabbing. Biting. Tugging. Hands and fingers clawing everywhere. Our breaths turned loud. If anyone walked by on the way to the restroom, surely they'd hear my moans of desire.

I didn't care.

Not with the way his lips consumed me, taking over these bruising, needy, dangerous kisses that felt like tipping over. Like I was losing what little control I had of my feelings for him. I was poised, teetering on the edge of something. This week had been so sweet, so delicious, so like a perfect courtship that it made me remember how deeply I'd been in love with him before. The way he'd treated me stirred up all those feelings I'd forced out of my mind and shoved into a box for the last ten years. They were resurfacing, breaking free of the past, and fighting their way up my body. Terrible, dangerous feelings that threatened to take over my mind.

I moved faster, harder, kissed more deeply, my desire climbing higher.

But then he placed his hands on my shoulders and gently but firmly pushed me away. Forcing me to look at him.

"Shan, why don't we get a room?" he asked, his eyes hazy with lust. "You know I want you so much. You're driving me wild, and we're practically fucking with our clothes on in a photo booth. C'mon," he said, tipping his forehead to the curtain as if to say *Let's go.*

And then, like the bastard it was, the past in all its shapes and colors grabbed my throat. Like a slingshot, it snapped me back to the girl who had felt too much.

Who needed to control her wild emotions.

I clenched my jaw, grabbing his collar. "I can't just go have sex with you because we're hot and bothered."

"Why not? Isn't that pretty close to what we're doing now?"

I swallowed hard, and let it out in a harsh, broken whisper. "Because it was never just sex with you."

Gently, he kissed my shoulder, making me shiver. "What was it with me?"

I cupped his cheeks and looked him in the eyes. Spoke the truth. "It was everything," I said, as I moved against him, the friction sending another powerful wave of desire through me. "All of it. This. You. Us. You were everything to me."

He laced a hand through my hair. "Do you have any idea how much I want to be everything to you again?"

I nodded, barely able to speak. "I think I do. That's what scares me."

"Why, babe? Why?" he asked as he kissed my neck.

His lips were barely there, just the flutter of a hummingbird's wings.

"Because it's too good right now," I admitted.

"What's too good?"

"Us. You and me," I said.

"Shan," he said, chiding me. "Assume the best."

"I'm trying," I admitted. "But it's hard."

I leaned my head back and succumbed to the strange combination of kissing and confessing. Of touching and talking.

He ran his fingers across my cheek. "I know it's hard. But I have your back," he said, holding my face and forcing me to look him in the eyes.

And as I did, something inside me cracked open. The ice that I'd packed around my heart, that he'd been chipping away at day by day, thawed completely.

"This is what scares me," I said, my voice breaking. Try as I might to be an optimist, I couldn't escape the painful truth of who I was. I stared fiercely at him, keenly aware of both the intensity of this conversation and our position. "I've already had my heart broken. It was splintered into a million pieces one night in a driveway, then again ten years ago when I lost you and a small, tiny person I was just starting to love. And it can only sustain so many breaks before it's shattered."

I let the tears slide down my cheeks, as they'd done so many times with him.

He gathered me close in his arms and stroked my hair. "I won't break your heart again. I promise."

I wanted to believe him. I wanted to believe myself too.

Because I was falling madly in love with him a second time, and I was terrified.

Heels clicked against the floor. Someone was walking past us. The sound of the footsteps sped up. I covered my mouth and widened my eyes, and he laughed silently.

It was time to go, so we left, holding hands.

As our fingers threaded together, the weight of my worries lessened. Maybe simply voicing them was what I had truly needed to move on. Oh, how I wanted to move on.

In every way.

And that meant letting him in. "Brent," I whispered.

"What is it, babe?"

"Sometimes I worry. That it could happen again. That the shooter is in touch with people on the outside. That he knows people who could do things for him. That he wants revenge for being locked up. I worry so much that something could happen to my family," I said, my throat closing tightly.

He stopped, set his hands on my shoulders, and leveled me with a serious gaze. "Let me ask around. See if I can find anything out for you."

He wasn't placating me. He wasn't saying, *Shhh, baby, everything's going to be okay.* Grateful he wasn't feeding me a line, I asked, "Do you know anyone who might know?"

"I can't promise I'll find anything, but I can promise I'll ask."

That was a damn fine promise.

25

BRENT

I did know someone.

I knew someone quite well.

But first, we had a card game to play. Because that was how it worked with Mindy—cards and chatting, in that order.

Today, the ace of diamonds winked at me, a mate to the ace of clubs that the dealer revealed next at a blackjack table at the Luxe. I flashed back to the card Shannon picked when I showed her my card trick. Same one. This was a lucky card, clearly.

"I'll split," I said to the goateed dealer. Together, my two aces were a bust. Torn apart, they gave me a second chance in the game.

"I've got a very important question for you," Mindy said, as the dealer laid a three on top of her eight.

"Hit me," I said to my friend, and she rolled her eyes at the pun.

Mindy adopted a girly, lovestruck tone. "Have you thought about what you're going to wear tonight to

Alvin Ailey?" She batted her eyes and squeezed my arm. "It's such a big decision."

"Bow tie. Seersucker suit," I said with a straight face, as the dealer slapped two new cards face up for me, and one for Mindy.

"And a panama hat. That'd be a nice touch," she added, as I stared happily at my new cards. Eight and a nine. Didn't get much better than that. But I wasn't just here to win a hand. I needed to talk to her. Mindy knew stuff about Vegas.

I called her the queen for a reason. She was the queen of this city.

"Or, call me crazy, I could just go with jeans and a nice button-down shirt," I said, as we finished the hand, with me winning.

"You lucky bastard," Mindy said with a low whistle.

Lucky. Was I lucky? In some ways I was. But I wanted to be more than lucky. I wanted to show Shannon I was determined.

Scooping up the chips, I tipped an imaginary hat to her. "And on that note, you ready to chat?"

"Sure. Thanks a lot. You killed me there, taking all the good cards. Now you want to steal my intel," she muttered, after we said goodbye to the dealer and weaved our way through the tables.

"Yes, that's what I want. Your brainpower. Got a price tag on that?"

26

MINDY

I would share my brainpower freely.

Because if there was one thing I craved deeply in life, it was justice.

And justice required knowledge.

In my field, I had to stay abreast of the goings-on in this city. It was my job, and it was my cause. "You know I'll tell you anything you want to know. There's never a price. Tell me what's on your mind."

He scrubbed a hand across his jaw and heaved a sigh. "Royal Sinners," he said in a hiss.

I'd had a feeling that was what he wanted to discuss. Since he'd started seeing Shannon again, I'd done my best to dig around so I'd be ready for this moment.

"You know people everywhere. Have you heard anything about them?" Brent added.

We slowed our pace, stopping by the cages as I answered, "They went kind of quiet for a while there. A few years ago. Were you aware of that?"

He shook his head. "I honestly hadn't tracked the comings and goings of the gang culture."

I flashed a *don't you worry* grin. "But I have. Here's what I know. Five or six years ago, it seemed like they'd kind of fallen apart." I continued, lowering my voice, "But I hear they're trying to become active again. Recruiting new members. Hitting the streets with drugs, tagging, fights over territory."

He clenched his fists, visibly seething. "Should I be worried? For her? For her family now?"

I squeezed his shoulder. "I don't think so. At least not yet."

"Why?" He sounded so desperate, and I had to help.

I took a breath. "When you started seeing her again, I did a little digging into Stefano with some of the guys I know on the force."

"You did?"

"Don't sound so surprised. You know I have your back," I said, and I did. I always had the back of my friends, and Brent Nichols was solid. After my tour of duty ended, when it was my fiancé's turn to serve and he never came home, Brent saw me through the heartache and the loss. He helped me find some semblance of happiness again, through friendships, cards, and his comedy routines.

"I know you do," he said, offering a fist for knocking. "And I'm damn grateful."

I knocked back, then told him all I knew. "A couple of my friends on the force were active when it all went down. I checked in with them, and they say that, yes, Stefano was tight with some of the Sinners at the time, a few in particular, but there are some rumblings now that maybe that's changed."

Brent nodded, processing this detail. "Sure, prison changes things," he said, coolly, taking it in.

I dialed down the volume even more. You never knew who might be listening. "My sources also said Stefano's girlfriend disappeared too around then. The authorities wanted to question her to see what she knew about the Sinners, but couldn't find her. Anyway, those were just the things I was told. There *is* some noise that not everyone's entirely happy with what's gone down since Stefano was locked up, but it doesn't seem to be over Thomas Paige, and no one is looking to take vengeance on the Sloans."

He sighed deeply. "That's all?"

I patted his shoulder, wishing I could be 100 percent reassuring. But stone-cold certainty was unlikely, especially with this type of criminal.

Bars didn't hold them back when they knew people on the outside. And when people might not be happy with the guys on the inside.

Or vice versa.

Still, I gave him my best reassurance and advice, what I believed. "Let's hope so. But let's also keep our eyes open."

"Yeah, that's what we have to do."

27

BRENT

I headed to my office, needing the relentless focus on contracts, deals, and plans to erase the cold, metallic taste that the discussion of gangs had left in my mouth. Nothing against Mindy—I'd rather know the details than not know them. But I was ready for that part of Shannon's past to stay firmly closed and never interfere with her future.

Focus on the present. Focus on today. Focus on tonight.

The trouble was, the conversation gnawed at me. I opened a browser window and searched Google for news on "Royal Sinners." I read a few articles—drug busts and convictions here and there. I dug around some more, dropping in every permutation I could find for "Jerry Stefano and girlfriend," but the internet wasn't serving up anything about the two of them from nearly two decades ago.

Like Mindy had said, the gang seemed to have petered out for a bit. This had to be a good thing—the gunman Shannon's mother had hired hailed from a gang that had dwindled in power and was now focused on drugs, something completely removed from Shannon's father's death.

Maybe this would be enough to give Shannon some solace, though I wasn't sure she'd ever have any.

But at least I could give her something I hadn't been able to in college. The night she wanted.

I shut the browser, parked my boots on my desk, and rang my buddy who ran the Luxe hotel chain. After Nate and I caught up briefly on work and business, I made my request. "Hey, man, you know anyone at this hotel who can score me a nice suite last-minute on a Saturday night in Vegas? Happy to pay top dollar."

Maybe it was wishful thinking. Maybe it was just some mad hope. Or perhaps I simply wanted to be prepared for any and all possible outcomes tonight.

Nate laughed loudly. "You hoping to get lucky at my property this evening?"

"I'm always hoping to get lucky," I said.

"I'll take care of you. Stop by ops on the way out to see my property manager. Alfonso will get you a key," he said.

"I owe you," I said.

"I owe *you*. Your club is driving up business like crazy. It's like a goddamn slot machine that pays off every time," Nate said, and I grinned. That was what I liked to hear. Edge was indeed the golden goose. I zeroed in on that thought while I worked for another hour, then checked the time. I needed to head home and get ready to pick up my date in a town car.

On the way out through the casino, Tanner's name

flashed across my phone screen. I nearly crossed my fingers, praying the man wouldn't say something to ruin my Saturday.

"Hey, Tanner. What's up?"

"Meeting was moved up. Gotta do lunch instead of dinner," Tanner barked.

My shoulders tensed. "Tomorrow? What's the deal?"

"The neighborhood association president, Alan Hughes, has to drive his daughter to summer camp on Sunday night, so dinner won't work. Only lunch. But listen, I think I've got him fluffed nicely for you."

Fluffed. The man actually used a porn term. "So he's leaning our way?"

"It's looking like that. See? I told you I'd be good for you. I bet you want to pay me extra on the lease each month, don't you?" Tanner said with a raspy laugh.

This man was a piece of work. "Glad to hear it's looking promising with Alan," I said, avoiding the other comment. I flashed briefly to the conversation with Bob from the comedy club, who'd been getting fleeced by his landlord too. Fingers crossed that this meeting tomorrow would send us all down the right path. I could continue the expansion of Edge, and Bob would have the new job he needed to pay his bills.

"Be here by noon, got it? Same location. McCoy's."

"See you tomorrow," I said, then sighed heavily in frustration as I hung up.

This would put a crimp in my plans.

I called my assistant and asked her to change my flight from the morning to the midnight red-eye to

New York. That gave me two hours with Shannon after the show ended.

Make that one hour, since I'd need an hour to get to the airport and through security. I set an alarm on my phone just in case, then picked up a key from Alfonso.

Wishful thinking for sure at this point. But sometimes you had to roll the dice.

28

———

SHANNON

My oldest brother finished screwing in the hinge on my loose closet door, then flipped the screwdriver in the air like a cocky juggler, and dropped it in his pocket.

"Good as new," he declared.

"Rock star," I said, then curtsied.

"I am indeed." He looked at his watch. "Speaking of, I better get going. I have a set tonight," he deadpanned.

I laughed. "You wish."

"I did wish once upon a time to be a rocker," he said, serious now.

I squeezed his arm. "I know you did. And now you're the best damn security guy in the country."

He blew on his fingernails. "True that. And no regrets."

I gave him a hug. "Seriously though. Thanks for stopping by. I appreciate it."

"I'll be your handyman as long as you need me, Shan." He fixed me with an intense stare. "How is everything going with the partnership? You managing that okay?"

Tension ramped up in me. Michael had been out of town for work for the week, and I hadn't had a chance to tell him Brent and I were seeing each other again.

I hadn't said a word to him last weekend at my grandmother's house, but I hadn't known then that I'd actually be dating—seriously dating—my ex-fiancé. Now I was, and I didn't like cloaking my life in lies around my brothers.

Colin knew, and it was time to tell Michael too.

I steeled myself for his reaction. Of all my brothers, he'd been the biggest fan of Brent, and then hated him the most when we split.

I could still hear the sting of Michael's comment in the airport when I flew home to see him that night. *Bastard.*

I cleared my throat. "I'm going out with Brent tonight. I'm seeing him again."

He froze. Furrowed his brow. "Pretty sure I just heard you wrong," he said slowly. "Say that again."

"I'm seeing Brent. Dating him," I added. I didn't need to add that tonight I planned to sleep with him.

"I thought you were just doing business with his clubs," he said, taking time with each word, as if he could re-stitch them into a pattern that made sense.

"I thought so too. But then it turned into something more."

"How? How did it turn into something more? Last time we spoke, it was just an apology for walking away, and it became . . . dating again?"

I swallowed roughly, then spoke the truth. "I care deeply for him. And he does for me. We're trying to do things differently this time around."

He blew out a long stream of air. "I'm . . . surprised. You were pretty damn clear ten years ago that you never wanted to see him again. You told all of us—me, Ryan, Colin. You made it abundantly clear he was persona non grata."

"I didn't want to see him then. But that was ten years ago, Michael. Things have changed. I told you that the other night."

"I get it. But what about everything else?"

I didn't want to serve up all my feelings for everyone to judge. It was hard enough to say them to Brent, let alone to my big brother. Some things were personal. Some things were private. Like the fact that I was falling again for someone who was tender and kind, rough and fiery, funny and sexy, and who only had eyes for me.

Someone who was putting me first.

But I didn't have the luxury of keeping this entirely to myself. Michael had looked out for me, and I owed him honesty.

"Everything else is what's changing," I said, nerves swirling inside me, hoping he'd see where I was coming from.

"Shan," he said in a heated whisper, as if that was the only thing keeping him from shouting, and he never shouted. He never raised his voice. He stayed in control of his emotions at all times. "If he hurts you again . . ."

I shook my head adamantly. "He won't."

"He better not," Michael said, then wrapped his

strong arms around me. "If he does, he'll have to answer to me."

I smiled as I rested my face against his chest. "And no one wants to have to deal with you."

"Damn straight."

29

BRENT

Cool white lobby. Etched glass on the double doors. Sleek blond wood floors and stairs that matched.

I drank it all in.

Her building. Her home.

In the light of day, I recorded the details, wanting to remember them.

It was as if I'd gained entry to a secret castle, to the tower at the top of it. Follow this path, take the fork in the road, and climb all the way up. At the top, there she will be.

The woman I wanted.

The *only* woman for me.

The soles of my shoes echoed on the steps as I walked up the three flights to her place, staring left, then looking right, inhaling everything. For so long, I'd searched for her. I'd tried to picture her, to imagine her life, her home, and her place in the world.

Right here. I was in it. Mere feet from where Shannon Paige-Prince had lived for the last few years.

Only a handful of miles away from my home. I turned the corner on the next landing and lifted my foot on the step, then I froze.

I didn't move. I was stuck in a sliver of stalled time.

Michael walked down the stairs. His eyes were like razors. His jaw twitched. The sound of his shoes clanged loudly in my ears, snapping me back to attention.

I unfroze.

"Hey, Michael," I said, doing my best to keep it casual, keep it chill. "Good to see you again."

I hadn't spoken to him since he'd helped me get the ring from his grandmother a decade ago.

Michael's dark eyes stared at me. He raised his left hand, clapped it on my arm. But it wasn't at all a friendly pat. It didn't say *Good to see you too, man.* His hand sent another message: *Do not fuck with my family.*

Michael spoke, low but powerful. "My sister is one of the most important people in the world to me. I swear . . ." he said, letting his voice trail off like the smoke from a fired gun. I parted my lips to say something, anything, but Michael left me no room. This was not a conversation. It was a speech. "You have no idea how devastated she was. I'm not even talking about for herself. I'm talking about *you*. When you didn't fight for—"

I held up a hand. "I know, man. And I am sorry. And I have told her that."

Michael didn't even acknowledge the words. "And if you do it again, you will know a new kind of hell. I will not hurt you with fists, because I am not that kind of man, but I will make sure you are *fucked* in this town. I will do whatever it takes to protect my sister from getting hurt again, from you, and from anyone. Is that clear?"

I raised my chin. "Message received, Michael. But I want you to know two things. One, I'm not the same guy I was ten years ago, and I'm doing everything to prove that to your sister," I said, then paused, because as much as I didn't intend to get pushed around, I also knew I had to show some respect to a man who looked out for his own. "And two, I'm going to prove it to you."

Michael didn't answer. He lifted his chin slightly, a nearly imperceptible nod, maybe even an invitation to say more. *I'm listening,* his expression said.

"And that means," I said, drawing a deep breath as I seized this opportunity, "I'm keeping tabs on the Royal Sinners. I'm looking into Stefano as best I can. I'm talking to friends in security who know people. I'm doing everything I can to make sure Shannon is always safe."

His lips were as straight as a ruler, but then they twitched. The tiniest sliver of a smile appeared. "You're doing that?"

"Damn straight. I won't try to pretend I understand what your family has been through, but, brother . . . I respect you. I respect your role, and I know what I'm getting into with Shannon. This is not something I take lightly."

Michael nodded, his voice barely registering as he said, "Thank you. You do that."

He resumed his pace, walking down the stairs, and I felt like I'd done my part with the head of the family.

But now I was ready to see my woman.

Mine.

She felt like mine.

I made my way to Shannon's door, knocking twice. When she answered, that encounter with her brother whooshed away. There was no real estate in my brain for anything but her.

Her eyes sparkled, and she jutted out her hip. The dress she wore looked like it had been painted on. The color of champagne, and with some kind of shimmer to the fabric, it hugged her hips, her thighs, her flat belly, and her beautiful breasts. I wished I had been there to watch her slip it on and zip it up. More than that, I hoped I'd be taking it off tonight.

I forgot about everything else in the world—schedules, plans, flights? Gone.

"Wow." I'd never been at a loss for words.

But she knocked the breath from my lungs and stole the words from my tongue. "Wow."

"You like?"

I shook my head. "I love."

I loved everything about her. The dress that was caressing her body. The bare legs boldly on display. The red leather shoes that I'd bought for her.

Her heart.

Her mind.

Her.

She stepped closer to me and ran her hands down the front of my shirt. Her touch was electric. "You look so handsome tonight," she said, and there was softness in her voice, an affection that hooked deeper into me.

And I was already so far gone.

"Thank you," I said, once again robbed of quips and wit.

She raised a hand and cupped my cheek. "So damn handsome," she repeated, and the vulnerability in her voice made me want to handle her with care. To shove all this lust and desire aside and give her whatever she wanted, whatever she needed. "And tonight, you're mine again."

Yes. That was all I wanted. Her in every way.

"And you're mine." I threaded my hands up through the back of her hair, letting the soft strands spill all over my fingers. She closed her eyes and sighed contentedly. Oh hell, I stood no chance. I didn't *want* to stand a chance of fighting anything I was feeling for her.

Because I felt everything. "Shan," I whispered.

She whispered something better. "Kiss me."

I ran the pad of my thumb over her bottom lip. She murmured and melted into my arms. She fit me so perfectly, sliding against me, our bodies like magnets, seeking their opposite, finding their way home.

I kissed her, soft and tender, and I could have gone on all night. Could have kissed her forever. But I wanted to take her to the theater too. To prove I'd changed. That I could put her first.

And it started by telling her what I'd told Michael.

On the way over in the car, I took her hand. "Listen, I told you I'd look into the Sinners, and I've only just started, but what I found out is they're mostly focused on drugs, tagging, and fights over territory," I said, sharing what Mindy had told me.

She nodded a few times, taking deep breaths. "Less about violence? Less about hits?"

"I think so, babe. I'm not positive, since I just started, but that's what Mindy and I are trying to figure out. She's keeping her ear to the ground. And I'm going to ask around. See what else I can learn."

She pursed her lips, holding in emotions, I suspected, then she nodded. "Drugs," she said, like she was processing the word. "That's okay. My mother didn't order the hit for drugs. She ordered it for money."

She nodded again, taking this in, when her phone bleated. Rustling around in her purse, she grabbed it, then showed me the screen with her brother Ryan's name on it.

"Hey, Ry," she answered. After a pause, she said, "I'm heading out to see Alvin Ailey." Another pause. "You want to talk now?" Another pause. Then a heavy sigh. "Fine. Tomorrow. I'll see you tomorrow."

When she hung up, her shoulders were tight again, her breath sharp. "What is it, babe?"

She took a moment before she answered. "Last time I saw him at our grandma's, he mentioned something about an attorney visiting Stefano. He says he has some more info. But he doesn't want to talk about it on the phone," she said, breathing out fumes of frustration.

I squeezed her hand. "That's smart though. That's a conversation best had in person."

"I know," she said, resigned. "I just wish I knew enough to protect myself fully."

My heart squeezed. This was the hardest thing. Would she ever feel safe? But I didn't know if she could in a world where attorneys were visiting the man who'd killed her father.

I wrapped an arm around her. "Listen, what Ryan tells you might be private, and I get that. But if you want to share, know I'll be here for you. Okay?"

She nodded. "Okay."

"I'll keep looking. See what else I can learn to ease your mind. And I'll protect you."

I wasn't entirely sure it was an offer I could make. But it was also one I couldn't *not* make.

She lifted her face, then pressed a kiss to my lips. "Thank you. Thank you for doing that."

In her kiss, I felt her gratitude.

I loved that too.

That she was giving it to me. That she was feeling it.

But I couldn't shake the sense that as we walked into the auditorium, she was scanning left and right, on alert.

And I wished I'd been more helpful.

I wished I truly could promise her the world.

30

SHANNON

I didn't want to think about seeing Ryan tomorrow. I didn't want to think about gangs or attorneys or visits to prison.

I wanted beauty. And passion and art.

And that was what I got tonight.

My mind was officially blown.

I'd seen countless ballets and watched thousands of modern dances, but Alvin Ailey had been my favorite since I was a girl—and also my fantasy. While other dancers dreamed of becoming a prima ballerina, I had pictured myself in a starring role in the Alvin Ailey American Dance Theater. The company's modern ballet style and athleticism had always spoken to me. As a young kid on the outskirts of town, growing up in a broken-down neighborhood, I'd been determined to dance my way out of my circumstances, and to win a spot in a prestigious company.

That had never happened, and while I'd moved on, picked myself up, and carved out a career that I loved, a small piece of my heart still longed to be the one onstage, still wished to captivate an audience as I myself had just been captivated.

As they neared the end of the show, the dancers moved with such passion, such exuberance that my heart was full, overcome with their joy in movement. I squeezed Brent's hand in the darkened theater. He'd been such a trooper. I knew he wasn't innately a dance fan. Most men weren't. Hell, my own brothers didn't go to the theater with me. And while I doubted Brent had personally delighted in the production, the mere fact that he'd taken me, watched with me, and focused on the stage meant the world to me.

He had stepped up from the second I'd shown up at his club last week to apologize. He hadn't been kidding when he'd said he'd do whatever it took to win me back. He'd been honest and open and giving, and everything I'd known him to be.

And I'd done my best to be what he needed. Open, honest, and as positive as I could be.

That was what second chances were about.

Showing you'd changed, and I truly believed we both had.

And tonight I wanted all of him.

I was ready.

Hell, maybe the dance was turning me on.

I smiled privately at the thought. Dance was foreplay for me in many ways.

I wanted the man by my side.

Wanted him in every way.

I had no desire for this date to end. I wanted it to

unfurl through the darkness and roll on into the sunrise.

After the euphoric finale on stage, I was the first to my feet, clapping and calling out, "*Bravo!*" Then I threw my arms around Brent's neck and planted a quick kiss on his lips.

"Thank you. I loved every second of it," I said, standing on tiptoes. "I feel like I'm floating on cloud nine." A dancer's high.

"I'm so happy to hear that," he said, his expression earnest. There was no teasing, no joking. He really had wanted me to be happy, and hell, if that didn't make my heart beat in overdrive for him.

We clapped once more during the final curtain call. I picked up the thread of our conversation as the audience started to shuffle out, the bright lights flickering on in the Luxe Theater. "Even if it did make me feel the tiniest pang of regret right here," I said, tapping my chest. More honesty, more openness.

More proof we could do this.

"I hope it wasn't too hard for you."

I shook my head. "Nope. Just makes me a little sad every now and then that I can't do that anymore. But that's all," I said, as I ran my fingers along his arm. I squeezed his hand as we exited the row, replaying my words—*can't do that anymore.* While I might not have been able to dance like those performers on stage—leaping, stretching, soaring beyond the atmosphere—there were other ways to dance. Oh yes, there were many other ways to move.

I tugged him close to me against the edge of the aisle

seat. The crowds filtered by as I leaned in, whispering in his ear, "But I can dance for you. The way you like."

Noise filled the theater. The chatter and hum of the crowd. The music that ushered the patrons out the door. The sound of shoes on carpets, of seats folding up, of phones buzzing. But beneath all that, I heard the sexiest groan escape his lips, a low rumble that came from deep within his chest. It touched down in my nervous system and sent the desire that had been on a simmer all evening to a boiling point.

My pulse doubled. My belly flipped. Want engulfed me.

"Now," he said, his voice husky.

"Do you want to come back to my—"

He produced a gleaming white key card from his back pocket. "I was hopeful," he said, raising an eyebrow.

I adored that hope in him. I adored it for so many reasons. Because he had so much of it, because he could call on it whenever he needed to, and because he'd always freely shared it with me. His brightness, his happiness, his luck.

"Your hope will be rewarded, you handsome man."

I'd take some of his luck tonight and make it ours.

31

BRENT

The elevator doors whooshed shut.

I was a tightly wound coil. I grasped her face and kissed her hard as I backed her into the corner, in clear view of the camera.

I didn't fucking care. I didn't care about anything but this moment. But her.

We were alone.

She sighed, she gasped, she moaned as the elevator chugged higher into the sky. Somewhere it slowed and stopped. I glanced briefly at the number keypad. Twelve. Not our floor. I returned to her lips, red and full and eager. The doors opened while I fused my mouth to hers, dropping my hand to her ass, gripping her soft flesh with the kind of hunger that came from knowing there'd be no stopping tonight.

"Um, we'll catch the next one," someone behind me said, and the doors shut again.

She reached for my hands, setting them on her hips. "Want to know something about that dance?"

"I sure do."

She pressed her body to mine. "It turned me on. Made me want to dance for you."

I groaned, barely able to form sentences. Shannon dancing for me before we fucked was the hottest thing ever.

That was music to my ears. And my dick. And my balls.

And my brain officially took the night off.

Inside the room, she grabbed my shirt and furiously began unbuttoning it. She didn't bother to glance around the room, to take in the surroundings, to comment on the thread count or the mood lighting or the unparalleled view of the Strip from the floor-to-ceiling glass windows. Nor did I.

I saw nothing but her as we made our way to the couch by the window, where she pushed me down as she finished opening my shirt. She stood in front of me, bent forward, and let her long hair tickle my chest.

Fire burned in my blood. I needed her. Desperately.

"Watch me. Watch me dance for you," she said, a filthy twinkle in her eye.

"I can't look anyplace else," I rasped out as she began to sway, her hips moving seductively from side to side. Oh, holy hell of a hard-on. She was doing it. She was going to become my fucking fantasy. I loved nothing more than when she did her stripteases. Made me feel like she was all mine, like she belonged only to me.

She trailed her fingernails down my chest. "How about a little music, handsome?"

I grabbed my phone from my pocket and scrolled through my music at the speed of light. In seconds, Marcy Playground's "Sex and Candy" blasted from my phone.

"Perfect for you," I said as I grasped her hips, and she wagged her index finger, tsking me.

"Perfect for *us* tonight." She spread her palms over my chest. I inhaled deeply, my body rocketing with pleasure at her touch. She glided her talented palm over the hard ridge of my erection, setting off fire after fire inside my body. She was an arsonist. And she was a tease. She took her hand away, hiking up her dress and straddling me.

My cock throbbed in my jeans. What I wouldn't give to have her touching me right now. Hands, mouth, pussy—any or all of the above, please.

My breathing turned erratic as she moved on me, a stripper's dance, grinding and teasing to the music.

Swiveling around, she arched her back, her long hair spilling down her spine. Lust pinballed through me with every succulent move she made, every bump of her ass, every sway of her hips, every press of her against every part of my skin.

"Did you ever get off to this image? To me dancing for you?" she asked.

"All the fucking time," I growled, holding tight to her hips as she moved on me.

"Then let me give you your fantasy." She shifted off me, and I nearly grabbed her and slammed her back down. *Contact.* I needed contact with this red-hot woman who sent the mercury in me soaring to record highs. Who had fried my brain of all rational thoughts.

But she was running the show. She stood and brushed her hand from her breasts, down her belly, to her thighs. I groaned loudly, my right hand dropping to my erection.

"Yes. I love that. Do that," she said, eyeing my crotch. "That's my fantasy."

I narrowed my eyes. "You want me to jack off?"

She arched a naughty eyebrow. "Yes. It's called fore-play. I want to watch you touch yourself as I dance. I want to witness how turned on you get just from looking at me."

"You're a fucking vixen seductress," I said.

"I know, and you love it."

"I do," I said in a hoarse whisper, motioning for her to come closer. "C'mon. I want your hands on me. I want your lips on me. I want to feel *you.*"

"You will. But right now, give me this," she said in a pleading tone, running her hands along my thighs as she wiggled her ass high in the air. She unsnapped the button of my jeans, and there were no more questions. She was winning. She was having her way. My dick ached with the need to be touched.

I unzipped my jeans, freeing my erection.

The look in her eyes was one for the ages. Her lips parted and she breathed heavily, sighing in admiration as I wrapped my hand around my cock. The chorus of the song built, and she backed away, returning to the center of the room, inching up her skirt, revealing her panties.

Moving. Dancing. Swaying.

So fucking sensual. So incredibly seductive.

Her body was a dream.

Her eyes feasted on me with each thrust of her pelvis, each sway of her hips. The way she gazed at me unleashed tremors of pleasure inside me, knowing she was savoring the sight of my hand on my cock. My fantasy—her stripping for me as I enjoyed the view— was her fantasy too.

I stroked harder, faster, not needing much right now because I was so damn aroused already. She unzipped her dress, sliding the straps down her arms, then to her waist, revealing those naked twin globes of gorgeous flesh.

"Bring those beautiful tits to me," I growled out, and she came to me, sinking down on my thigh, rubbing herself on me as she brought her breasts closer.

"Anything for you," she whispered as she pushed them in my face. My tongue darted out, sampling a rosy peak. "Mmm," I murmured as I licked her nipple, then drew her deeper into my mouth.

She pulled away to slide her dress past her hips, showing me the top of her panties. White lacy panties. Blood pounded in my cock as I gripped myself.

"More," she said, tipping her chin to my crotch. "I love watching you."

I shuttled my hand harder, working my fist over my dick. "You get me so crazy with wanting you. You love turning me on. You move your hips—I'm hard. You walk into the room—I'm ready to take you. God forbid you bend down to pick up something that dropped on the floor. You don't even want to know what would go through my head."

"Oh, I do. I do want to know," she said, sliding the dress past her panties, letting it fall to the floor.

My hand tugged harder. My breathing grew unsteady. "I'd grab your hair, push you against a chair. Lift your ass in the air, and sink deep into your sweet, wet pussy."

It was her turn to moan, a throaty, feminine sound that made my balls tighten. She returned to me, clad only in her panties and the shoes I'd bought for her. "I love watching you touch yourself, knowing you're thinking of fucking me."

"I'm always thinking of fucking you, Shannon," I said, on an upstroke. My spine tingled as she resumed her lap dance, her heat mercilessly close to my dick. "Fuck, Shan. I need you so much. Need to be inside you." I set my dirty words aside for a moment to say the kind I needed in this moment. "Let me make love to you, babe."

She leaned in, her breasts pressed to my chest, her mouth on my jaw. "I need that too, Brent. Need it so much. Need all of you again."

Finally.

We were finally going to come together the way we'd been dying to.

Clothes flew off, and the woman I adored straddled me, positioning herself over my cock.

I groaned so damn loudly from the expectation of

pleasure, from the absolute otherworldly bliss of reuniting with her like this.

Of fucking and making love.

Because that was what it was with my woman.

She rubbed against the head, then unleashed the sexiest moan of pleasure in the world, chased by my name. The way she said it, full of lust and love, left me with no doubts.

"You," I moaned, ready to thrust up into her when my phone beeped.

An alarm.

Tension swept over me. What the hell was that?

She raised a curious brow. "Is that a sex alarm?" It came out playful.

And when my tardy brain finally reminded me of my fuck-up, I dropped my head against the couch, cursing, then I muttered, "I have a plane to catch."

32

BRENT

She was a statue.

She didn't move for ages.

Then, in slow motion, her lips parted. "What did you say?"

Holy hell. What did I say? What *didn't* I say?

I smacked my forehead, and my own sheer idiocy mocked me. I hadn't told her I had to leave tonight.

I had forgotten to tell her I had to move my departure.

And on top of that, I'd practically forgotten my flight too.

With the weight of twelve tons of bricks on me, I dragged a hand through my hair. "I have to catch the red-eye."

She stopped moving. "When did you get the room?"

"Earlier today," I said, rewinding briefly to the call with Nate. And then, holy shit. *Fuck me with a chainsaw.* The call with Tanner.

I heaved a sigh. I'd packed a bag and tossed it in the

trunk of the town car on the way to pick her up, but had promptly forgotten about my flight the second I'd laid eyes on Shannon. Hence the alarm.

"When were you going to tell me you were leaving tonight?"

I groaned my frustration. "I was going to tell you when I saw you. But . . ."

"But what?"

"I got distracted by you," I admitted.

She laughed, but it was a mirthless sound. And it was made worse when she wriggled off me, grabbed her clothes, and yanked on her panties.

"You were distracted?" she asked, like it didn't compute. "Now I'm really confused. You knew I wanted to be with you tonight. Knew I wanted to make love, and you were just going to bang me and catch a flight?"

I heard worse than shock in her words. I heard self-loathing. Like she couldn't believe she'd be with someone who'd do that.

And honestly, it was a dick move.

But I hadn't meant to do it. "Shan, it's not like I wanted this," I said, standing and grabbing my clothes too.

Well done, brain. Well fucking done.

"Right, but it seems like you could have remembered at some point. Like, at my house or in the car or during intermission or in the elevator."

"It seems that way, but we were talking about important stuff in the car. Remember?"

She rolled her eyes, holding up a hand. "Don't. Don't go there."

"Look, I'm sorry. I should have said something, and I didn't," I said, frustration laced through every word, stringing them together. "And now I have a plane to catch in sixty fucking minutes."

As she tugged on her dress, she shot me a sharp stare. "Then you should go."

"Don't be like that," I said with a sigh.

"Like what?" she fired back, then dropped her voice. "You *should* go. That's the reality. You set an alarm. You have a flight. Go." Her tone was too cool for my taste.

"Shan," I said, zipping my jeans. "It's the New York club. Remember the guy who called earlier in the week when we were at lunch?"

She nodded as she grabbed her shoes. "Yes."

"I told you I had to go to New York for dinner tomorrow night to meet with the head of the neighborhood association, but I just found out this afternoon, after I booked this room, that they had to move the meeting to lunch tomorrow instead, so I have to catch a red-eye tonight instead of a morning flight. But I didn't want to miss anything tonight with you. It's not like I wanted this."

She exhaled, taking her time. "And it's not like I wanted to be taking it slow, getting to know you again, falling hard for you, and then tonight to be ready. It's not like I wanted to be naked, on top of you, about to make love to you for the first time in ten years, and then have to cut the night short."

When she put it like that . . .

I shoved my phone in my jeans.

Tension twisted in my chest, squeezing my lungs.

The last thing I wanted was to fight with her, not when she'd been melting in my arms moments ago. And I didn't want to miss my flight either. "I'm sorry. But I have to go."

Her green eyes were like stone. "I get it. I do. It's important. You should leave."

And I knew what she *wasn't* saying. That work came first again. I didn't know how to tell her that it wasn't true.

Because it looked true. It felt true to her.

But even if I didn't know how to ask for absolution, I had to try my best. "Look, I forgot to say anything about the change in my flight. It happened this afternoon at four o'clock. This guy is running me around, working me over, ragging my ass about my rep and the club. He's looking for reasons not to do business with me. The neighbors are worried I'll bring trouble to the neighborhood. They didn't like my late-night show or something, and now I have to be squeaky clean. I have a lot on the line. I've promised jobs to people. I have to show up. It's not like I *want* to go to New York at midnight—I'm just trying to do it all."

"They think you'll bring trouble to the neighborhood?" she asked, latching onto that detail.

"Yes," I said.

"That's not who you are." Her tone was defensive, like she was protecting me. It was an odd sound, but not an unwelcome one.

"I know," I said, though I didn't know what she was getting at.

And once again I wasn't sure where we stood.

All I knew was I had to leave. I stepped toward her, setting a hand on her cheek. "You're not second best. You could never be second best."

"Thank you." She swallowed and looked away, then put on some strange sort of smile. "You should go."

I put her in a cab to take her home, but the expression on her face was unsettling.

The look said she was checking out of us.

33

BRENT

Focus did not come easily.

But I didn't have the luxury of fucking up.

I didn't have James with me to save my ass.

And I was the goddamn boss.

So I had to man up and take care of business in New York.

When I landed in the morning, I sent her a message telling her I missed her and she replied *Same here,* but that was it.

I'd have to be okay with that. This time around, we were figuring out how the hell to navigate what this was.

At least I hoped so.

But now it was time for business.

* * *

Turned out the head of the neighborhood association had a guilty pleasure.

Vegas.

"Love the city, love the Strip, love to gamble," he said in a confessional whisper over lunch on Sunday.

"No better place to lose money than Sin City," I remarked as I tucked into the prime rib.

"What was it like growing up there?" Alan asked, hungry for details. "You must have stories to tell."

Over steak, I entertained Alan and Tanner with stories of the Strip, tales of mob bosses, and details about shows and neon and gambles won and lost.

Alan was enrapt. "But there's a seedy underside too," he said. "Don't you think there's a very seedy underside?"

"Sure," I said, a little wary now because what did this have to do with anything? "But that's the case with any city."

"Right, but Vegas has its very own Crips. What are they called?"

"The Royal Sinners," Tanner supplied.

Tension shot through me. Why the hell was he bringing them up? "Yes, but gangs aren't unique to Vegas."

"That is true," Alan said with a laugh, then a shrug. "And hey, what do I know about gangs? I'm just a guy with a bit of an obsession with true crime."

The tension dug deeper into me. Did he know something about Shannon? Was he going fishing on this *tell me about Vegas* expedition?

"True crime is all the rage," I said, adding a smile, trying to keep my comments general, like this discussion could only ever be about pop culture.

"Man, it sure is," Tanner said, jumping in. "There's a podcast I've been listening to, and the theme this season is the most cold-blooded murders for hire . . ."

My head clanged, and *my* blood chilled.

I gritted my teeth as they talked, trading stories about their favorite episodes. No one mentioned the Paige-Prince family, and for that I was grateful.

Still, my skin prickled with every word they said. Even though the conversation was simply circumstantial.

Finally, Alan cleared his throat. "But let's get down to business. You want to win over the neighborhood association, and that's not going to happen by talking about true crime." He slapped on a smile.

"No, it's not," I said, pasting on a grin too. Were both of ours fake? I didn't know, but I sure as hell wanted to move on to other topics. "Talk to me about who I need to win over, Alan. Tell me what you see in your neighborhood," I said, dead set on shifting gears.

Alan clucked his tongue. "Look. As much as I love shooting the breeze about Vegas, that's just between us guys. When it comes to the neighborhood, you need to present a different side. We're all about families. We want to see that you're a family guy. That's what matters. You need to meet the people in the neighborhood. Show you care."

"That's easy, because I do care."

"Good. We've got a big picnic coming up in the park. Fundraiser for some neighborhood services. I'll get you the date. You could come by and say hello. Meet the neighbors. Talk to them. Let them know you're a family guy at heart. Don't say much about comedy. Don't tell dirty jokes. And all that shit we just riffed on?"

"The Vegas stuff. The true-crime stuff," Tanner added, like I could forget it.

"What about it?" I asked.

Alan made a slashing sign across his throat. "Don't say a word."

I furrowed my brow, wanting to point out that I wasn't the one who'd brought up the subjects in the first place. But I didn't want to rock the boat. Instead, I said, "I have a million other things I can talk about."

"Good. Because Vegas is verboten."

I couldn't help but wonder why.

* * *

But after another hour with the two of them, I left the meeting figuring that they were simply playing their parts.

Alan and Tanner were two men who liked to swear like bros, talk like pigs, and then act like choirboys.

They weren't my favorite people, but I'd learned their rules and had figured out how to play their games.

Alan had asked me to swing by and meet his wife and kids that evening, and I'd said yes, so I'd do that later.

Back at my hotel, I unknotted my green tie and tossed it on the king-size bed. Making quick work of the buttons on my crisp white shirt, I stripped that off next, grateful to be rid of it. I grabbed my phone, scrolled to my messages, and clicked open the photo

Shannon had sent me a couple of days ago—one she'd snapped at the photo booth on Friday afternoon. She'd added a bushy black mustache to my face, and planted a purple wig on her own head.

I ran my fingertip across her face. Even in a silly shot like this, she was beautiful. I dropped my head onto the pillow. "I'm so screwed," I muttered.

I was more than crazy about her. I was completely under her spell, hypnotized, and I never wanted it to end. It hadn't taken much for me to fall back under. I was nearly there before I'd even started seeing her again. But then she did things like this—things that were so goofy, so silly, and so utterly us. Things that made me want to hold on tight and never let go.

But she'd seemed so out of sorts last night. Understandable, but still, I'd felt her drifting away.

And that was not going to fly with me.

An arrival text wasn't enough.

I had to be the man she needed.

But more so, I had to be the man I wanted to be.

Even if work got in the way now and then, I needed to let her know she was first in my mind and my heart.

Out of the corner of my eye, I caught a glimpse of pink and purple on my upper arm. The tattoo she'd given me was still there. That was as good a reason as any to call her.

"Hey," she said when she answered on the second ring. The background noise told me she was in the car.

"Hey you. Guess what I just learned?" I asked, as if I had a big surprise.

"Tell me." Her voice sounded light, and I hoped that meant I was forgiven.

"Those temporary tattoos last at least two days," I said.

She laughed. "Admit it. You just haven't showered since the day at the photo booth."

I heaved an exaggerated sigh. "You're right. I'm a pig. Also, I am not a mustache guy. Remind me to never ever grow one because I look stupid as hell like this. You, on the other hand, are hot in a purple wig."

"Why, thank you. I do have mad Photoshop skills, don't I?"

"Could be another career path for you," I said, parking my free hand behind my head, thinking how epic it was to slide right back into this kind of comfortable banter with my woman. "By the way, have I mentioned I was sorry for jetting last night?"

"You have," she said softly. "And it's fine. We're good."

"But I'll say it anyway. I'm sorry for letting you down. And for taking off early."

"We are all good. I swear."

"So I'm forgiven?"

"You were never *unforgiven*. That was just a speed bump. We made it over."

I grinned. "We sure did, and I will make it up to you. I promise."

"Anyway, how was the meeting? I keep thinking about what you said when you left. How they were worried you'd bring trouble to the neighborhood. Did that come up today?"

Ah, the heart of the matter. Do I tell her they mentioned one of her least favorite topics? Or do I keep that to myself?

Keeping things to myself wouldn't help us move forward.

Still, I figured treading lightly was best. "Mostly good. He made it clear he'll go to bat for me as long as I don't bring any baggage to the table."

I was met with silence on the other end of the phone.

Dead silence.

"Sorry," she said in a quiet voice, sounding strained. But her reaction didn't compute.

"Why are you sorry?"

"I'm sorry he said that," she added.

"Oh. Sure. Me too."

"Did he explain what he meant by it?" she asked, as the beep from her turn signal echoed in the background.

Staring at the ceiling, I asked myself if this was the moment to be fully honest. After last night, though, I needed to do just that. "Turns out they aren't too wild about me being from Vegas," I said, starting with that.

"That's odd."

"The guys were into it, but they don't want me to talk it up when I meet the neighbors. They want all the Vegas connection on the down-low. And the weird thing is—they brought up the Royal Sinners."

"What?" Her voice rose.

"They're true-crime junkies. It was nothing specific,

babe. Just general questions. They both listen to true-crime podcasts."

"But why would they bring up the Royal Sinners?" she asked in a rush.

"I think it was just curiosity. They were asking all sorts of questions about Vegas and the mob and gangs."

"That has nothing to do with your clubs."

"I know that. I absolutely know that." I settled into the soft covers on the bed. "But what can I do? I need New York. The location is perfect, and New York is the centerpiece of our expansion plans. I'm meeting the neighborhood association president's wife and daughter tonight to say hi, so that should help. I just have to jump through their hoops."

"It's insulting what they're focusing on. Like that's what makes a difference in whether they approve you or not," she said harshly.

"Couldn't agree more, so let's talk about something else. How is your day?"

She cut the engine. "Fine. But I need to go. I have a rehearsal. Then a meeting with my assistant. And then I'm going to see Ryan. Let's talk later."

I blinked. I hadn't expected that. "You're a busy woman," I said, and when the call ended, I scratched my jaw, wondering once again if she was slipping through my fingers.

34

SHANNON

Rehearsal was exhausting.

And it didn't entirely clear my head either.

Nor did my meeting with Christine.

Questions still raced through my mind when I reached the gun range, where I was meeting Ryan, several hours later.

Questions about my family.

My baggage.

My hometown.

And I was here to understand all of that.

I crossed my arms and watched my brother mow down targets with clockwork precision. Huge earphones covered Ryan's head, muffling out the sound as he fired with one hand. A sure shot. I knew how to fire too, though I rarely did. I owned a subcompact Glock 42 that Ryan had bought me when I'd moved back to Vegas.

"It's your housewarming present," he'd remarked when he took me to the gun store.

"You afraid the Royal Sinners are coming for me?" I'd asked, joking but not joking.

He'd squeezed my shoulders reassuringly. "They're not coming for you. But you never know who is." He'd filled out the paperwork, plunked down his credit card, and handed me the weapon, and said, "Welcome home."

Then he'd taught me how to handle a gun.

Sometimes I joined him at the range, sharing his focused intensity, his cold concentration. Other times, I'd wished I'd never learned to shoot, never imagined that I might need to. Even if you were skilled in how to fire, a gun couldn't always save you. If my father had carried a gun, he'd likely still be dead. He'd been shot in the back, and never saw it coming.

Guns were useless when someone put a price tag on your head.

That was the cold truth of true crime.

Ryan took aim at another black-and-white cardboard cutout. I counted off in my head with each bullet.

One target. Two targets. Three targets. Now, four. Now, five. He landed the last one too. Straight down the middle. He lowered his arm, his revolver solidly in his right palm. After he tugged off the earphones and goggles, he turned around and flashed me a bright smile. He blew on the end of the gun and winked.

Show-off, I mouthed, watching him from just outside.

He waved me into his lane, gesturing for me to join him. "You hit half of what I did, I'll buy you lunch," he said.

I rolled my eyes, but accepted the challenge. He positioned the earphones over my head, placed the goggles on my eyes, and set his Smith & Wesson in my palm. I planted my feet wide, peered down the lane, and raised both hands, keeping the weapon steady, solid against my flesh. I peered at the target at the end of the range, a black-and-white sketch of a body with a bullseye on his chest.

I tried not to think of Stefano ending my father's life. But that trick never worked. I *always* pictured that man, that fucking scum who took a job from my mother.

That killer.

I burned.

I raged.

If I didn't see Stefano at the end of the barrel, I'd imagine my mom. I couldn't go there. I couldn't live in that land of hate for the woman who'd raised me, taken care of me, kissed me good night. If I pictured my mom, I'd be just the same as her.

My hate was reserved for the triggerman. For the man who had shed my father's blood. My jaw tightened, and I watched the reel. Each unlived moment played before my eyes. My father would never know where I'd gone to college, what I did for a living, if I was happy, if I was in love. He'd never walk me down the aisle, and he'd never tuck his grandchildren into bed or take them to the park.

He'd never enjoy a day of fishing as a retired man—his dream.

He'd never celebrate his fiftieth birthday. He was eternally thirty-six, and always would be.

He'd never grow old.

They took all that away from him.

From my grandparents.

From my brothers.

From me.

And they were still taking. They were fraying my nerves. They were circling me, it seemed. I *hated* that people were talking about crimes like they were pop culture.

I hated that gangs were a topic of discussion at a meal across the country.

And I hated the judgment of those who'd never known how a bullet could fracture a family.

How a cold-blooded choice could nearly destroy your heart.

But mine wasn't shattered.

Not all the way, not yet.

I stared, ready.

My teeth were clenched, my lips were like a tightrope, and my hands belonged to a surgeon. Steady, practiced, perfect.

Jerry Stefano.

I fired three shots to the heart.

Adrenaline surged through me, lighting up my bloodstream with wild energy. I could lift a car, fight a man twice my size. My chest rose and fell; my fingertips tingled. Then those endorphins were chased with a dose of red-hot anger, with the madness that comes from the black hole of loss.

I pressed my fingertip to the trigger, wanting, wishing, eager. Itching to fire again.

Before the anger consumed me, I lowered the gun. I handed it to Ryan.

"Lunch is on me," he said warmly.

"I'm not hungry," I said coldly.

* * *

Minutes later, we sat in his car in the parking lot. The engine was off. The radio was on. The National, Ryan's favorite band, crooned about missing the one you love. Such a moody song. Fitting too.

"What's the story?" I asked, cutting to the chase. "Is Stefano facing more charges?"

Ryan shot me a quizzical look. "No. Not that I know of."

I rolled my hands, as if to jog his memory. "You told me your friend in the DA's office said they visited Stefano in prison about other crimes or something. You called last night wanting to talk."

"Right, but even if he has intel about other crimes, that won't change his sentence."

"I know that," I said, but then I realized—Ryan hadn't called me to discuss the latest news about the shooter. He hadn't mentioned Stefano last night. I was the one obsessed with Stefano. He was obsessed with someone else. "So *this*," I said, gesturing from him to me, "isn't about Stefano?"

"No," he said, forming an *O* with his mouth. "Not at all. It's about someone else. I talked to Mom."

RYAN

My sister's jaw dropped. I hadn't intended to shock her, but the evidence was on her face.

"She called you?" Shannon whispered, as if she couldn't quite wrap her mind around the concept of the phone and how people used it to stay in touch.

Scanning the parking lot through the window, I made sure we were alone. No one was wandering around. I turned up the music a little more, just in case. I'd always believed it was best to have these kinds of conversations in person, with plenty of background noise. "She called me collect the other night. She told me a lawyer came to see her."

Her eyes widened. "The one who represented her at the trial?"

I shook my head. "Nope. That guy is long gone. He went into private practice. But the guy who came to see her is also a public defender. She said she contacted him, and he went to Hawthorne to visit her."

Shannon cleared her throat and swallowed, then

spoke in a clipped, controlled voice. "What does she have to talk to a lawyer about? Is she trying again to get them to re-open the case? Is she rehashing the details over and over like she did the last time we saw her? The evidence against her? The phone records showing she *repeatedly* called Jerry Stefano for two months before the murder?" Shannon asked, smacking the dashboard for emphasis. "What if Stefano is in touch with someone on the outside? What if he gets pissed she's stirring the hornet's nest? What if he wants revenge?"

I dragged a hand through my hair, hating that Shannon was getting worked up. But I understood her what-ifs. I completely got why she was concerned—her demon was the shooter.

Her demon had always been the shooter.

Understandable.

"Shan, I can't promise you a damn thing about Stefano. But that's not what Mom called about."

"Did she call with more lies? Because the lies she told about those calls were ludicrous. The prosecution saw right through them. She couldn't even come up with a decent reason for them."

But I knew why she'd lied.

I knew she had a decent reason to fashion all sorts of fables about her calls with Stefano. The truth would have made her look guiltier, so she'd gambled. Honesty would have tethered her more closely to Stefano and his Royal Sinners.

I knew some of those truths. She'd shared them with me, begged for my help, and I'd kept them locked up in my head. I'd never uttered a word of them. To a soul.

The best way to protect a secret was to never tell it. Seal your mouth, zip it shut, and don't breathe a word. That was the one guaranteed method, and I kept secrets like a champion.

But I hadn't asked my sister to meet me so we could revisit the chain of evidence that had landed our mother behind bars. I'd called Shannon because she was the only one of my siblings who hadn't closed the door on our mom. I needed strength in numbers, even if that number was two.

"Mom and I didn't talk about the phone calls with Stefano," I said, trying my best to reassure her. "He's locked up, Shan. He's not getting out."

Her jaw ticked. "So why did she see a lawyer?"

I drew a breath, wishing I had more to tell. "She said she'll tell us in person when we come see her. We've got to go see her."

Shannon held out her hands in frustration. "See? She can't even tell you why she's talking to a lawyer. She's manipulating us into visiting her."

"She's our goddamn mother!"

"I know," Shannon hissed, and pointed two fingers back at her eyes. "I damn well know. I look in the mirror every day and see her eyes. I have her eyes. I look like her. I have her goddamn cheekbones and chin too."

"You are your own woman. Doesn't matter what color your eyes are."

She dropped her head in her hands, breathing out hard. "Ryan. I feel like I can't live a normal life," she whispered.

I rubbed a hand against her back. "Same for me, Shan. It's the same for me. But look, maybe Mom has something that needs to be said in person. Maybe it's important," I said softly, but in a firm tone that brooked no argument. "We need to find out what's up. She's writing to you a ton. She's calling me. Something could be going on. We need to know. Don't you think?"

She didn't answer. But I saw the tacit yes in her eyes.

"End of the month. Her hours were cut, but she gets her final two hours the last day of June. We need to plan for it. Take the day. No excuses. Are you in?"

"Probably." She shoved her hand through her hair, yanking it back into a ponytail. "Why are you so deter-mined to believe she might be innocent?"

My lips parted, but I took my time. My mother wasn't an innocent woman, not by any stretch of the law. She might not even be a good person. But I believed there was a difference between the things she'd done, and the things the district attorney had said she'd done.

I believed that with my whole heart. "Because we need to be certain."

She closed her eyes, the conversation clearly paining her. Hell, it pained me. When she opened them, the look in them was one of defeat. Even so, she nodded. "I'll go with you."

"Good. I need you there," I said, and flashed a small smile.

"Now there's something I need your advice on."

"I'm all ears."

"But first, you need to know I'm with Brent again."

I flinched. I'd be less surprised if she told me she could levitate. "What the hell is that about?"

She tapped her heart. "It's about this. So respect my heart, please. And no big-brother act."

I sighed heavily. "I'll behave," I said, because I understood what it was like to be unable to let go of something.

"Brent met with some business partners in New York, of all places. They brought up the Royal Sinners. They talked about Vegas. They talked about baggage."

"Shit," I muttered. "They know he's with you again."

"Maybe. But even if they don't, I'm afraid I'm damaged goods. Like my history is going to affect his present."

She told me more, and I hated to agree, but it sure as hell sounded like someone didn't want to associate with anyone involved with the former Paige-Prince kids.

As far as I was concerned, anyone who felt that way could fuck all the way off.

And I told her as much, but I also told her to be careful, because between this and our mother's urgent phone call, there was definitely something brewing, and we seemed to be in the center of it all once again.

36

SHANNON

I cranked up the volume to "You're the One That I Want" on the radio in my cherry-red BMW as I drove home. I needed the upbeat, dancy number to reset my mind. Belting out the celebratory tune as I turned onto my street, I let the lyrics fill the hollow and angry space between my conversation with Ryan and the rest of my day.

Between Brent's news and my evening.

The music was my buffer, and as I sang, I choreographed the number in my head, the dance and the movement ushering out the negative thoughts. Dance had always been a way through tough times for me. Today I would lean on it even more during the second rehearsal—Christine and I were seeing the dancers at Edge to review that choreography.

And maybe that would help settle my mind after the crazy day.

And settle the debate raging in my heart.

Because I was baggage.

I was trouble.

I was so damn checkered.

And somehow that was going to affect Brent.

The busy day would keep my focus off my mom and off Stefano and off my relationship.

As I turned along the road to my condo so I could grab my favorite dance shoes, I spotted a strange car I'd never seen before parked just outside the gate to my building.

A Buick.

An old one at that.

It looked like it was from last century.

I was used to Audis, BMWs, SUVs, hybrids, MINI Coopers, and plenty of electric cars at my building. This vehicle was the answer in a *one of these is not like the other* game. Buicks weren't common cars. Though I hadn't memorized the rides of all my condo mates, I was sure I'd have remembered this earthy brown vehicle that hailed from days gone by.

I didn't remember it.

A young guy in jeans, boots, and a worn black T-shirt leaned against the trunk of the car, his elbows resting on the metal.

Watching.

Like all my fears.

Casing the joint? Doing recon?

This guy was simply staring, looking, scanning.

Technically, he was doing nothing wrong. *Technically.*

But cars didn't park by the gate. Young guys dressed

like that didn't wait by my building. He didn't look familiar at all.

Stefano probably hadn't looked familiar to Dad either when he scoped out our house.

My spine crawled with fear.

Better safe than sorry.

I heeded the warning bell. The automatic gate rose for me as it picked up on the transponder in my car that gave me access. Rather than sliding into my regular parking spot in the garage—a garage that someone could easily enter by foot—I made a loop around the cars on the first level and exited on the other side.

The guy was still there.

The hair on my arms stood on end. Fear tripped through my blood. Was I overreacting or under-reacting?

I couldn't tell if he was watching me, or just waiting.

But that was precisely why I left.

By the time I slowed to a stop at a red light near the Luxe, my heart hammered in my chest, and my hands were clammy.

And that was precisely why I called Brent.

"I'm about to go into a dead spot. What's going on?"

I gritted out the words that tore through me. "I'm damaged goods, Brent. You're better off without me."

"What are you talking about?"

My voice shook. "You said the guy you met was asking about Vegas. He mentioned the gang that shot my father. You shouldn't get involved with me. I'm only going to bring you down."

"Shan," he said calmly, "you could never bring me down. But can we talk about this in person?"

My throat tightened. "If you want to."

"Let's discuss this in person," he repeated. "I promise I will see you soon."

But that was the last thing he said, because his line went dead.

In the parking lot at the Luxe, I cut the engine, dropping my forehead on the steering wheel and letting the tears rain down.

When I got out of the car, there was a text from him.

Brent: You are everything to me. Do not cut me out of your life.

Shannon: You're everything to me too.

But that was all I could say.

It was only part of the truth. I called my grandmother. I needed to talk to someone who'd understand.

She didn't answer, so I walked into Edge, understanding only dance.

37

BRENT

Once upon a time, I let work get in the way.

I let my desire to get ahead push me into corners.

I made choices I regretted.

I didn't do enough, say enough, fight hard enough.

I wasn't that twenty-two-year-old anymore.

I knew what I wanted. I knew what I needed. I needed *her*.

And that was why I left New York after lunch. As soon as I'd gotten off the phone with her after seeing Alan and Tanner, I made a choice.

Go to her.

Because she wasn't herself.

I could feel it.

I could tell. I'd been able to tell since our call after my lunch.

And I wasn't going to let her slip through my fingers.

No way.

And when I landed, and the shuttle was rattling through the airport, she called.

And, as I suspected, she tried to push me away.

Saying she was baggage.

Saying she was damaged goods.

Saying she'd bring me down.

No.

No way.

As soon as I got off the tram and service came back, I called her again. She didn't answer.

But I knew where she was.

My club.

I'd be there in mere minutes.

38

SHANNON

The lithe, pretzel-like redhead swung upside down on the gauzy swath of fabric that hung from the ceiling of Edge in a room that wasn't in use tonight. Her hair spilled below her like a sheet of fire, as she held on with only one ankle twisted around the cloth.

As the lush music pulsed, she twirled in gorgeous circles, captivating me with her contortionist skills.

I zoomed in on her with my phone camera, capturing Cassidy's finale of the dress rehearsal as she curved her body into impossible shapes. Then, along with a trio of other dancers, she slid in a wild rush upside down to the floor. I stopped recording and clapped proudly.

Cassidy flashed me the bright, magnetic smile of an entertainer who'd nailed it.

"You were amazing," I told her, grateful that I could do this—my job—without fear. That I could choreograph shows without worrying too much. Everything else I wasn't so sure about. "Absolute perfection. No changes."

"Thank you, Shay. I'm so happy you liked it," the girl said, beaming as she and the other dancers took off for the dressing room.

I finished my notes from the dress rehearsal and said good night to Christine, when my phone rang at last. The person I needed to talk to. I stepped away from the noise, heading into the ladies' room at Edge, where it was quieter.

"Hi." My voice sounded hollow to my own ears.

"You rang. What's going on, baby? Your message didn't sound good," Grandma said.

"I don't feel good," I said, wobbly.

"Do you want me to come by? Bring you some tea? Chicken soup?"

"No. It's not my body that hurts." I slumped against the wall.

"Sweetheart. What's going on?"

"I don't know how to love like a normal person," I whispered, because talking over the lump in my throat felt impossible. "How do you do it? Tell me. Because I don't know."

She sighed sympathetically. "There is no secret. You just love. From your whole heart. Like your father did."

My chest ached at the mention of the man I'd looked up to. "But I don't want to hurt the people I love. And I don't want them to be hurt because of me."

"We can't protect ourselves every second of the day, and we can't protect the ones we love either."

"But I'm like a black sheep. And Brent needs a white

sheep or something," I said. "He's trying to get this business deal, and I'm just worried that any association with me is going to ruin it."

"Oh, honey."

"I mean it."

"I know you do, but you didn't do anything wrong. The people who did are locked up."

"But are they?"

"Shannon," she chided. She'd always cautioned me against these kinds of questions. Questions that would hurt, she'd said. "There is only so much you can control. You are trying to control the present and the future. You are trying to control people. You can't. You can only control your choices. What are you choosing here exactly?"

I drew in a shaky breath, looked up at the ceiling, then in the mirror, and studied my face. My mother's eyes. *My* eyes. What was I choosing? That was the question. Was I choosing retreat? Was I choosing safety?

Or was I choosing fear?

"I just wonder if he's better off without me."

"Why don't you let him decide that? Because that's his choice. Yours is this—are you better off with him?"

I flashed back on the last week or so we'd spent together. On the dates, on the talks, on the times we'd had.

On the moments. The connection.

And even our argument last night.

Even his forgetting didn't bother me that much.

That was minor in the scope of things. I understood it. I accepted his explanation. I was fine with it.

What was major, though, was how I felt for that man.

And I felt all the things for him again.

So much I didn't want to hurt him. "I am better with him. But I told him I thought he was better off without me."

"And is that true?"

"I hope not," I said, my throat tightening. "I hope he's not better off without me, because I need him and want him and love him."

Her voice grew intense. "Then find him. Talk to him. Say you love him, say you want to be with him. As long as he's not gone, you can keep making up. We live and we love and we hurt each other. We don't always say the right thing or do the right thing at the right moment. Sometimes we need space and distance, and sometimes words fall from our lips that shouldn't have been said. Sometimes they seem untenable, and sometimes they are," she said, then stopped to take a breath. "And we always hurt the ones we love most. If we didn't love so much, it wouldn't hurt so much. But you keep going. You keep loving. You keep working on that love every day. The only time you won't have a chance at making up is when one of you is gone. Since he's still there, it's not over. Not in the least. So love him. Show him that you love him."

I squared my shoulders, gathered my thoughts, and called up my courage. I stepped out of the bathroom, saying, "I do. I do love him."

"And he loves you."

I looked up to the man who had spoken. "Brent?"

39

SHANNON

This was a time warp.

That was the only explanation.

Either that or my eyes were playing tricks on me.

The man I loved stood in front of me less than twenty-four hours after I'd last seen him. And a mere thirty minutes after we'd spoken on the phone. I hung up quickly with Grandma, then turned to Brent.

"How?" I asked, startled. "How are you here?"

His smile was wry and warm. "I would have been here sooner, but traffic was terrible on the way over from the airport."

I shook my head, shock coursing through me. "No, how are you here?" I asked, pointing to the floor, as if to indicate Las Vegas itself. "In Nevada. You were in New York a few minutes ago."

He arched a brow. "Wings?"

"*Brent.*"

He stepped closer, setting his hands on my arms.

"You're not giving up on us, and you're not scaring me away. I won't let you."

"But I don't want to hurt you."

He ran his palm down my bare arm. "The only thing that could hurt me is you leaving me. And sorry not sorry. But I'm not going to let that happen."

I tried to rein in a grin. It was a futile effort. "You're not?"

He shook his head adamantly. "Nope. I came back to tell you that."

I looked at the clock on the wall. "Isn't it a five-hour flight?"

He nodded. "It is. And as soon as we talked on the phone earlier, I could tell you were fading away. I wasn't going to let you."

"But you said you had a meeting tonight?"

"Ditched it," he said confidently, like he had zero regrets. "I left early. Switched my flight again. I came home early to tell you"—he stopped, paused, locked his eyes with mine—"*no*."

I laughed at his comment. "You did?"

"I did. Because I don't care what those guys say about trouble or baggage or what-the-fuck-ever. I care about *you*. You don't bring me down, Shannon Paige-Prince. You raise me up. You make me better. You make me want to be the man I should be. The man for you. I let you get away once, and I am not ever letting that happen again. Do you get that?" His brown eyes were hard, intense, and his touch was hot and confident.

"I do," I said, amazed he'd done this. Amazed he was here. "But does it ever bother you that you've had such a normal life and I have this . . . *crazy* one? I have so much baggage, and you have none."

He shook his head. "Baggage doesn't scare me. I told you I'm strong. I will carry it. I will carry you."

I pressed my lips together, then spoke once again, because I needed to make sure. "You bake pumpkin pie for your parents every year at Thanksgiving. What could I possibly ever do for you?"

"Don't you realize? I want to give what I have to you. I'm lucky. I know that. I have an overflow of luck, happiness, all that stuff. I will be by your side as you deal with every day, no matter how positive or how troubling. *Always.*" He slid a hand into my hair, making me tremble. "And you have no idea what you do for me."

"Then tell me. I can't even imagine what I could ever do that would compare."

"You send me a selfie of us, and I'm ecstatic. You give me a pony tattoo, and I'm over the moon," he said, and his voice was filled with a sincerity that made my heart beat faster. He was the easiest person to please, and I loved that about him. "Think of me like a cactus. I don't require much. A little water, some sun, and I'm good."

"I'm a hibiscus, then. They require a ton," I said, as a smile spread across my face.

"Good. I've got a lot to give. But what I don't have to give is a single fuck about what those two assholes in New York think of me. I don't care if they think Vegas is a city of ill repute. I care about you. Ten years ago, I missed the chance to be there for you. I'm not missing a thing anymore," he said, and my heart soared. "I came here to tell you I love you." He cupped my cheeks. "I love you, Shay Sloan. I love you, Shannon Paige-Prince. I love you."

Joy.

That was all I felt.

So much joy.

It was all I wanted to feel as I pressed a soft kiss to his lips. "I love you, Brent Nichols."

Then I kissed him harder, showing him how much I adored him.

When he broke the kiss, he wiggled a brow. "I was wrong. There is one thing you can give me."

"What is it? Name it."

"All I want is you. Give me you," he said, and his words warmed me from the tips of my toes to the ends of my hair.

"Have me."

40

BRENT

I shut the door of my office on the second floor of Edge. The sound of it clicking made my dick even harder. It was the noise that signaled the start of what I'd been waiting for ever since I'd laid eyes on her at the Waldorf Astoria.

But my desire dug deeper than the past week.

It unspooled over years.

It had grown roots in the last decade.

There was no way out of this. The only way was through it. I was finally going to have her. To take what was mine—this woman I adored to the ends of the earth and back.

The woman I loved madly. All the time. For all time.

I locked the door without looking away from her beauty. She wore a sleeveless dress and black sheer stockings that made me think only one thing—how far up did they go?

Then there were those shoes. Those black leather

pumps that I was going to have wrapped around my back so damn soon.

"Now why on earth would you say you're not giving?" I backed her up against the wall. My hands were already on her. Goosebumps rose on her skin as I touched her. "Because *this* is the best gift I've ever had. You. In my office." I brushed my fingers along the fabric of her dress, and she trembled. That telltale sign of her lust scorched my blood. "The woman I intend to fuck. The woman I'm going to make love to."

She licked her lips. "That's who I am. For you, only you."

I leaned into her neck, kissing her, inhaling her honey scent. I bit down gently on her flesh. "All day," I growled. "All day I've thought about you. If you were okay. What I could do for you. How I could make things better."

"You can do me," she said, all sexy and playful.

"That's what I want." I buzzed a path along the column of her throat. She made the sexiest little whimpers and sighs. I pressed my body against hers, my hard-on making contact with her belly. She moaned in response.

"That's how much I want you. All I can think about is having you again," I said as I began lifting her dress.

She grabbed my shirt collar, tugging me closer. Her eyes were on mine, hazy and full of heat. "It's the same for me. You're all I think about too."

My blood was on fire. I dragged my fingers up the sheer fabric of her stockings, groaning when I reached the lacy top that hit the soft flesh of her upper thighs. I didn't stop though. I was in hot pursuit of her pussy. "Let me test that for sure," I said, then slid my fingers against the panel of her panties. She was soaked all the way through. I dived in, sliding my fingers inside the black lace, gliding them across her sweet flesh that felt like heaven to my touch. I brought my fingers to my lips and sucked her off. "You are so ready for me."

Her lips parted on a sexy sigh. She looped her arms around my neck and arched her hips against me. "Please. Please take me now. I can't wait anymore."

I scooped her up and stalked over to my desk, setting her down. "There is no more waiting. And tonight isn't ending, Shan. I promise you."

She reached for me and began unbuttoning my shirt, her gaze pinned on me as she spoke in a sexy purr. "Good. Because I want you to fuck me now, and I want you to fuck me again tonight. At your place," she said, working her way down the buttons on my shirt.

"All night long, babe. I will be having you all night long."

She grasped my shirt and pulled me closer. "Good, because I don't think I can get enough of you."

And I'd thought I couldn't want her any more than I already did. She'd just proven me wrong with those words. I wanted her even more.

And I knew I wouldn't ever be able to have enough of her.

41

SHANNON

I was ready.

Nearly. There was something I had to say. Something that couldn't wait any longer. I placed my hands on his chest, so firm and strong and solid. "Wait."

He froze on my command. "What is it?"

I cupped his cheeks. "There's something I have to tell you."

"Okay," he said tentatively.

He sounded worried, and I was going to nip that worry in the bud. He'd shown me he'd changed, he'd become the man I wanted, and he said he was willing to give himself to me.

I hoped I'd done the same too.

"Brent," I said, stroking his stubbled jaw, loving his five-o'clock shadow. Loving his deep brown eyes. Loving all of him.

"What is it, Shan?"

I wasn't scared. I didn't need liquid courage or a

hearty dose of guts. All I felt was an incredible joy, an iridescent passion that tripped through my bones and sparked along my skin. "I've never fallen in love with anyone but you," I said, my lips curving into a grin.

The expression in his eyes changed from lust to wonder. He parted his mouth, but I shushed him, pressing my fingertip over those soft, delicious lips that I'd be kissing in seconds. I felt so vulnerable, but so sure. He was the one true thing in my life.

"You're the only man who's ever had my heart. And I don't just love you. I am so unbelievably madly in love with you."

He arched an eyebrow playfully. "Yeah?"

"It's only ever been you," I said, loving telling him this, thrilled that I could. I was no longer scared of what was happening between us. It was everything I wanted.

Everything I almost gave up.

"Shan, it's always been you." His eyes sparkled, full of a passion that matched mine. He clasped my hand and kissed my palm, and when he looked at me, he was grinning like a fool in love too. "I'm madly in love with you. I never stopped, Shannon. I never stopped loving you. Not once. You are the only one for me."

Happiness raced through my veins. Hope flooded my body. Love was all I felt. Heart, mind, and body, I was all in. "I want to be with you forever."

"I'm never letting you slip away from me again," he said as he brushed his thumb along my cheek. "You belong with me."

I held his face, not wanting to look elsewhere, not

wanting to break the hold he had on me. "Fuck me, take me, make love to me."

"When I fuck you, you are always the woman I love. You always have been. You always will be," he said as he pushed up my dress and yanked off my panties. I ached between my legs, pulsing with heat and want.

He gazed hungrily at me. "Beautiful," he murmured on a low rumble, his hot stare making me wetter. He unzipped his pants and pushed down his briefs, freeing his gorgeous cock. It was beautiful—long, thick, hard— and I knew what it could do. I knew the depths of pleasure he alone could deliver. He could take me to heaven and back.

He trailed his fingers along the inside of my thigh, and I trembled with desire, watching the path of his hand as he slid his finger through my folds. A current surged through me at his caress.

"You're so fucking turned on, I can coat myself in you," he said, rubbing my slickness on his hard length. I burned fever hot as I watched him.

Groaning savagely, he spread my arousal on the head, then back down all along his length. His eyes floated closed as he stroked—a long, lingering, tantalizing stroke meant to tease me to the point of no return.

It worked. Oh hell, it worked. I was an inferno.

I couldn't wait. Seconds seemed too long. I had to have him inside me. "*Please*," I begged, as he rubbed the head of his cock across me now, teasing me with that first touch, tempting me with so much more. I desperately longed to feel him slide into me. To have him so deep inside me that the world faded away, that day shaded into night, and night melted into day. And that *this*—the connection between the two of us, the intensity of our need for each other that spanned years—became all that existed.

Because this was everything good in the world.

"Take me," I said. "Take me now."

Every atom in me buzzed. My cells were no longer made of molecules. They were comprised of desire and lust. There was no more waiting, no more time. I needed only this, only now. Mercifully, he sank into me.

"Oh God," I cried out, and roped my arms around his neck. His eyes blazed darkly at me, so hot, so full of the same raw and primal need. He stilled himself when he was all the way in, letting me feel him, letting me adjust to his size.

"It feels so good," I moaned. "I want you so much."

"I have never wanted anyone like this," he said, moving in me.

"Me neither," I said, gasping with each thrust.

"I have never been so in love with you."

I gripped his neck, digging my nails into his skin. "*Never.* I've never felt like this." My world spun silver and gold. The intensity of him inside me drove me wild. My heart beat in a frenzy.

"I fucking love you more than I did the first time," he said on a powerful thrust. My head fell back on my shoulders, and I squeezed my eyes closed. I rocked my hips up into him, chasing even more pleasure.

"The same," I said, barely able to form words anymore. Fire roared through me. "I feel the same."

He grabbed my hips and yanked me up to him, deeper, harder. "You are like coming home."

My body jolted with each delicious thrust. My heart pumped wildly as he drove into me, burying himself. "Deeper," I panted. "More."

Pressing a hand on my chest, he lowered my spine to his desk. I grinned wickedly as I hooked my legs up on his shoulders, wrapping them behind his neck. He practically climbed onto the desk, his knees on the wood, and he took me. He just fucking took me.

My spine dug into the desk. His hands curled around my head as he drove into me. His cock hit that spot inside me that sent me galloping closer to the cliff. I felt him everywhere.

Every thrust consumed me. He filled me completely, and he owned my body with his. The world rotated on its axis again as Brent Nichols fucked the last ten years without him right out of me.

Time was crushed to pieces in the way he took me.

I could barely move, and I didn't care. Couldn't care. All I wanted was to give myself to him.

My back scraped the desk as the friction drove me to the edge. "Please," I called out. Tremors of lust slammed into me, assaulting me with pleasure and sending me flying as my body detonated.

The world slipped away into bliss, into ecstasy, into the end of missing-the-love-of-your-life.

This was everything.

I was back.

We were one.

He held me harder, gripping my head. "I love you," he grunted as he thrust, reaching his own release. "I love you so much."

And I felt that love everywhere.

42

___

BRENT

The stars twinkled against the inky black night as I pulled off the highway, en route to my home in her car. Shannon had told me about the guy she saw outside her condo, and how she didn't want to spend the night there.

No way was I going to let her. Especially since I told her I'd seen someone suspicious there the other week. It sounded like the same guy in the same car.

We'd stopped at her place to pick up some clothes for her.

Now, we were nearing my home. I pulled up to the curb and turned off the car.

"A sleepover at last," I teased as we walked inside, and I dropped my bag from New York by the door.

I flicked on the lights and led her straight to the bedroom.

And we wasted no time.

"It's been ten years. Once is not enough," I said.

"Couldn't agree more."

In minutes we were naked, tangled up together, making love. Making promises. So many promises of love and passion and togetherness.

She was worth flying home for.

She was worth everything.

In the morning, we didn't want to get out of bed. I'd already planned on taking the day off, since I'd worked over the weekend. Shannon said she could play hooky.

And then we did our two favorite things.

Talking and touching.

Touching and talking.

This was who we were. This was who we'd be again.

"Why don't you move in with me?" I said.

"You think I should?"

"I'd feel better if you did. I don't like the idea of someone watching your place. I have a security system, but I can also get you a security detail for when I'm not here."

She smiled and ran her fingers down my arm. "I do have two brothers who run a security firm."

"Then let's put them to use."

She dropped a kiss to my nose. "Do you just want me to move in to keep me safe?"

I tossed my head back and laughed. "Woman, I want you to move in with me because I want to be with you all the time. Get that straight."

She tackle-hugged me. "Fine, fine. Twist my arm." She held out her arm, but instead of twisting, I kissed it, and as my lips trailed along her skin, she tossed out a question. "What's going to happen in New York, Brent?

You've been so eager to expand there. I hate that you might lose this chance."

"Don't know anymore."

"Do you think the deal can still happen?"

"Maybe. I'm honestly not sure," I said, and the funny thing was, I didn't care as much as I'd thought I would. I'd been so damn keen on that club and that location until yesterday. The two men I had to deal with didn't seem to want to deal with me. That was a bit of a turnoff. "They aren't at the top of my list of people I want to do business with," I said, pressing a kiss to her wrist.

Gently, she tugged her wrist away, then propped her head in her hand. "I don't want you to lose business because of me."

I scoffed. "The meeting was over. Lunch was done."

"But you were supposed to meet that guy's wife and daughter last night and you got on a plane," she added. "And my past, it's like it's haunting you too."

"If I lose the deal, it's not because of you, Shan."

"Isn't it though?"

I shook my head, owning this. "It's because of *me*. I made a choice. I had someplace else to be. And they don't really like my past either, but I am who I am. I have no regrets about that."

She frowned. "I want to help you."

I stroked her cheek. "You are helping me."

"How?"

"By listening. By caring. By being here. That's all I want."

"*You're* all I want." She kissed me, and my mind

turned hazy, and my body responded instantly. With her lips on mine, pleasure ricocheted through me.

I laced my hands through her hair, curling my fingers around her head as we kissed harder.

Then she broke the kiss, slid down my body, and took me in her mouth. I groaned appreciatively at the sight. Shannon, between my legs, her head bobbing up and down, her tongue a wicked instrument of carnal pleasure. She was a vision, with her hair spread across my thighs and her lips full and ripe.

"Take me in deep," I rasped as I traced my fingertip over her top lip. "I need to own that pretty little mouth of yours right now."

She looked up at me as she wrapped her hand around my shaft, her other hand playing with my balls. "Own me, Brent. You already do."

She drew me in. The head of my dick hit the back of her throat. I gripped her hair, drawing her closer so she had to take me all the way.

"I can't hold back anymore," I groaned as I pushed her hair away from her face, giving me a perfect view of her lips, filled with my cock. "I'm going to fuck your mouth hard now. Can you handle it, babe?" I asked as I thrust. She nodded, and that was all I needed. Permission to take over her mouth completely.

To occupy every inch of her.

This wouldn't last long. Thirty seconds, a minute tops. I was damn near there already.

"You're so fucking beautiful. So fucking perfect . . ." I said, the words trailing off as my spine ignited, pleasure crackling through my bones.

Another deep thrust, and I was there. "Coming. Coming so fucking hard," I gasped, my fingers curling around her skull. Lust slammed into me, tearing through every cell in my body. I closed my eyes, and the world turned black and brilliant.

And when I opened my eyes, there she was, looking as satisfied as I was.

She wiped the back of her hand across her mouth. "I've got an endless store of those for you, handsome. Because you know what?" She tap-danced her fingers up my abs.

"Tell me."

"You deserve all the blow jobs in the world."

I parked my hands behind my head. "I like the sound of that. Tell me why I'm so damn deserving."

She moved up the bed, dropped a kiss to my lips, then said, "Because you're you."

That afternoon, we finally made it out of bed, and I gave her a proper tour of my home. I watched as she drank it in, walking around my place in the light of day, checking out the couch, trailing her fingertips over it, surveying the coffee table, looking at my books.

Her eyes landed on a vase on the table, and she tilted her head. "You have sunflowers." She pointed to the bouquet of yellow flowers.

I banded my arm around her waist. "What can I say? I was hopeful you'd come over soon."

Her smile was reward enough. "So you got them for me?"

"You seem to have a thing for sunflowers," I said. There was a time when I was reluctant to ask her, when I didn't want to press. But we were all in, and I wanted to know everything. "Want to tell me why?"

"How about I show you?"

The grass was spongy under my feet, and the late-afternoon sun cast golden shadows across the headstones.

The oaks and elms rose stately and green, their lush leaves forming canopies. Flowers burst to life everywhere, some wild, many in bouquets laid on the ground. It was an odd juxtaposition—all that verdant life in the midst of those markers of death. But that was what cemeteries were for—for the living to remember the dead.

With her hand in mine, we neared her father's grave.

As the simple stone came into view, I saw yellow. So much yellow.

"My grandma was here this week. She brought those," Shannon said, gesturing to the sunflowers along the headstone.

I read the etching. *Thomas Darren Paige. Loving father.* My throat hitched, and I swallowed it away as I wrapped an arm around her shoulder.

"I bring them here too," she continued.

"They're beautiful," I said softly as we stood a few

feet from the grave. "It's a beautiful way to remember him."

"They're not only for him," Shannon said, looking up, meeting my eyes.

"Who are they for?" I asked, but then I knew the answer. In a flash, everything made sense—the photos in her home. The ultrasound picture behind them.

I inhaled sharply, walloped once again by something unexpected. "For the baby we lost?" I asked, setting a gentle hand on her belly.

"Yes, our baby. I don't know if we would've had a girl or a boy," she said, and the fact that she was saying *we* tugged at all my heartstrings. I wanted that with her—a family. I wanted everything. "But I like to think his or her soul is with my dad. That they keep each other company in the great beyond."

I swallowed roughly and spoke softly. "I believe that too."

"I started to bring the flowers when I moved back from London. I was struggling and I needed to find a way through all that sadness. There was this hole inside me," she said, her voice soft but steady. I could hear her strength in it. I could hear all her resilience, all her survival. "And soon, the pain lessened. Time did what time is supposed to do. But I'd still come here when I was in town, and I'd leave more sunflowers, and soon I realized I wasn't leaving them for the baby anymore."

"You weren't?"

She shook her head, then met my eyes. "They were for you."

"After what you thought? How we split?" I asked carefully.

"Yes. For what you'd meant to me. Sunflowers always reminded me of you."

"Why?" I asked, my throat dry as the desert, choked with emotion.

She didn't answer with words at first. She answered through touch. She pushed up the sleeve on my right arm, revealing my ink—the black sunburst I'd gotten with her in Boston, when she'd told me it fit my sunny disposition. "Because you were like the sun to me. You made my days better. You were my warmth and my happiness. And I wanted to remember all the good times we'd had. I wanted to have hope again."

My heart stopped. My breath fled my chest. My life narrowed to a before and an after.

To this moment in time. It marked the man I was, and the man I was becoming. The man I could be for her. In that second, those words became the epicenter of my life. "I never knew how far and deep it went when you said I was like the sun to you."

She ran her fingertip over my sunburst. "You were all my sunny days, Brent. You were always so happy and so upbeat, and you never let anything get you down. And you gave all that to me. You turned my days around when I met you."

I closed my eyes and swayed closer to her, trying to take all this in, to digest the enormity of what she was saying. Then it hit me, with the clarity of a thousand suns. There was life and death, and the thinnest thread separated the two, like the edge of a razor. Life was for the living, and for the loving.

I dropped down to one knee for the second time. I had no ring. No plan. No speech. I grasped her hand in mine. "Marry me."

She blinked, a look of utter disbelief on her face. "Are you proposing to me in a cemetery?"

"I am," I said. Hoping. Praying. Wanting that yes. "Life is precious, Shan. Life is for this. For us. For living again, for loving again. Marry me now. Because I make you laugh, and I always will. Because I make you happy, and I promise to make that my greatest mission for the rest of my life. Loving you is the best thing I've ever done. I love everything about you—your body, your heart, and your mind. I have been in love with you for more than a decade, and I've spent most of that time without you. Let's pick up where we left off and spend the rest of our lives together. Let's do what we were supposed to do ten years ago. Let's do it now."

Her eyes lit up with mischief. "Yes. Vegas, baby."

She held out her hand and tugged me up.

"Vegas, baby," I replied.

That was our new vow.

43

BRENT

There were no flowers. There were no rings. But the bride did wear white.

She stopped at a store she liked and grabbed a new white sundress, while I snagged a white shirt and jeans from my house. We raced over to the marriage license bureau and signed the paperwork. Plunking down our IDs was nothing short of thrilling.

I pulled up in her car to a drive-through chapel, its orange neon sign lit up and flashing. The officiant came to the window. I had called earlier to book a quickie ceremony, and that was exactly what we got. No Elvis impersonator, no Johnny Cash stand-in, no Vegas theme package of mobsters or starlets or showgirls. At the end of the two-minute ceremony, the officiant said the words I had longed to hear years ago. "I now pronounce you husband and wife. You may kiss the bride."

No one needed to tell me that twice. I laced my fingers through Shannon's hair and dropped my mouth to hers, kissing her softly at first, savoring the sweet taste of her lips, memorizing every second of the first kiss with my wife.

Mrs. Shannon Nichols.

The name played in my head, and it was so perfect, so damn sexy, and everything I'd ever wanted in my life. In mere moments, the kiss climbed the heat scale as I kissed her furiously, and she tangled a hand in my hair, consuming my lips with her fire too.

I kissed her harder, even as the officiant clapped and cheered and wedding music played from the chapel.

Click.

Click.

Click.

I opened my eyes to see her cell phone held in one outstretched hand. I broke the kiss.

"I know you love selfies of us, so this is your first wedding present from your bride. Our first picture as husband and wife."

"I love it, Mrs. Nichols," I said in a low, dirty growl in her ear. "Now, I need to fuck my wife for the first time."

"Then put on your seat belt, handsome. I see a parking spot over there that's got our name written all over it."

"Mr. and Mrs. Nichols?"

"Yes. Those names," she said, wiggling her eyebrows.

"Love those names."

A minute later, I pulled into the farthest spot in the lot, away from other cars and lights. In a quick tango we'd practiced years ago in college, I moved to the passenger seat, lowered it, and lay back, bringing her on top of me.

"We have ten years of lost sex to make up for."

"We're going to be pretty busy," she said, her eyes sparkling with equal parts naughtiness and love, then with heat and want, as I hiked her skirt to her waist.

"My beautiful wife." I brushed my fingertips along the front of her white panties. She trembled into my touch. I traveled lower, my fingers on a luxurious path to her center. Her mouth fell open in a sexy gasp as I felt the first evidence of her desire. "Hmm. Seems getting married to me turns you on."

"Nothing has turned me on more," she said, her breath already coming fast.

I unzipped my jeans, yanked her panties to the side, and lowered her onto me. Sparks spread across my skin as I savored both the intensity of sliding into her gorgeous body, and the sweet, blissful knowledge that I had a lifetime ahead of me to be with her like this.

She took her time, rising up and down and swiveling her hips in a way that drove me wild. I watched her, raking my gaze over her face, her body, her hips. She was mine now, completely mine. I reached for her hair, threading my fingers into the strands, pulling her nearer.

"Closer," I said on a groan. "I need more of you."

She rocked faster, harder, her hands grappling with my hair, her breathing turning frantic.

She said my name in the most desperate, ecstatic voice I'd ever heard, and it sent us both over the edge.

After, I wrapped my arms around her, her heart

beating wildly against my chest, her cheeks flushed. I stroked her cheek, amazed she was here with me. *"Mrs. Nichols."*

She smiled. "You like saying that?"

"I've wanted to call you that for ten years."

"I've wanted to hear it, and it was worth waiting for."

When we returned to *our* home, I carried her over the threshold, knowing I was now truly home at last.

44

———

SHANNON

Several days later

I kissed Brent goodbye at the door. "I'll see you tonight," I told him.

"I'll be counting down the hours till you knock on Room 1204 dressed as a sexy room-service French maid."

I furrowed my brow. "Just exactly what kind of hotels do you stay at, Brent?"

He winked. "The kind where my wife shows up in the evening. The Cosmopolitan." He'd booked a reservation at my favorite restaurant, then a room at my favorite Strip hotel tonight just for fun. I liked that kind of Friday fun with him, and I planned to make it worth his while with his favorite kind of dance.

"But how do you know I won't be in a sexy nurse costume?" I teased.

He growled. "Nurse, French maid, cop. It all works for me as long as it's you."

I swatted him. "It better be me."

"It's always you."

Sliding an arm around my waist, he kissed me. "Have a great rehearsal." He swooped in for one more kiss. "See you tonight."

I shooed him out the door. "Go to your meeting. I can't wait to hear what you decide."

He and James were seeing their real estate attorney to regroup on the expansion plans. The New York deal had fallen apart. But it was by choice. The day after we tied the knot, Brent had called Tanner and said thanks but no thanks.

He didn't want to deal with those guys.

But he did feel bad about his friend Bob, and he wanted to find a gig for him.

I wanted to help out too, so when I went back inside, feeling safe and secure, thanks in part to the security detail he'd hired, I made some calls too, hoping I could figure something out for him.

I didn't know if I'd have any luck, but I had to try. More importantly, I wanted him to know his job mattered to me. That it wasn't a source of friction as it had once been, and that we were in this together now.

As I spoke on the phone, I finished getting ready for work, pulling on a pair of black leggings, a tunic tank top, and heels, then tossing my favorite scarf around my neck—the blush-pink silk scarf that Brent had given me. A thin, wispy thing, it was perfect for the summer heat.

And because it reminded me of him.

I had a final Vegas rehearsal today with the dancers who'd be working at his San Francisco club, and I wanted to make sure everything was perfect.

Then tonight, I'd meet my man for a date night.

We had a busy weekend too, including dinner tomorrow night with my grandma and grandpa to celebrate. We'd told them the news the day after we said *I do*, and my grandma had berated me for a full minute, then smothered me in hugs before sliding into post-wedding party planning mode, insisting on a barbecue in a few weeks. My grandpa had promptly welcomed Brent into the family, then asked if he knew how to grill. Now, Brent wanted to take them out someplace fabulous, so he'd snagged a reservation at a swank new eatery at the Bellagio, and then we were taking them to Cirque du Soleil.

At the end of the weekend, Ryan would return from his business trip, and the two of us would depart at the crack of dawn on Monday for the five-hour drive to Hawthorne, a small town with a big prison.

Whew.

I was exhausted just thinking about everything on the agenda, though it was all good stuff. But maybe I was mentally drained too, in advance of the visit with my mother. As I finished applying mascara, I fast-forwarded to visiting day at the Stella McLaren Correctional Center. My stomach churned as I heard my mom's voice in my head, as I imagined that desperate, manic look in her green eyes.

The fact that she'd met with a lawyer still gnawed at me.

It was that little detail that twisted my gut. Surely a lawyer wouldn't have come just to have his ear bent with my mother's latest obsessive claims. If a lawyer had visited, something was up, and I needed to know what that something was.

As I slung my purse over my shoulder, my phone bleated from inside the bag. I fished it out to find an incoming call from an 800 number, one I didn't recognize.

"This is Shay Sloan."

The phone was silent, and I was ready to hang up when I heard a tinny voice say, "This is the operator. Will you accept a collect call from the Federal Bureau of Prisons?"

My stomach plummeted. I managed to say yes, and five seconds later, my mom was on the line.

Cooing.

My mother actually cooed when she heard me say hello.

She launched into rapid-fire chatter. "I can't wait to see my sweet babies. Are you and Ry-Ry on your way? Will I see you any minute? I've been waiting all morning for my babies. I even put on lipstick today. I can't wait to see you. I was so excited I had to call. I hope you don't mind."

I sighed, a sad, wistful sound. She couldn't even get the date right. "Mom, it's Monday. We're coming on Monday. When Ryan is back in town."

My mother gasped. "No, no, no. It's today. Did he tell you Monday?"

"You did, Mom. You told him, and you told me in your letters. Last day of the month. That's what you said. June thirtieth."

She gasped. A fearful sound. "I meant today. It's today. Last Friday of the month. Friday, baby, Friday," she said, with the speed of an express train. "Today, today, today. They gave me my final two hours today. Mondays are bad. No one likes Mondays. It's today. By five p.m.," she said, her voice turning into a low wail.

"Ryan's not even in Vegas, Mom. He's in California right now for work."

"Then you need to come. Please. There's so much to say, baby. So much to say. I have to see you. It's urgent. You have to come, you have to come today, you have to come today. It could change everything."

Everything.

There was no way this could change everything.

My mouth tasted bitter. My skin felt clammy and cold.

But that desperate, frantic tone clawed into me. I pressed my palm against the door, pushing firmly.

What if? What if? What if?

That question echoed in my mind, in the house, across the whole damn expanse of time. I didn't believe for a second that anything had changed, and yet . . .

What if it had?

I glanced at my watch. It was eight thirty. I could rush over to Edge for fifteen minutes, since it was on the way out of town. The valet could babysit my car so I wouldn't lose much time there. I could be on the road by nine fifteen and at the prison by one thirty, two p.m. at the latest.

I'd be back in time to see my husband for our date. It was *just* a date, but even so, I didn't intend to cancel. He'd been there for me when I'd needed him. I was going to show up for us.

45

BRENT

We strolled past a machine crooning "Pure Imagination" as a cartoonish Willy Wonka presided over the slots. "You feel good about the plan?" James asked as we left our meeting with the real estate attorney.

"I do. We'll find another venue in New York," I said, but a small pang of guilt nagged at me as I thought of Bob. "I'd just like to do it sooner rather than later."

"Same here. I'll make some calls today. See what we can figure out."

"Sounds like a plan. I've got some paperwork to go over and emails to power through," I said, and I planned to be head down with work today so I could lavish attention on my wife tonight.

When we reached the offices, I said goodbye to James right as my phone rang. I grinned like the happily married man I was, since Shannon was calling.

"Hey, babe. Do you miss me already? Fine, fine. I'll

meet you for a quickie if you insist. Be at my desk in thirty minutes."

"Actually," she said with a heavy voice, "I wanted you to know I won't be around today."

Something inside of me tightened with worry. "What happened? Is everything okay?"

"My mom called. The date was wrong. I'm going to see her today."

My spine straightened. "You are?"

"Yeah. She was pretty worked up that I wasn't there this morning with Ryan. I guess there was a mix-up with the date. She said she has something to tell me that will"—she paused and I could practically see her sketching air quotes—"*change everything.*"

"Shan," I said softly as I sat on the edge of my desk. "You can't go alone. Ryan's not even in town."

"It's okay. I called him right after she called me to tell him about the mix-up. He's frustrated because he wanted to go, but we talked and we're on the same page, and I've got this. I can handle it," she said in a cheery voice. "Seriously. Don't worry about me. I'm sure it's nothing new. Nothing I haven't heard a million times before."

"Hmm," I muttered.

"Hmm, what?"

"I don't think you believe what you're saying."

"Brent, it's fine. I've got it all under control. I will see you as planned tonight, and I'm not going to tell you whether I'll be a naughty nurse or a French maid or a schoolgirl. It'll be a surprise."

But even the thought of her dressing up for me didn't lighten my unease.

I didn't like the idea of her driving five hours through the desert on her own. To a prison. Then five hours back. That was not sitting well with me at all.

"Shan—"

From her phone, I heard a car horn honk in the distance.

"Let me call you back. Traffic to Edge is getting dicey. Need to pay attention. Bye." She hung up, and I stared at my phone with narrowed eyes, as if there were an app to reveal how she really felt, and whether she could truly handle this meeting with her mom all by herself.

Well, of course she could. But should she? The things her mom had been saying lately seemed to suggest the woman had a plan to be freed. What if she'd uncovered some key piece of evidence? What if it was the kind of evidence that turned on its head everything Shannon and her brothers had ever believed about the conviction?

I headed to James's office and rapped on the door.

He looked up. "Everything okay?"

"Everything is great. But I need to take off for the day. I'm going to catch up on emails and contracts over the weekend."

"You're the boss," he said with a smile. "You set your own hours."

"Keep me posted on your calls?"

"Absolutely."

I left.

46

SHANNON

"Go!" Christine pushed my arm playfully. Or maybe not so playfully.

I held up my hands in surrender. "I'm going. I swear."

"I have this under control," she said, gesturing to the final rehearsal. The dancers were glorious, moving like waterfalls, lush and sumptuous, as the music played loudly overhead.

"Are you sure?"

"You go take care of things," Christine said. I hadn't given her the details on my upended plans, and I was glad my second-in-command wasn't nosy enough to pry.

I took a deep breath and nodded, then waved to the scene unfolding in front of me in the empty club. "You're right. Everything looks amazing."

"I will text you and keep you updated. I can even send you pictures and video," Christine said, as she continued to shoo me away.

"Yes, please do," I said, and then walked out of the club.

I race-walked past the shops of the Luxe and threaded through the slot machines and card tables on my way to the exit. Handing the ticket to the valet, I tapped my foot as I waited for my car. I lowered my shades and grabbed my phone from my purse, finding several missed calls from Brent. The music was so loud in Edge I hadn't heard the phone.

Quickly, so I could get out of Dodge in a jiffy, I opened the GPS app, keying in the address of the Stella McLaren Federal Women's Correctional Center in Hawthorne, Nevada. Four hours and thirty minutes away, since traffic was light, the app predicted. That was doable. Very doable. I plugged in my headset and dialed Brent.

"You looking for me?"

I stared at the screen. The voice didn't seem to be coming from the phone. It was coming from . . . I looked up and saw my husband walking over to me.

I parted my lips to speak, but he went first as another valet pulled up with my little red car.

"I'll take it from here," he said to the valet. "I'll drive."

"But . . ." I said, sputtering.

"No ifs, ands, or buts about it. No wife of mine is driving five hours in the desert, then five hours back by herself when I'm here. I'm going to be by your side. That's the promise I made to you, and I'm keeping it," he said, his eyes fixed on me, his gaze so strong as he opened the passenger door for me.

My heart thundered in my chest, swelling with

emotion as I slid into the car, the surprise of seeing him still working its way through me.

He walked behind the vehicle, tipped the valet, then got in on the driver's side. After adjusting the seat and the mirrors, he pulled out of the Luxe's portico.

"Did you just literally walk out of your office?" I asked, still trying to compute that he was here. That he'd decided in mere minutes to join me. I hadn't even asked him to.

But he'd done it. Just like he'd flown home from New York last weekend for me.

This man.

He was everything to me.

He showed me his love every day.

"Sure did. Turns out emails can be answered tomorrow," he said as he flipped on the blinker to turn right.

"Even though you can't go in? They only let family and approved visitors in."

"I'm going for you, Shan. I'm here for you. Whatever you need. I'll drive you, and wait for you, and be there for you."

I brought my hand to my chest, overwhelmed by what he'd done. How he'd chosen me yet again.

I squeezed his thigh. "I love you, Brent Nichols. Have I told you that lately?"

He made a show of peering at the clock on the dash. "Earlier this morning you did. But I like hearing it."

"I love you," I said again with a smile.

"Music to my ears." He pointed to the radio. "Speaking of, let's crank up some tunes. You got a desert driving playlist? We need something to rock out to."

I raised an eyebrow. "Would 'Folsom Prison Blues' be too ironic?"

"Irony is my middle name."

I turned on Johnny Cash and held my husband's hand the whole way through the desert as the sun rose high in the sky, blazing through the windshield, the road unfurling before us in a slate ribbon. My heart was full, in spite of where we were headed.

* * *

The air-conditioning hummed, blasting out sheets of coolness in the stark visiting room. I rubbed my bare arms, wishing I'd brought a sweater. I didn't remember it being so chilly the last time I was there. Perched on the edge of a hard plastic chair at a table inside a small room, I waited.

I tried to conjure up an image of my mother, tried to remember how she'd looked at Christmas, but the images that paraded before my eyes were older ones, so much older. Sewing my leotard, the corner of her lips screwed up in concentration as she threaded. Placing a Band-Aid on my knee when I'd skidded on my bike. Holding my hand as she walked me to school. So young, so vibrant, so blonde. Just like me. She'd had the same bright blonde hair. Absently, I raised my hand to my now-brown strands.

Someone opened the door.

I rose. Nerves skittered across my flesh. The corrections officer appeared first, a tall, sturdy woman with dark hair in a braid. Holding the door open, the guard nodded and grunted a curt "Hello."

"Hello," I said to Clara, the word feeling strange on my tongue. Even after all these years, it still never felt normal to be conversing with a corrections officer.

My mother entered next, and I did my best impression of a sealed-up box. Otherwise I'd fall to pieces. Keeping my chin up, my muscles steady, I managed a simple "Hi, Mom."

My mother was a shadow of the woman she'd once been. Her hair was the color of dishwater, her cheeks were sunken, and her emerald eyes were a shade of sallow. Even so, she smiled. Her lips, with their cracked red lipstick, quivered as she held out her arms for a hug.

"My baby," said the woman in orange.

I walked into her arms, embarrassment and shame smacking me from all directions. I wasn't ashamed this woman was my mother. I was ashamed for what she'd become, for the choices she'd made that led her to this. Thin arms wrapped around me, arms that had once been strong and maternal.

"Oh, baby. My baby. It is so good to see you again," she said, her mouth closer to my neck than I would have liked.

"It's good to see you too, Mom," I said, lying, but knowing it was only a white lie. It wouldn't hurt anyone for me to say that.

"I'm so happy you're here." Another firm grip, then I felt a drop of wetness. A tear had fallen on my bare shoulder as she embraced me harder and tighter, as if she could graft her body onto mine.

"All right, Prince. That's enough," the CO said, her command clear.

My mom pulled away and shot the woman a contrite look. "Sorry. I just missed my baby girl so much. She's a dancer. Isn't she lovely, Clara?" My mom held out her arms to me as if she were presenting me on *Wheel of Fortune*.

"Mom, stop," I said, embarrassed now for a whole new reason. I glanced at the woman. "We're fine. We'll sit down now."

"Behave, Prince," the woman warned as she shut the door, leaving me alone with my mother.

47

DORA

They always told me to behave, but what did they know? Had Clara spent eighteen years without her babies?

I didn't think so. I had, and I would damn well hug my daughter. My angel girl.

But I had to play the game, because that was what this was here.

A game.

A system.

And I was figuring it out.

Shannon sat at the gray plastic table, and I spat out the first thing that I had to tell her.

The indignity of all this. How the guards were punishing me for fighting for my rights.

Fighting for freedom.

"Baloney," I said, embarrassed and frustrated all at once.

"Baloney?"

"That's what they fed me the other day. Baloney on

white bread. Can you believe it? Baloney." I brought my hand to my eyes, covering them, the memory of the cold cuts too much to bear. "I hate baloney."

"Tell them you hate it," she said calmly.

That was my girl. So smart. She knew what to do, but so did I. "I tried. I asked for turkey. They don't think I deserve turkey."

"Did they say that?"

I raised my face, whipped my head back and forth, then whispered the cold truth. "They don't have to. I can tell. They don't like me here. They don't like me at all."

"Mom," she said, so comforting and caring. "Why would you say that?"

"Because I'm trying to—" I wanted to say more. Dear God, I did. But I couldn't. I knew I couldn't. The temptation though . . . it was so strong. I clamped my lips shut, refusing to speak. The guards didn't like me yearning for true justice, trying to find it. So they fed me barely edible food and ignored my requests for more. Another punishment.

"Because why?" Shannon pressed.

"Because," I said through my fingers over my mouth. "Because. Because. Because."

My baby girl held up her hands in defeat. "It's okay. You don't have to tell me."

She was here. For me. I didn't want her to feel defeat. If I could only say something. How I longed to speak the truth. "Because of what happened," I snapped out, a tornado inside me.

"Because of why you're here?" she asked gently.

But that wasn't it. That wasn't the reason.

I shook my head, whipping it back and forth so rapidly it started to hurt. Everything hurt. "No. Not that. Not that at all. It's because of the—" I stopped talking and jammed my fist in my mouth, biting hard on the knuckles.

Keep it inside, Dora.

Keep it inside.

Don't say a word.

Don't ever say a goddamn word.

My girl cringed and reached for my hand, trying to remove it from my mouth. But I was her mother. I was tough. She had no idea how strong I was. No one did. I was so damn strong. I wouldn't budge.

She tried again. I bit deeper, my teeth digging into my own flesh.

"Mom, stop that," she said in a terrified whisper. "Your CO will come back and you'll have to go. You're making a scene."

But I had no choice. I had to shut up. I couldn't chance it. This was the only way. I crunched down, digging into the flesh of my hand.

"You're going to draw blood. Stop!"

The door swung open.

"Enough, Prince," the corrections officer barked.

I dropped my fist from my mouth, shoulders sagging, body limp, so tired. Clara held up her hand and raised her index finger. "One more shot, Prince. One more shot."

If only.

"Okay," I muttered, numb now, only numb.

I looked up at my baby. She stared at my hand. It had deep grooves in it, red and raw, on the cusp of bleeding.

"What was that all about?" she asked, bewildered, horrified.

My stomach clenched, and my heart—it ached so bad. So painfully. Full of the desire to tell her. I'd thought I could. But looking at her face, I couldn't.

"Nothing," I mumbled. *Keep it inside.* "Just nothing."

"Okay, then. Are you still watching *General Hospital*?"

Something happy. Something light. I felt a spark inside me as she asked about my favorite show. I rattled off couples, and plotlines, and twists and turns. "It's okay that I'm spoiling it?"

She laughed lightly. "It's okay, Mom."

I told her more and more.

But after fifteen minutes, I stopped. I couldn't waste time on a soap. She was here. I needed to know all about my baby girl. "Tell me about work. How are your shows? I want to know everything." I was desperate for something good. For anything good. And Shannon was all the good in the world.

I listened as she told me about her shows, and I pictured her dancing, imagining it, seeing it.

Even if she wasn't the one onstage anymore, I always saw her dancing. I saw her as she was *before*. I saw her as the thirteen-year-old girl I'd had to leave.

My reasons.

As she spoke, she looked happy, so happy, but then she turned serious, meeting my eyes. "You said earlier you wanted to talk about something that would change everything. Is the case being reopened?"

I sat up straight, hope springing up in me. Could it be? Was that even a possibility. "Is it?"

She sighed. "Mom, I don't know. I thought that's why you wanted to talk. You told Ryan on the phone, and you told me earlier today that you had news that would change everything."

She placed her hands on the table, and I reached for them, gripping hers, needing the connection. "I do have news."

"Tell me," she said, desperate. "Did someone find new evidence? I heard the DA was talking to Stefano. Is there something going on? Tell me, Mommy."

Mommy.

She hardly ever called me that.

I hadn't heard her say that word in years.

I loved it so much. It was my heart.

But I didn't have an answer to her question.

"I don't know anything about Jerry," I said.

"What did you see your lawyer about, then?" She squeezed my fingers, like she was urging me to speak.

Like she wanted to know what I had to say.

Like she might believe me.

My chest rose and fell. I breathed heavily. Then faster. A lone, silent tear streaked from my eye. I could tell her this. Yes, I could tell her this. This was what I wanted her to know. "It's about Luke."

48

SHANNON

I flinched. I hadn't heard that name in years. There had been no reason to even think of Luke Carlton. He was long gone. The local piano teacher my mother had had a brief affair with when I was thirteen was ancient history. The police had questioned him after my father's death, but it had been perfunctory. He'd never been a suspect. He'd had no connection at all to the crime.

"What about Luke?" I asked carefully. I wasn't wild about the man, not by any stretch, but there was a big difference between sleeping with a married woman and being a killer. There was no evidence to show my mother's lover was involved in Dad's death in any way, except by loving the wrong person at the wrong time. "The police cleared him, Mom. In just two days after the murder, he was cleared of any suspicion."

Her face pinched, her eyes welling with something like long-lost love. My God, did she still long for the man?

"I know he didn't do it," she said protectively. "He's

not that kind of man. He's not the one who shot your daddy in the driveway. And it wasn't me either. It was a robbery gone wrong," she said, sticking chapter and verse to her age-old defense, as if the open wallet and stolen bills proved her innocence.

I sighed deeply, my heart cratering as my mom toed the old party line. After the baloney obsession and the *General Hospital* chatter and the gnawing on her own damn fist, we were back to this? After all the begging and the letters and the madness, we were at square one. "Then why are you bringing up Luke?"

My mom peered at the door, making sure it was shut, then looked back at me. She lowered her voice to a feather of a whisper. "He said he'd wait for me. He promised he'd wait for me. That's what he told me. He meant it. I know he meant it. Don't you believe me?"

I sucked in a heavy sigh, then reminded her of the bitter truth. "You're in for life. He's going to be waiting a long time."

She stabbed the table with her finger. "Not if they find the real killer."

"If they were going to, it would have happened already. It's been almost eighteen years since you came here," I said, reminding my mother that time was not on her side. I didn't bother to bring up the powerful evidence that had put her here in the first place, including the shooter's own testimony that she'd hired him.

For a moment, she looked smug, nodding confidently. "Oh, it'll happen. They'll realize."

I bit back all the things I wanted to say, all the truths

I wanted to remind her of, because I didn't want to rehash the case. I didn't want to play courtroom trial again. "What does this have to do with Luke?"

My mom leaned across the table, coming as close to me as she could, and said in a fast breath, "Because he promised to wait for me. He swore he would. And I just found out he got married. One of my girlfriends on the outside told me. Baby, he married another woman and he was supposed to wait for me. For me, for me, for me. And now he's with someone else, and I'm all alone." She dropped her head to the table, tears spilling like summer rain from her eyes.

I brushed a hand over my mother's limp hair. "That's what you talked to your lawyer about?"

My mom nodded her head against the table as she sobbed. "Yes. Because it proves something. And lawyers need proof."

"What does it prove?"

"It proves that Luke lied to me," she said, her voice breaking like waves. "He lied when he said he'd wait."

"And that changes everything?"

"Yes. It changes everything for me. Everything." My mom cried more, a river of tears flowing onto the plastic table as I stroked her hair, some kind of strange relief washing over me even in the midst of all this hollowness, all this hurt for the woman my mother had become.

Through it all, one fact remained starkly clear.

The case was closed. My mother's fate had been irrevocably sealed eighteen years ago, and now she was paying for her crime in so many ways. With her life, with her health, and with her sanity.

Dora Prince lived in her own world, and she'd done it all to herself.

49

———

BRENT

"Skittles? Salt and vinegar chips? Twizzlers?"

I plucked the snack foods from a dusty shelf, waving each bag in front of my wife.

She crinkled her nose. "I'm not that hungry."

"Yeah, these might be stale." I lowered my voice to a whisper. "I don't think many people come around here too often." I peered at the expiration date on the Skittles. "Whoa. These Skittles were past their prime two years ago."

She laughed half-heartedly as I dropped the unwanted snacks on the shelves.

"I'll just get a soda," she said, pointing vaguely in the direction of the fountain drinks at the Lucky Seven Gas & Go somewhere in the middle of the desert. As far as I knew, we were halfway between Hawthorne and Vegas, which meant two and a half more hours of cruising south on the highway to home.

"Shan, you need to eat. You haven't had anything all day."

"Maybe just some pretzels, then. Pretzels taste expired anyway."

I grabbed a pretzel pack with gusto, as if my enthusiasm for potentially out-of-date road-trip snacks would somehow buoy her spirits. She walked to the soda fountain, grabbed a cup, and pressed it against the Diet Coke spout. She leaned forward slowly, as if she was starting to tip over, then rested her forehead against the dispenser. She'd slept the whole ride back so far, slumped against the passenger seat with her shades on, after she'd left the prison and given me the Cliffs-Notes of her visit as we drove out of Hawthorne.

Crossing the distance in a second, I took the cup from her. "I'll do it."

This time, she rested her head against my chest. "Thank you."

It was only a soda. That was all I was doing. Filling a flimsy paper cup at a rest stop in the middle of nowhere. But it was something I alone could do for her right now. And she needed it.

I finished filling the cup and popped a lid on it.

"I'm sorry I made you drive me all the way there for nothing," she said.

"Hey. You did not make me do anything. I chose to. And it was not nothing." I set the cup down on the counter, and lifted her chin. "It was not nothing."

"But you took the day off, and we had to cancel our dinner, and it's just the same old stuff with my mom."

"Then that's something. That's exactly what you needed to know."

"The same old stuff?"

I ran my finger along her jaw, certain that this visit today mattered. That it could help my wife let go of the past. Let loose some of the stranglehold it'd had on her at times.

"Yes, the same old stuff. Because now you know. Now you know that nothing has changed. Now you can stop worrying that something is going to be different. This is the same stuff she did to you in college," I said, holding her gaze firmly. "She tried to work you over. She tried to get you to believe her madness. And you are good and loving, and you did the right thing by seeing her, Shan. You visited her; you listened to her. You did a loving thing without compromising who you are. And now, you can let it go. The past is the past."

50

SHANNON

I leaned my cheek into his hand, so strong and so soft at the same time. "How did you get to be so wise?"

"My wife taught me how," he said, planting a kiss on my forehead, then rubbing my belly. "Now I need to go pay for this stale nourishment I'm procuring for you."

He picked up the soda and pretzels and walked to the cash register. As I watched him, I couldn't help but feel an unexpected pang of guilt over all he was doing for me.

I wanted, desperately wanted, to do something for him.

And as he paid, I learned I might be able to.

An email landed on my phone from Michael.

And I grinned. It was full of names.

Names I'd wanted.

I sent them to James, since I had his email address. I tapped out a note as Brent paid, and then I crossed my fingers, hoping, wishing.

* * *

A few miles down the road, a sign rose into view, the rays of the dipping sun illuminating the battered wooden billboard. *Gateway to Death Valley, Beatty, Nevada. Established 1903. Population 1000.* It stood proudly amid the sand and rocks, the dryness and dust.

Twenty feet away, there was a sign for a Motel 6.

I touched Brent's arm and pointed to the sign, then wiggled my eyebrows. "It's not The Cosmopolitan, but . . ."

"But I get your drift, Mrs. Nichols. I get your drift indeed."

He cut the wheel at the exit, and we checked into a fifty-nine-dollars-a-night room at a hotel that boasted a coin-operated laundry, free local calls, and morning coffee on the house.

As well as a bed that squeaked. I pushed down on the springs of the mattress inside room number fourteen, on the first floor with a view of the parking lot.

"Are you tired?" he asked.

"Not anymore." I'd perked up after the potentially promising news I'd received at the gas station—and at the accumulation of my husband's incredible care for me today.

He arched a brow. "Then tell me what you could possibly have in mind."

I ran my fingers along the silky fabric of my scarf. "You. I have you in mind."

"I can give you me, no problem."

Soon he'd stripped me naked and tied my hands with the scarf, knotting the ends to the headboard of the creaky motel bed. "I knew this gift would come in handy."

"It's a multiuse scarf," I said, squirming as he began to kiss me.

No, he didn't just kiss me.

He worshipped me.

He caressed my breasts with his lips. He nipped my throat with his teeth. He adored my belly with his tongue, working his way across the landscape of my body, marking the territory of me with his lips and his sighs and his groans. As he traveled across me with his mouth, I let the day fall away. I gave myself over to passion.

My hips shot up, seeking more of him, begging with my body for him to work his magic.

But it was more than just magic. He was more than just my sweet drug as he consumed me and sent me soaring into a state of ecstatic bliss that had me singing his name to the heavens.

He untied me, flipped me over, and sank into me. I cried out, louder than I'd ever been, more aroused than I'd ever been, there on my hands and knees in a Motel 6.

Yes, it was so much more than mere intoxication. Sex with Brent flooded my brain with endorphins, filled my body with pleasure, and freed me from the past.

This connection, this deep and abiding love, was part of the letting go. As we came together in a mad carnal frenzy, the past crumbled to dust.

There was no more *before*.

It was done. It was over.

There was only the present, only love, only life. My life with my man, together.

51

BRENT

As I lifted my fork for a final bite of scrambled eggs and hash browns at a truck-stop diner an hour outside of Vegas the next morning, my phone rang. It rattled on the table, blinking James's name across the screen.

He didn't usually call when I took the day off. I showed the screen to Shannon. "I hope everything's okay," I said to her.

"Maybe it's good news?" she suggested.

"I'm sure he's calling to tell me I'll never get a club approved in New York. That Tanner has made sure the whole city will blackball me."

I slid my thumb across the screen and answered, "Hey, James."

"I've got good news."

"Do tell," I said, as a waitress in a starchy pink diner uniform stopped at the table, gesturing to her pot of coffee. I held up my mug for a refill.

"We've got a lead on a red-hot location in New York.

A nightclub is closing, and the landlord wants to talk about moving us in. It's in Soho."

"That sounds great," I said, whispering a *thanks* to the waitress. "How'd you find something so quickly though?"

"I didn't. Your wife did."

I blinked. "My wife did?"

"She sent over some names yesterday."

"Did she?" I asked, as a smile spread nice and slow.

"She did indeed. She said her brother sent her some contacts, so I made a few calls. Looks like we might be able to line something up."

"How thoughtful of her," I said, remembering her offer when she'd first heard there might be trouble in New York. I'd turned her down, but clearly she'd gone ahead anyway.

I caught Shannon's gaze as she brought her mug to her lips and drank some coffee. Her eyes were full of mischief. My heart raced. It tripped out of my chest and leaped into Shannon's hands.

"She's a keeper," James said dryly.

"She definitely is."

When the call ended, I switched sides and moved in next to her on the sky-blue cracked vinyl booth. "Seems like you were up to something," I said with a smile.

She shrugged happily. "You've done so much for me, it was the least I could do."

"And Michael didn't mind?"

She shook her head. "He's happy that I'm happy with you. He wanted to help. I'm just glad that you might be able to find a new location. I hope it's okay that I did this anyway, even after you said not to." A nervous quiver shook her voice.

"It's more than okay," I said, reassuring her. "You didn't have to do that at all. But I'm thrilled you did."

"You gave up New York for me, Brent. I wanted to help you achieve your dream," she said, all soft and vulnerable and so damn lovely.

"Shan," I said, cupping her cheeks and moving in for a kiss. "I already have everything I've ever wanted."

* * *

A few days later, I swung by Shannon's grandmother's house, picked up the ring, and took it to the jeweler. A week after that, I returned home one fine summer evening, with a bouquet of sunflowers and a brand new ring for my wife.

She was already Mrs. Nichols, but I got down on one knee anyway, at the dinner table, and proposed one more time.

"Shannon Nichols, will you be my wife?"

She laughed. "I already am."

But she held out her hand, and I slid on the diamond solitaire anyway. Then I kissed her forehead, her cheek, her lips.

When we broke the kiss, she said, "I have something for you."

"Lucky me."

She reached into a bag, wiggled her eyebrows and tugged out a new pink scarf. "It's just a scarf."

I shook my head, smiling. "No. It's a promise."

She nodded, her smile making it clear she never intended it to be *just a scarf*. "It's absolutely a promise. That we will always find our way back to each other. Every day," she said.

"And every night," I echoed, then I kissed her again, reminding her of that promise tonight.

EPILOGUE

Brent

A few weeks later

The delicious scent of barbecue wafted through the summer air. Ryan manned the grill, flipping burgers and chicken breasts, and turning cobs of corn.

Music played from an outdoor speaker. A string of red pepper lights hung along the wooden posts of the fence. Her grandparents had insisted on a wedding celebration, and everyone was here—my parents, my brother and his wife and their daughter, Mindy, Ally, Nate and his wife, James and his family, and Shannon's brothers, of course.

Everyone who mattered deeply to the bride and groom.

The first few weeks of marriage had been bliss, and I

was confident the next thirty, forty, fifty years would be too.

And soon we might be expanding. We'd been working hard on that project, though it was hardly work.

More like nonstop pleasure. In a few more days, she'd take a test and find out if baby would make three.

Oh, how I wanted that with her.

I wanted it so damn badly.

As I took a long swallow from a bottle of beer, my eyes found my wife. She relaxed in an Adirondack chair on the deck, bouncing Carly on her knee and making cooing sounds at my niece while chatting with Julia. The sight of my Mrs. Nichols holding a baby tugged on all my heartstrings, reminding me of a bright possible future.

I felt a hand on my arm and turned to see Mindy. "Hello, Queen."

"Hey there, subject."

Then I glanced around, and lowered my voice. "Did you ever find out anything about that guy? The pics I showed you?"

"Brent," she chided. "We're at your wedding celebration."

"This is important though." I'd given Mindy the pictures I'd taken of the guy in the Buick a few weeks ago, and she'd agreed to show them to some of her friends on the force to see if the plates—or as much as I'd captured of them—or the tattoos revealed anything. I couldn't dismiss the notion in the back of my mind that the ink meant something.

We hadn't seen him around since then.

Or anyone else for that matter.

Maybe, just maybe, he'd been nobody.

Mindy set a hand on my arm. "Truth be told, I don't have anything yet. They're pretty swamped, and can't really do license plate checks anymore for privacy reasons. But one of my guys said he'd take a close look and see if the ink looks familiar. I promise to let you know as soon as I hear."

I offered her a fist for knocking. "I appreciate you."

"You better," she said with a smile.

My gaze returned to Shannon as she handed the baby to Julia, then blew me a kiss. I returned it, and watched as she headed inside the house, her brothers in tow. They'd told me they had a special gift for Shannon, and I suspected they were giving it to her now.

I lifted my beer and tapped it to Mindy's. "Thank you."

"Anytime. Now, celebrate. Don't worry about the pictures. Have a great time with everyone here."

That sounded like a damn fine plan.

This was a good life indeed, and it was time to keep moving into the future.

EPILOGUE

As my grandmother refilled a pitcher of iced tea in the kitchen, Michael swooped in behind her and grabbed something from the counter.

"Told you we'd get you a wedding gift," he said, holding up a small white box with a silver bow tied daintily on it.

"I wrapped it," my grandma chimed in, with a knowing glint in her eyes. "That's why it looks nice."

I reached for the box. "Because these boys don't know how to wrap gifts. Yet another reason why you all require further domestication." I took my time giving each of my brothers a steely-eyed yet playful stare.

"Good luck on that front. Pretty sure I'm not train-able at all," Ryan said, tucking his thumbs into the belt loops of his shorts.

I patted him on the cheek. "There, there. Every dog can learn."

"All right, funny girl. Open your gift," Michael said, nodding at the box.

"You know I don't need anything, right? I hope you didn't get me a blender," I said as I removed the silver bow.

"The world's smallest blender," Colin joked.

Peering inside, I folded back the tissue paper to uncover a gorgeous platinum bracelet that matched the rose-gold and silver ones I already wore.

"It's so pretty," I said, admiring the simple and elegant design. When I spotted the date engraved in the center, I brought my hand to my heart. "My wedding date."

"Look at the inside too. It's also inscribed," Michael said, nudging me with his shoulder.

Turning the slender bracelet on its side, I read the engraved script. *To our wonderful sister on her happily ever after. Remember—live with love.* "Live with love," I whispered. Our father's words. His advice for us. Always.

A lump rose in my throat, fighting its way up. I clasped a hand over my mouth as a tear slid down my cheek.

That tear was a declaration. An announcement of our love, our bond, our unbreakableness.

The Sloans. We were the Sloans. And we'd worked hard to live up to our new name, to honor our father, to be who he believed we could be. I wrapped my arms around my guys in a big group hug.

"I love you guys. So damn much," I whispered in our huddle.

"We love you," they all said in unison.

When we pulled apart, I wiped the tears from my cheek and shot them a wild grin. "Hmm. Now who gets to go next? Michael, Ryan, or Colin?" I said, counting off my brothers as my grandmother laughed. "I have a feeling the next one of us to fall in love will be—"

The doorbell rang.

EPILOGUE

Michael

The sound of the *ding* cut off my sister's love prediction. So very like Shannon. Ready to pair us all off. With her big heart, it was no surprise she wanted to see her brothers fall hard and fast.

Not to mention soon.

But it wasn't going to be me. My heart was given to someone else a long time ago.

Right now, though, I wasn't focused on matters of the heart.

This was a gut moment.

Because when my grandmother headed to the door, saying, "That's probably our neighbors. I invited them too," I set a hand on her arm.

I had a feeling it wasn't the neighbors.

"I'll get it, Nana," I told her. She was mine to look out for. This whole family was mine to protect.

I peered through the peephole, eyes narrowing as I took in the uninvited visitors, then carefully opened the door to the two men.

They weren't neighbors.

My jaw clenched as my gaze traveled up and down, quickly registering who they were.

One wore a light-blue button-down. The other sported a gray striped shirt. Both wore loosely knotted ties and had badges at their waists.

Cops only knocked on the door if you were in trouble, or if someone you loved was dead.

I did a quick inventory of people, even though I already knew the answer—everyone I loved was safe and sound in this house.

Nearly everyone.

Still, my pulse spiked as I regarded the officers, because their presence didn't add up.

"What can I do for you gentlemen?" I asked.

I waited as the guy in the button-down cleared his throat. Waited for minutes, it felt, for him to break the unbearable silence.

Then he spoke. "I'm looking for Victoria Paige. Is she here?"

My grandmother stepped up next to me, nodded crisply, and held out a hand. "I'm Victoria. What can I do for you?"

He shook her hand. "I'm Detective John Winston with Metro. This is my partner," he said, but I barely heard the other man's name as blood pounded in my ears, and I *knew*. I knew there was only one reason they could be here.

"We wanted to let you know as the family of the victim, that in light of new evidence, the investigation into the homicide of Thomas Paige is being reopened."

THE END

Want to know what happens next to the Sloan family, now that the investigation is open again? Find out in Ryan's love story, told in MY SINFUL DESIRE and FREE in KU!

BE A LOVELY

Want to be the first to know of sales, new releases, special deals and giveaways? Sign up for my newsletter today!

Want to be part of a fun, feel-good place to talk about books and romance, and get sneak peeks of covers and advance copies of my books? Be a Lovely!

I've written more than 100 books! **All of these titles below are FREE in Kindle Unlimited!**

The Love and Hockey Series

<u>The Boyfriend Goal</u>

A roommates-to-lovers, teammate's little sister hockey romance!

<u>The Romance Line</u>

An enemies-to-lovers, player and the publicist, forbidden romance!

<u>The Proposal Play</u>

A brother's best friend/marriage of convenience romance!

The Girlfriend Zone

A coach's daughter romance!

The Overtime Kiss!

A single dad/nanny romance!

The Flirting Game!

A neighbors to lovers, fake dating romance!

Hockey Ever After

Just Breaking the Rules!

A brother's best friend/workplace/one who got away romance!

Just Playing for Keeps!

A grumpy sunshine, fake dating romance!

Holiday Romances

Merry Little Kissmas

Fake dating my brother's best friend at Christmas!

<u>My Favorite Holidate</u>

Fake dating the billionaire boss at Christmas!

Darling Springs

It Seemed Like a Good Idea!

An only one-bed-in-the-room, forbidden, small town bodyguard romance!

I've Got a Crush On You!

A grumpy sunshine, workplace romance where the boss has a secret identity!

The My Hockey Romance Series

Hockey, spice, shenanigans and cute dogs in this series of standalones! Because when you get screwed over, make it a double or even a triple!

Karma is two hockey boyfriends and sometimes three!

Double Pucked

A sexy, outrageous MFM hockey romantic comedy!

Puck Yes

A fake marriage, spicy MFM hockey rom com!

Thoroughly Pucked!

A brother's best friends +runaway bride, spicy MFM hockey rom com!

Well and Truly Pucked

A friends-to-lovers forced proximity why-choose hockey rom com!

The Virgin Society Series

Meet the Virgin Society – great friends who'd do anything for each other. Indulge in these forbidden, emotionally-charged, and wildly sexy age-gap romances!

The RSVP

The Tryst

The Tease

The Dating Games Series

A fun, sexy romantic comedy series about friends in the city and their dating mishaps!

The Virgin Next Door

Two A Day

The Good Guy Challenge

How To Date Series (New and ongoing)

Friends who are like family. Chances to learn how to date again. Standalone romantic comedies full of love, sex and meet-cute shenanigans.

My So-Called Love Life

Plays Well With Others

The Almost Romantic

The Accidental Dating Experiment

A romantic comedy adventure standalone

A Real Good Bad Thing

Boyfriend Material

Four fabulous heroines. Four outrageous proposals. Four chances at love in this sexy rom-com series!

Asking For a Friend

Sex and Other Shiny Objects

One Night Stand-In

Overnight Service

Big Rock Series

My #1 New York Times Bestselling sexy as sin, irreverent, male-POV romantic comedy!

Big Rock

Mister O

Well Hung

Full Package

Joy Ride

Hard Wood

Happy Endings Series

Romance starts with a bang in this series of standalones following a group of friends seeking and avoiding love!

Come Again

Shut Up and Kiss Me

Kismet

My Single-Versary

Ballers And Babes

Sexy sports romance standalones guaranteed to make you hot!

Most Valuable Playboy

Most Likely to Score

A Wild Card Kiss

Rules of Love Series

Athlete, virgins and weddings!

The Virgin Rule Book

The Virgin Game Plan

The Virgin Replay

The Virgin Scorecard

The Extravagant Series

Bodyguards, billionaires and hoteliers in this sexy, high-stakes series of standalones!

One Night Only

One Exquisite Touch

My One-Week Husband

The Guys Who Got Away Series

Friends in New York City and California fall in love in this fun and hot rom-com series!

Birthday Suit

Dear Sexy Ex-Boyfriend

The What If Guy

Thanks for Last Night

The Dream Guy Next Door

Always Satisfied Series

A group of friends in New York City find love and laughter in this series of sexy standalones!

Satisfaction Guaranteed

Never Have I Ever

Instant Gratification

PS It's Always Been You

The Gift Series

An after dark series of standalones! Explore your fantasies!

The Engagement Gift

The Virgin Gift

The Decadent Gift

The Heartbreakers Series

Three brothers. Three rockers. Three standalone sexy romantic comedies.

Once Upon a Real Good Time

Once Upon a Sure Thing

Once Upon a Wild Fling

Sinful Men

A high-stakes, high-octane, sexy-as-sin romantic suspense series!

My Sinful Nights

My Sinful Desire

My Sinful Longing

My Sinful Love

My Sinful Temptation

From Paris With Love

Swoony, sweeping romances set in Paris!

Wanderlust

Part-Time Lover

One Love Series

A group of friends in New York falls in love one by one in this
sexy rom-com series!

The Sexy One

The Hot One

The Knocked Up Plan

Come As You Are

Lucky In Love Series

A small town romance full of heat and blue collar heroes and
sexy heroines!

Best Laid Plans

The Feel Good Factor

Nobody Does It Better

Unzipped

No Regrets

An angsty, sexy, emotional, new adult trilogy about one young
couple fighting to break free of their pasts!

The Start of Us

The Thrill of It

Every Second With You

The Caught Up in Love Series

A group of friends finds love!

The Pretending Plot

The Dating Proposal

The Second Chance Plan

The Private Rehearsal

Seductive Nights Series

A high heat series full of danger and spice!

Night After Night

After This Night

One More Night

A Wildly Seductive Night

Joy Delivered Duet

A high-heat, wickedly sexy series of standalones that will set
your sheets on fire!

Nights With Him

Forbidden Nights

Unbreak My Heart

A standalone second chance emotional roller coaster of a
romance

The Muse

A magical realism romance set in Paris

**Good Love Series of sexy rom-coms co-written with Lili
Valente!**

I also write MM romance under the name L. Blakely!

Hopelessly Bromantic Duet (MM)

Roomies to lovers to enemies to fake boyfriends

Hopelessly Bromantic

Here Comes My Man

Men of Summer Series (MM)

Two baseball players on the same team fall in love in a forbidden romance spanning five epic years

Scoring With Him

Winning With Him

All In With Him

MM Standalone Novels

A Guy Walks Into My Bar

The Bromance Zone

One Time Only

The Best Men (Co-written with Sarina Bowen)

Winner Takes All Series (MM)

A series of emotionally-charged and irresistibly sexy standalone MM sports romances!

The Boyfriend Comeback

Turn Me On

A Very Filthy Game

Limited Edition Husband

Manhandled

If you want a personalized recommendation, email me at laurenblakelybooks@gmail.com!

CONTACT

I love hearing from readers! You can find me on Twitter at LaurenBlakely3, Instagram at LaurenBlakelyBooks, Facebook at LaurenBlakelyBooks, or online at Lauren-Blakely.com. You can also email me at laurenblakely books@gmail.com

www.ingramcontent.com/pod-product-compliance
Lightning Source LLC
Chambersburg PA
CBHW071351300726

48976CB00006B/1839